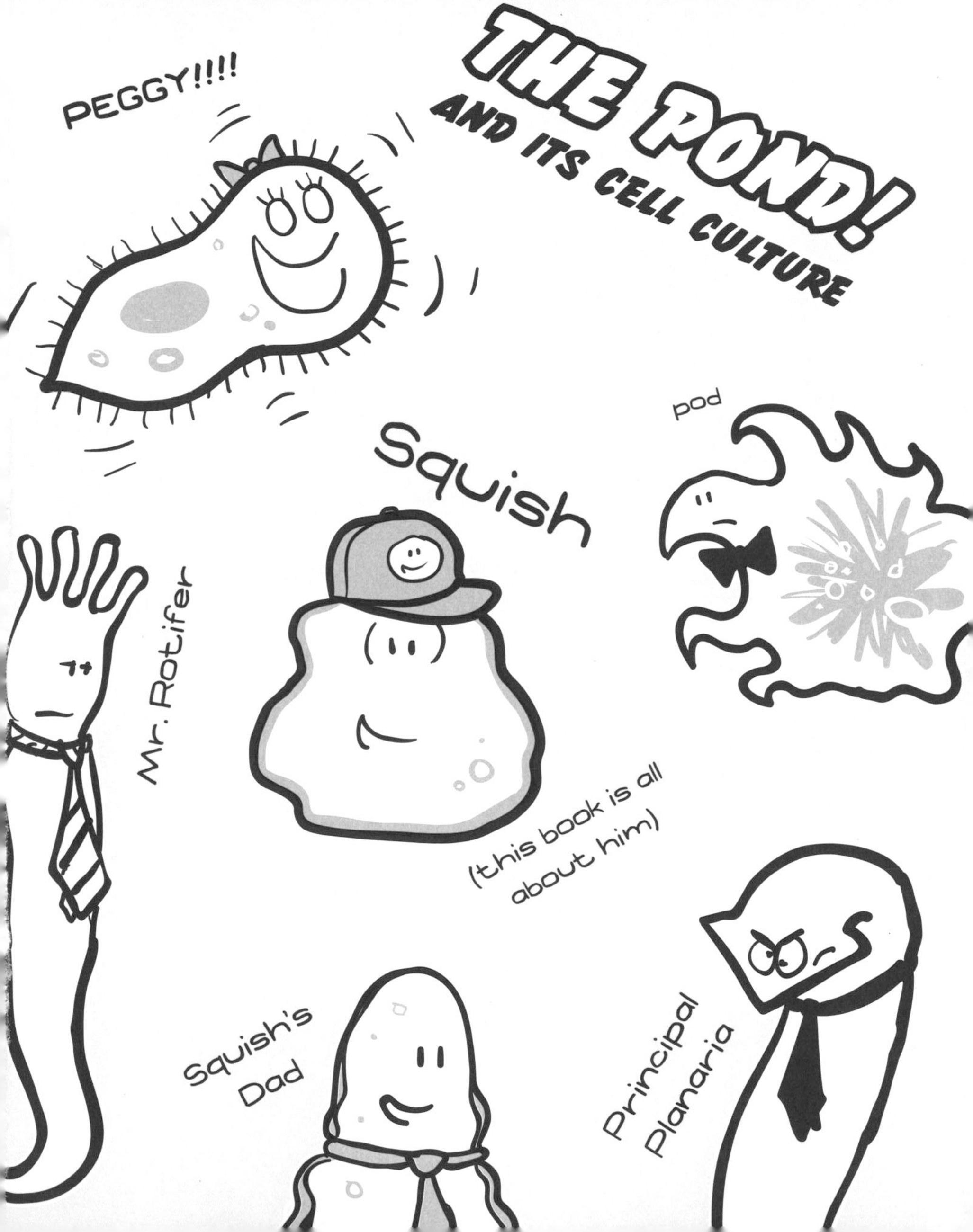
THE POND!
AND ITS CELL CULTURE
PEGGY!!!!
pod
Squish
Mr. Rotifer
(this book is all
about him)
Squish's
Dad
Principal
Planaria

★"HILARIOUS. IF EVER A NEW SERIES DESERVED TO GO VIRAL, THIS ONE DOES."

—KIRKUS REVIEWS, STARRED

Read ALL the SQUISH books!

#1 SQUISH: Super Amoeba
#2 SQUISH: Brave New Pond
#3 SQUISH: The Power of the Parasite
#4 SQUISH: Captain Disaster
#5 SQUISH: Game On!
#6 SQUISH: Fear the Amoeba

squish
THE POWER OF THE PARASITE

BY JENNIFER L. HOLM & MATTHEW HOLM

RANDOM HOUSE 🏠 NEW YORK

All rights reserved. Published in the United States by Random House Children's Books, a division of Random House LLC, a Penguin Random House Company, New York.

Random House and the colophon are registered trademarks of Random House LLC.

Visit us on the Web! randomhousekids.com

Educators and librarians, for a variety of teaching tools, visit us at RHTeachersLibrarians.com

Library of Congress Cataloging-in-Publication Data
Holm, Jennifer L.
The power of the Parasite /
by Jennifer L. Holm and Matthew Holm. — 1st ed.
p. cm. — (Squish ; #3)
Summary: At swim camp, Squish's new friend Basil helps him avoid learning to swim with pranks that sometimes go too far, but the comic book exploits of Squish's idol, "Super Amoeba," help him deal with Basil and conquer his fear.
ISBN 978-0-375-84391-4 (trade pbk.) —
ISBN 978-0-375-93785-9 (lib. bdg.)
1. Graphic novels. [1. Graphic novels. 2. Amoeba—Fiction. 3. Camps—Fiction. 4. Practical jokes—Fiction. 5. Swimming—Fiction. 6. Superheroes—Fiction.]
I. Holm, Matthew. II. Title.
PZ7.7.H65Pow 2012   741.5'973—dc23   2011024120

MANUFACTURED IN MALAYSIA   14 13 12 11 10 9 8 7 6 5
First Edition

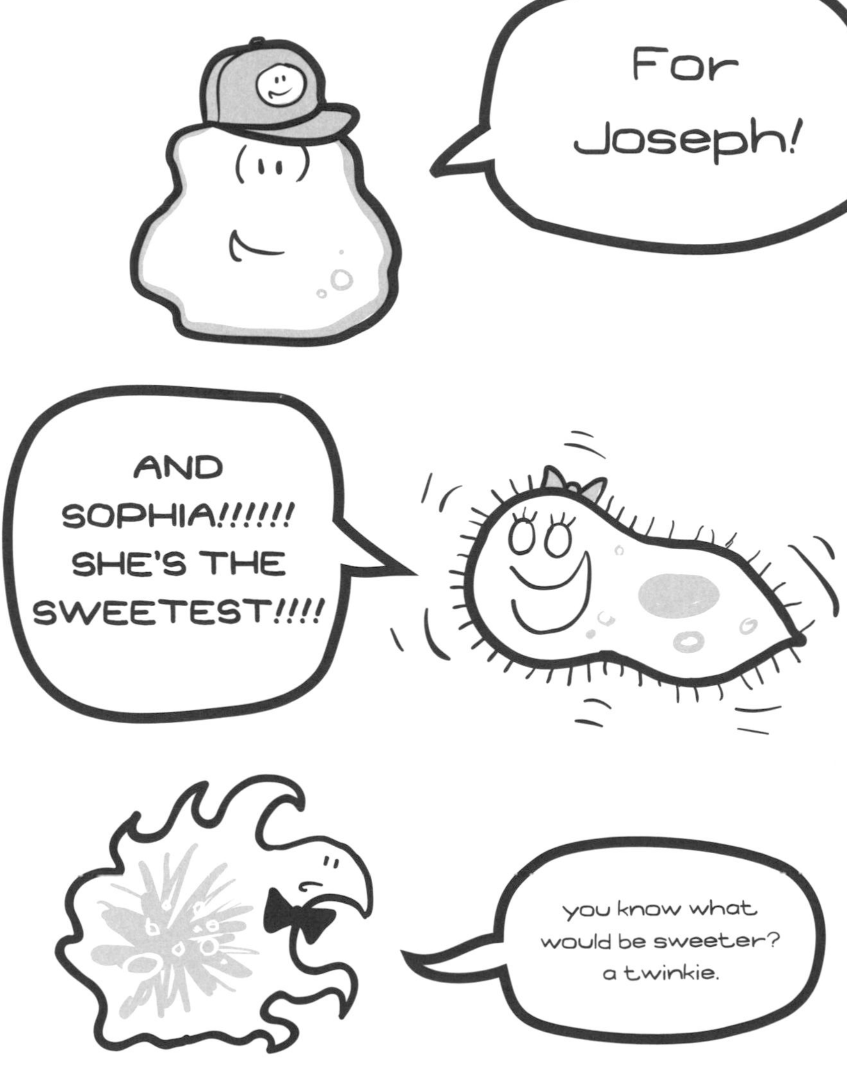
For Joseph!
AND SOPHIA!!!!!! SHE'S THE SWEETEST!!!!
you know what would be sweeter? a twinkie.

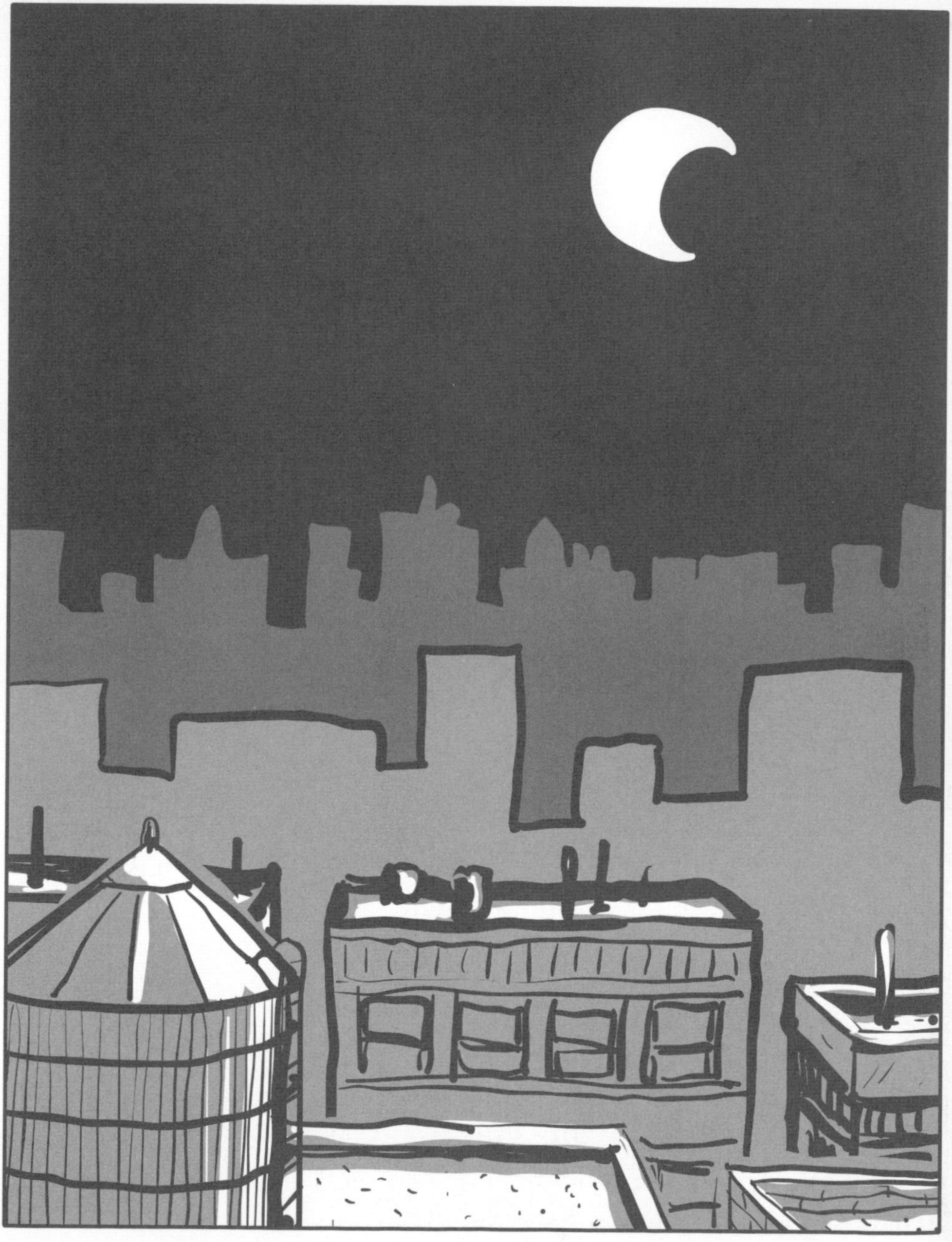

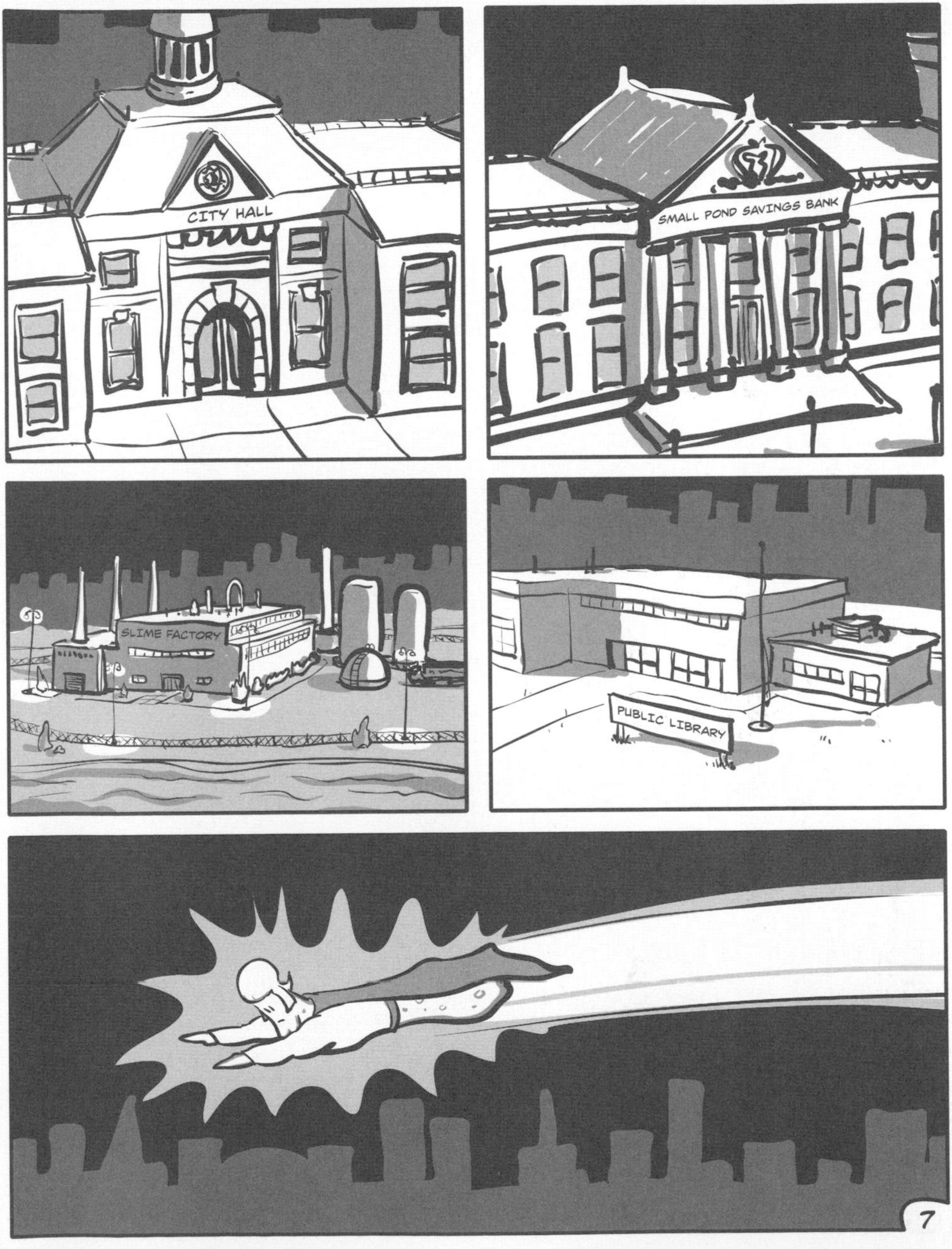
CITY HALL
SMALL POND SAVINGS BANK
SLIME FACTORY
PUBLIC LIBRARY

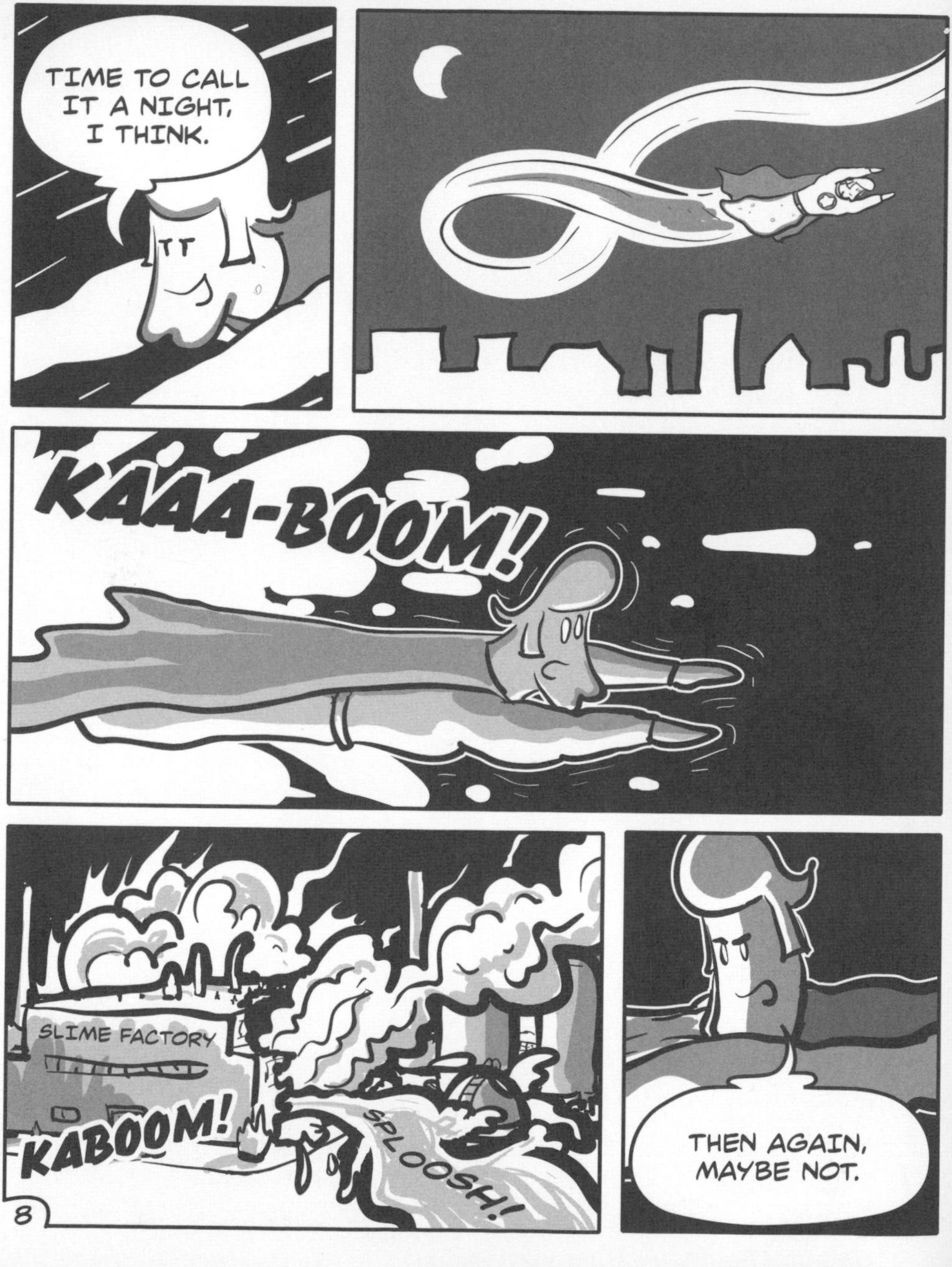
TIME TO CALL IT A NIGHT, I THINK.
KAAA-BOOM!
SLIME FACTORY
KABOOM!
SPLOOSH!
THEN AGAIN, MAYBE NOT.

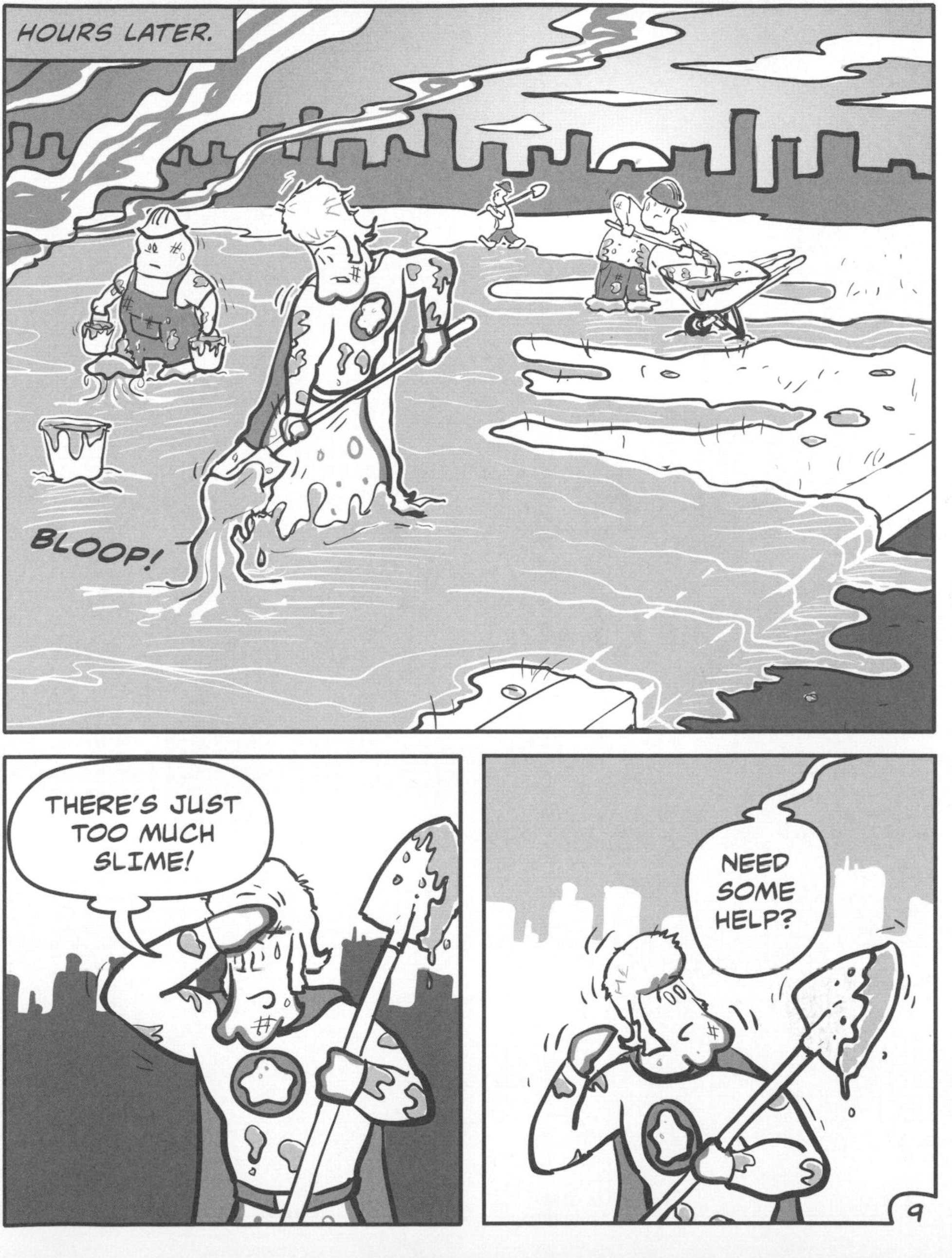
HOURS LATER.
BLOOP!
THERE'S JUST TOO MUCH SLIME!
NEED SOME HELP?

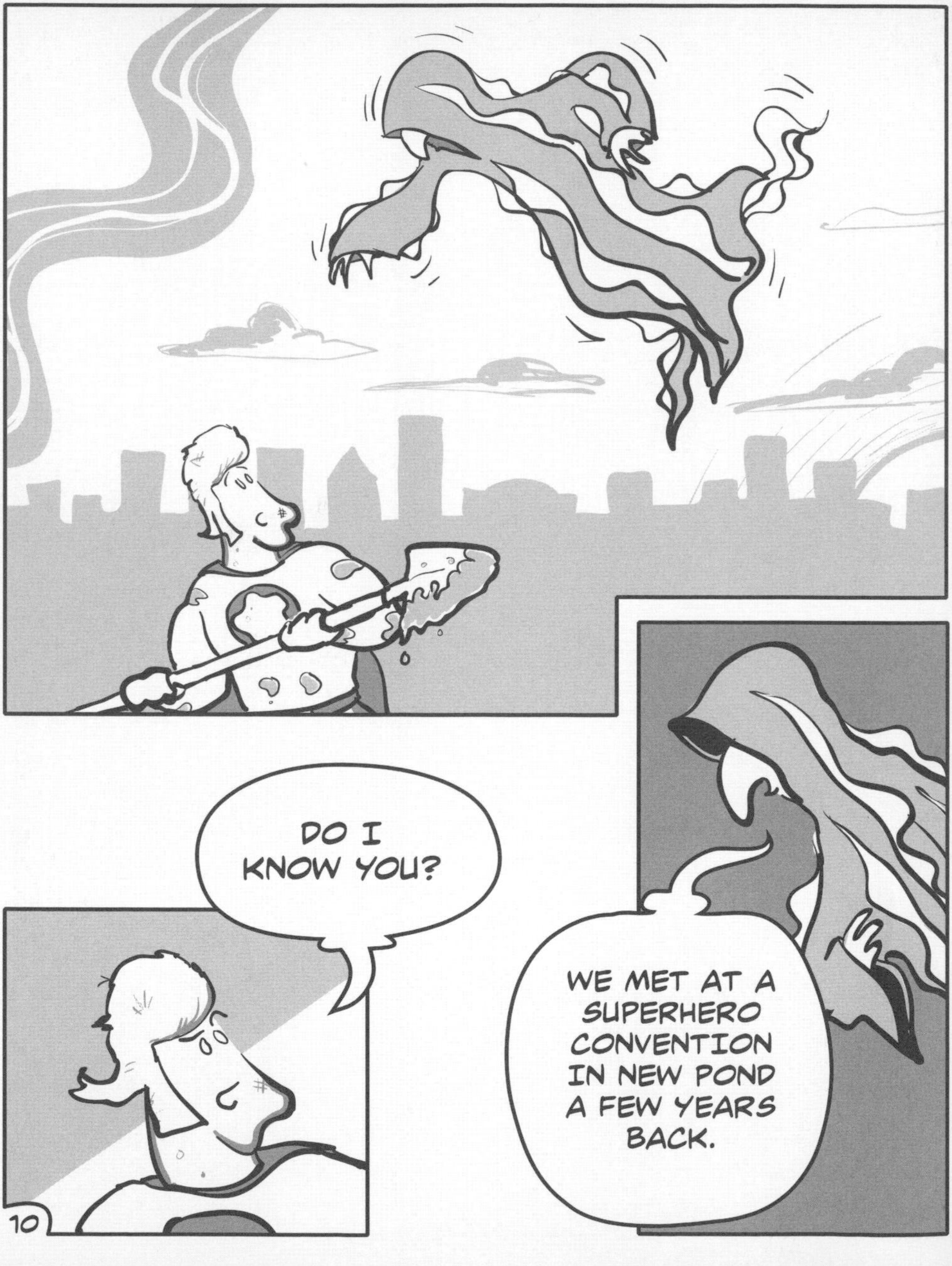
DO I KNOW YOU?
WE MET AT A SUPERHERO CONVENTION IN NEW POND A FEW YEARS BACK.
10

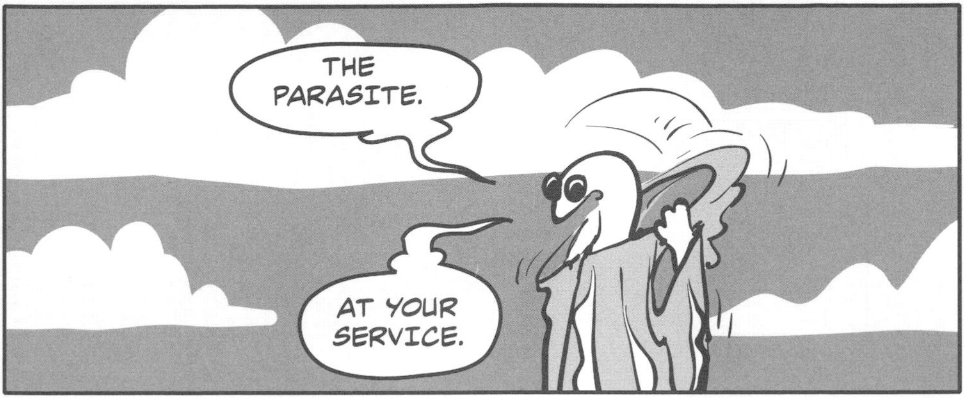
THE PARASITE.
AT YOUR SERVICE.

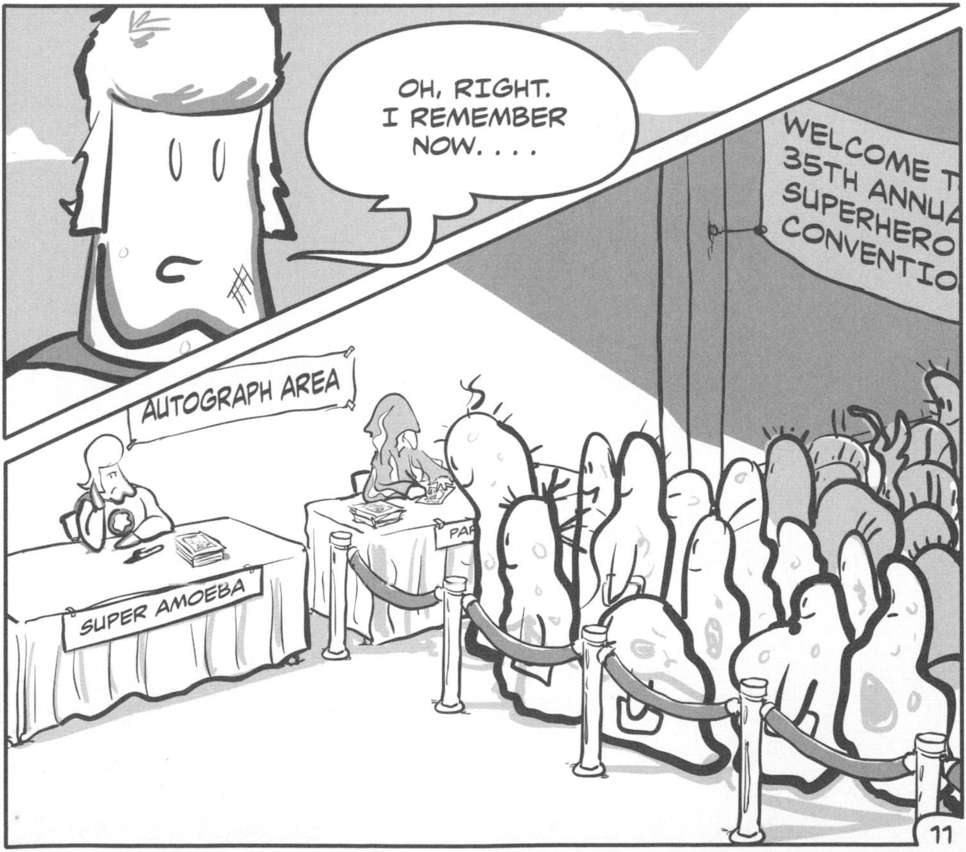
OH, RIGHT. I REMEMBER NOW. . . .
WELCOME T
35TH ANNUA
SUPERHERO
CONVENTIO
AUTOGRAPH AREA
SUPER AMOEBA
PAR

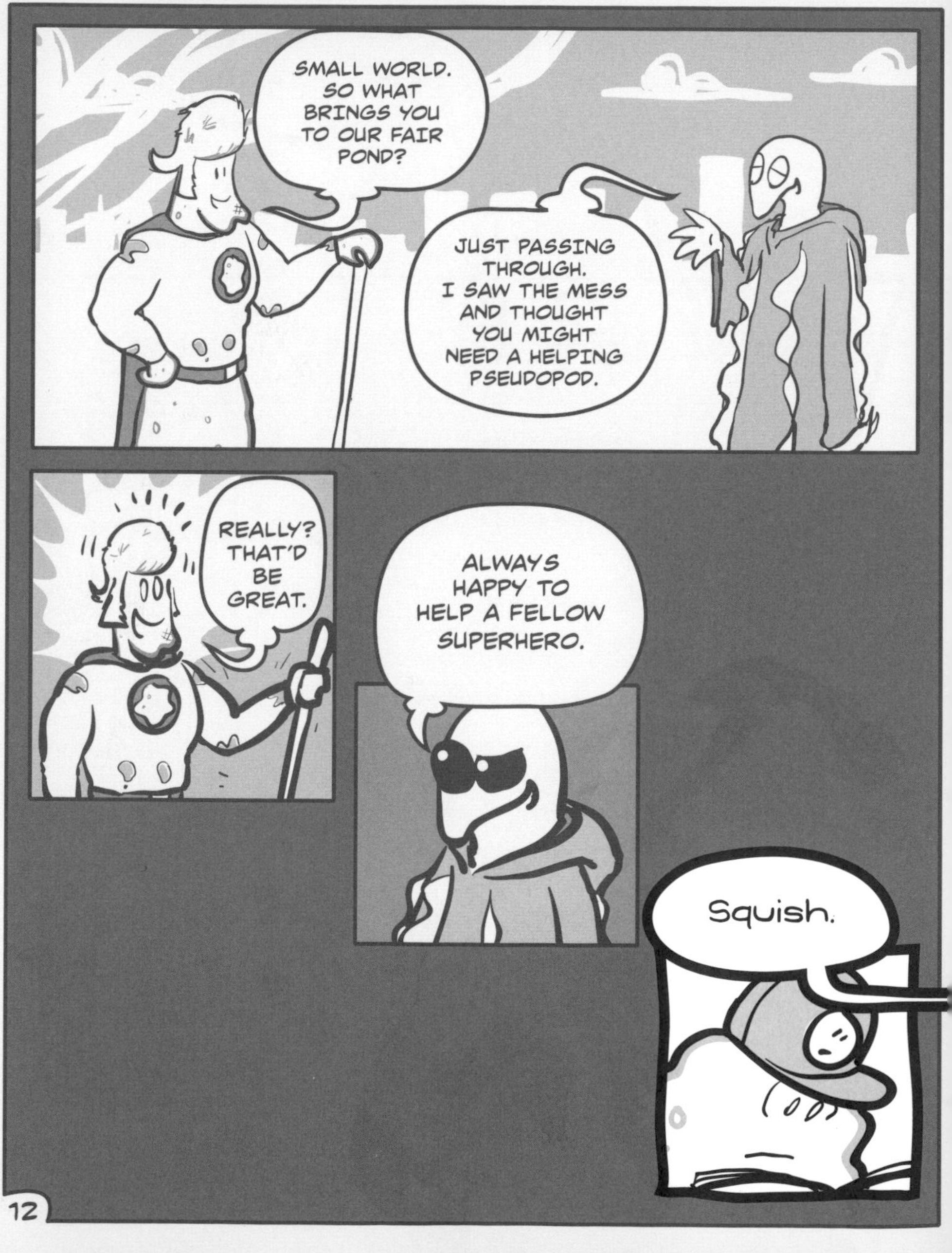
SMALL WORLD. SO WHAT BRINGS YOU TO OUR FAIR POND?
JUST PASSING THROUGH. I SAW THE MESS AND THOUGHT YOU MIGHT NEED A HELPING PSEUDOPOD.
REALLY? THAT'D BE GREAT.
ALWAYS HAPPY TO HELP A FELLOW SUPERHERO.
Squish.

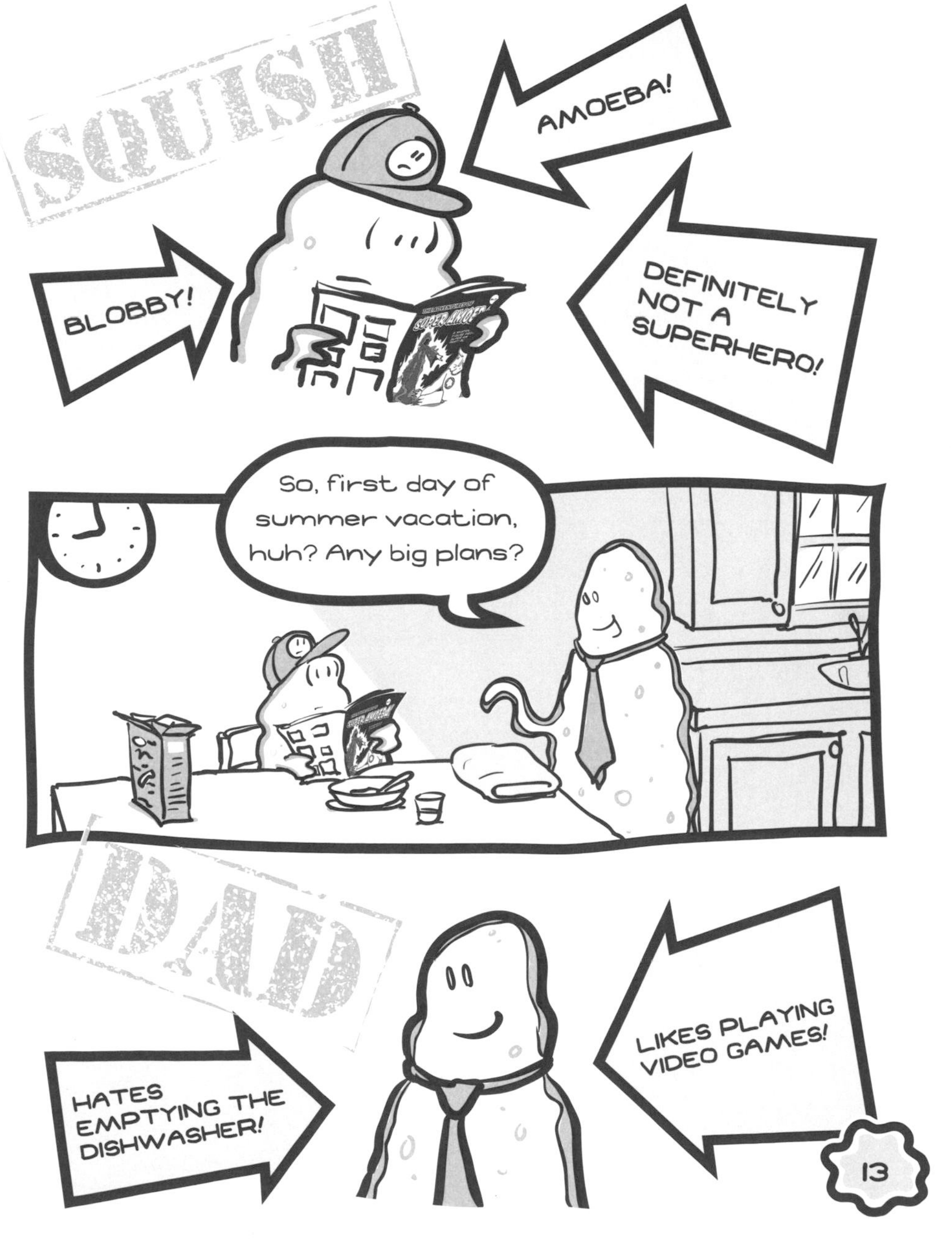
SQUISH
AMOEBA!
BLOBBY!
DEFINITELY NOT A SUPERHERO!
So, first day of summer vacation, huh? Any big plans?
DAD
HATES EMPTYING THE DISHWASHER!
LIKES PLAYING VIDEO GAMES!

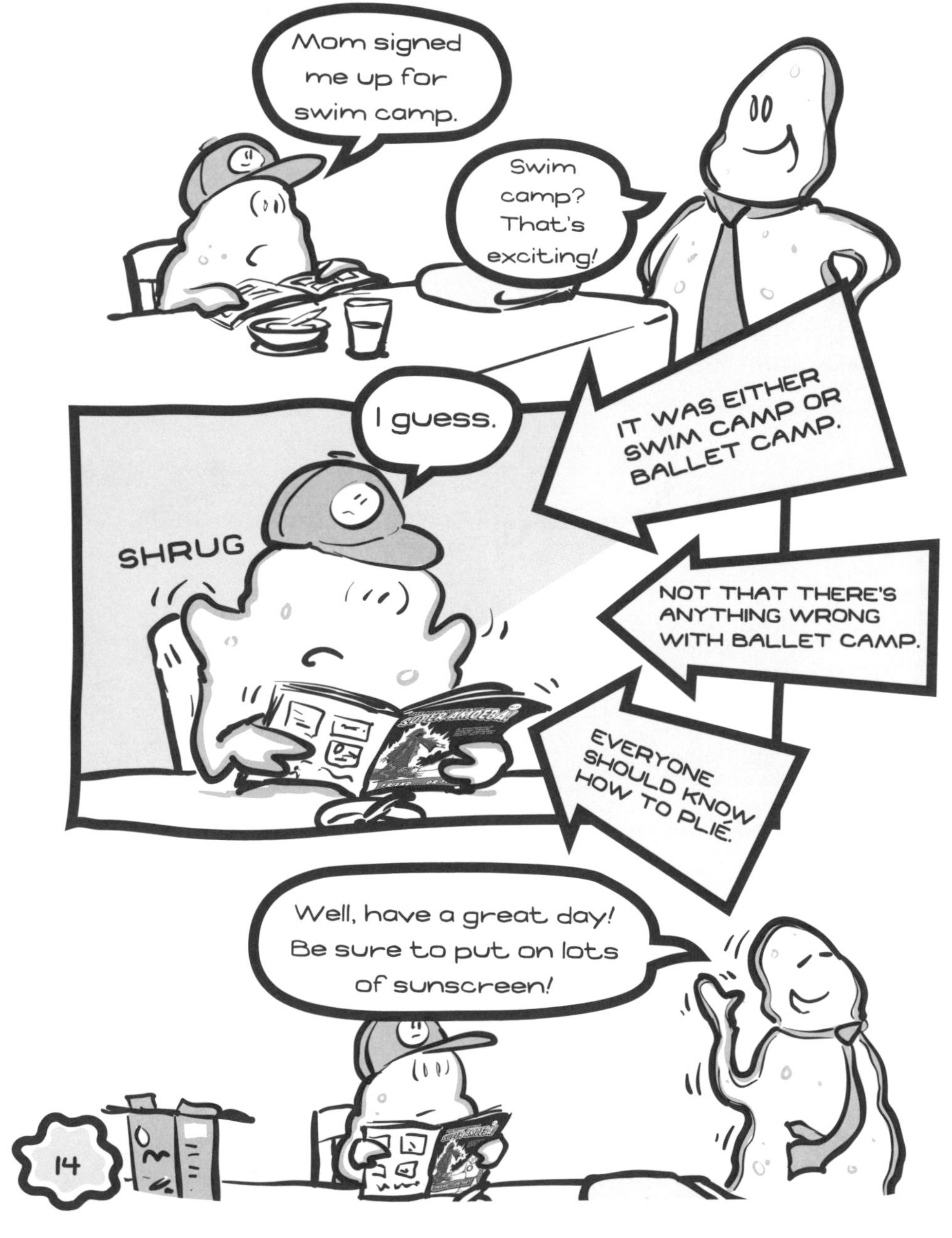

Mom signed me up for swim camp.
Swim camp? That's exciting!
I guess.
SHRUG
IT WAS EITHER SWIM CAMP OR BALLET CAMP.
NOT THAT THERE'S ANYTHING WRONG WITH BALLET CAMP.
EVERYONE SHOULD KNOW HOW TO PLIÉ.
SUPER AMOEBA!
Well, have a great day! Be sure to put on lots of sunscreen!

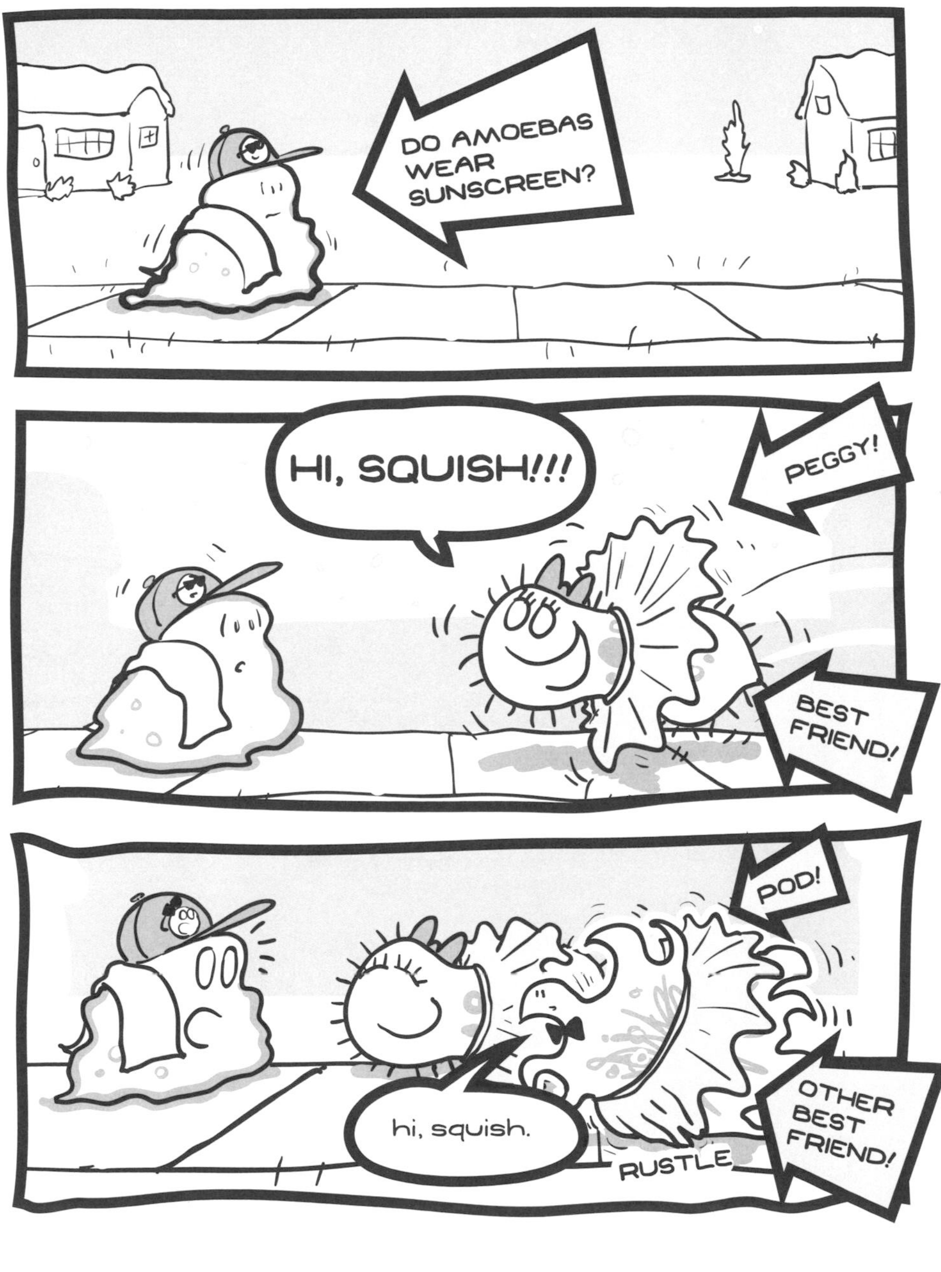
DO AMOEBAS WEAR SUNSCREEN?
HI, SQUISH!!!
PEGGY!
BEST FRIEND!
POD!
hi, squish.
RUSTLE
OTHER BEST FRIEND!

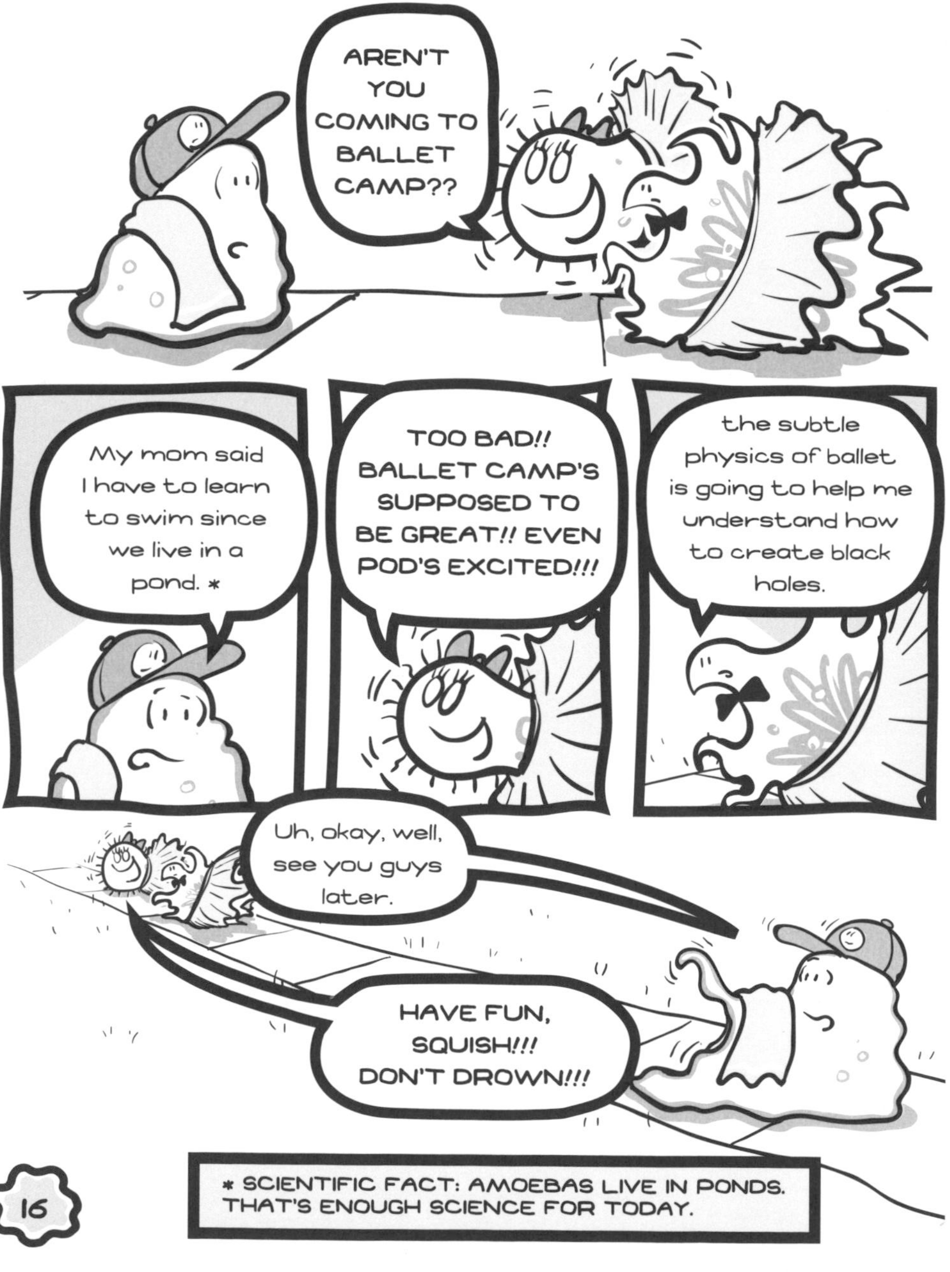

AREN'T YOU COMING TO BALLET CAMP??
My mom said I have to learn to swim since we live in a pond. *
TOO BAD!! BALLET CAMP'S SUPPOSED TO BE GREAT!! EVEN POD'S EXCITED!!!
the subtle physics of ballet is going to help me understand how to create black holes.
Uh, okay, well, see you guys later.
HAVE FUN, SQUISH!!! DON'T DROWN!!!
* SCIENTIFIC FACT: AMOEBAS LIVE IN PONDS. THAT'S ENOUGH SCIENCE FOR TODAY.

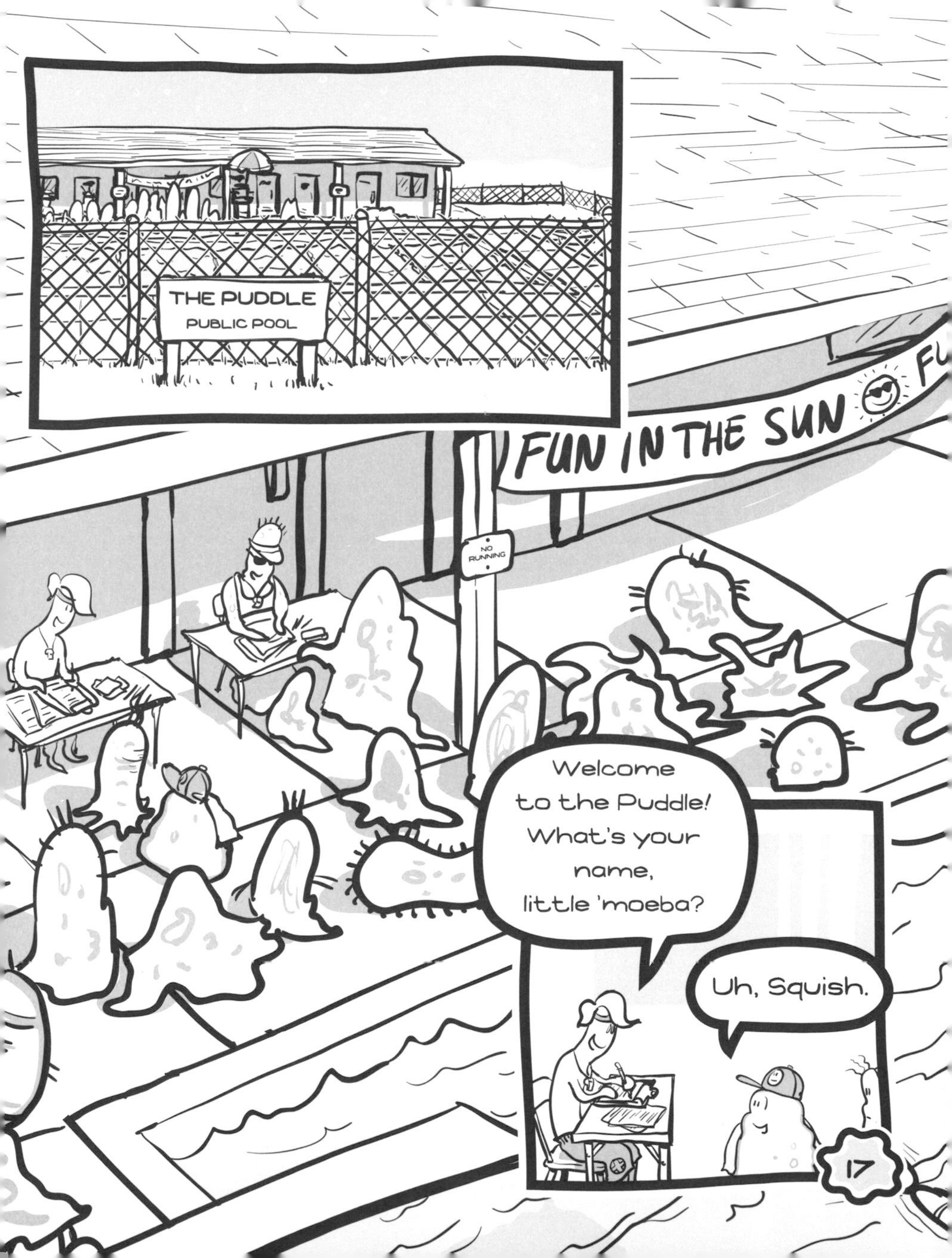

THE PUDDLE
PUBLIC POOL
FUN IN THE SUN
NO RUNNING
Welcome to the Puddle! What's your name, little 'moeba?
Uh, Squish.

Here you go, Squash. Go hang up your towel and grab some grass.

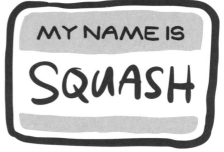

MY NAME IS SQUASH

Sigh.

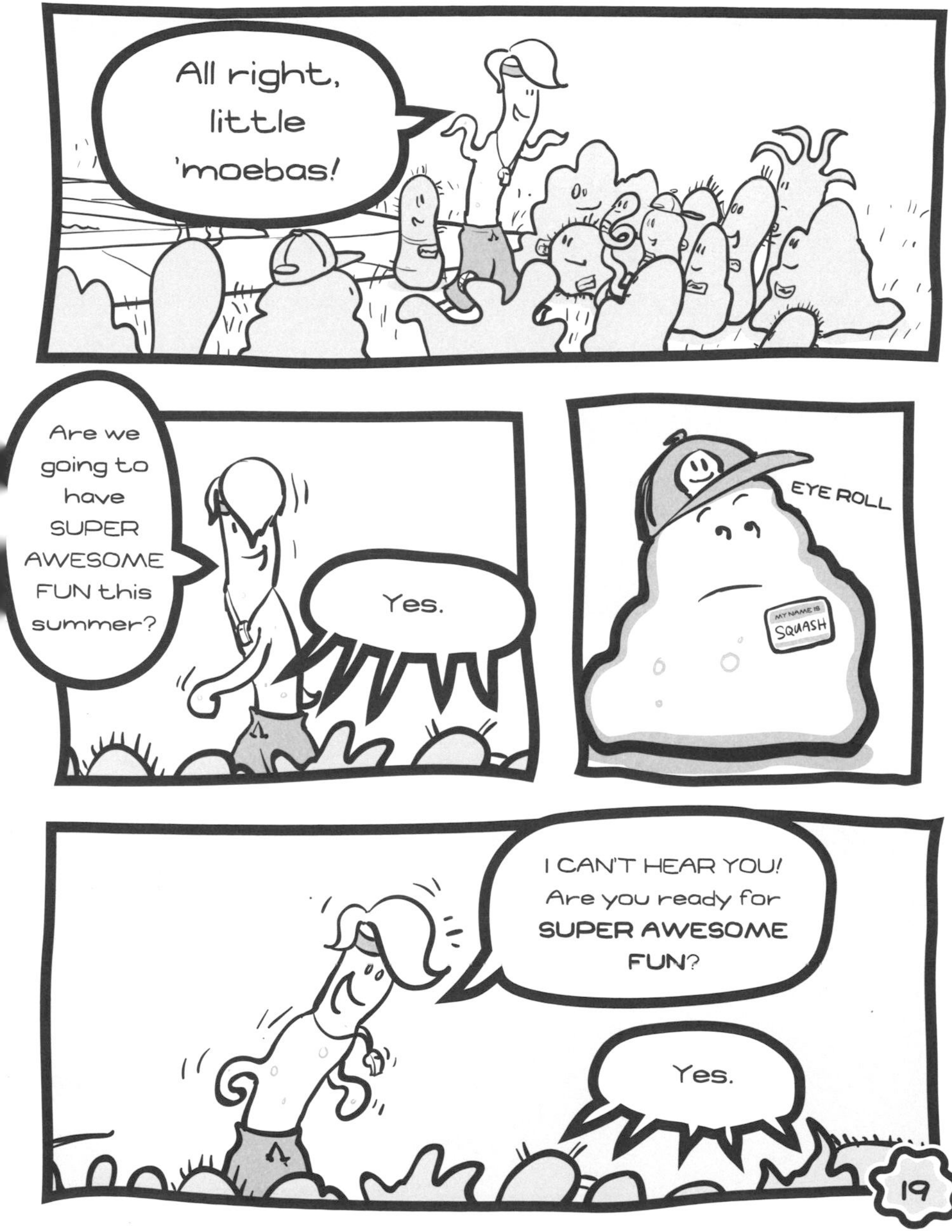
All right, little 'moebas!
Are we going to have SUPER AWESOME FUN this summer?
Yes.
EYE ROLL
MY NAME IS
SQUASH
I CAN'T HEAR YOU! Are you ready for SUPER AWESOME FUN?
Yes.

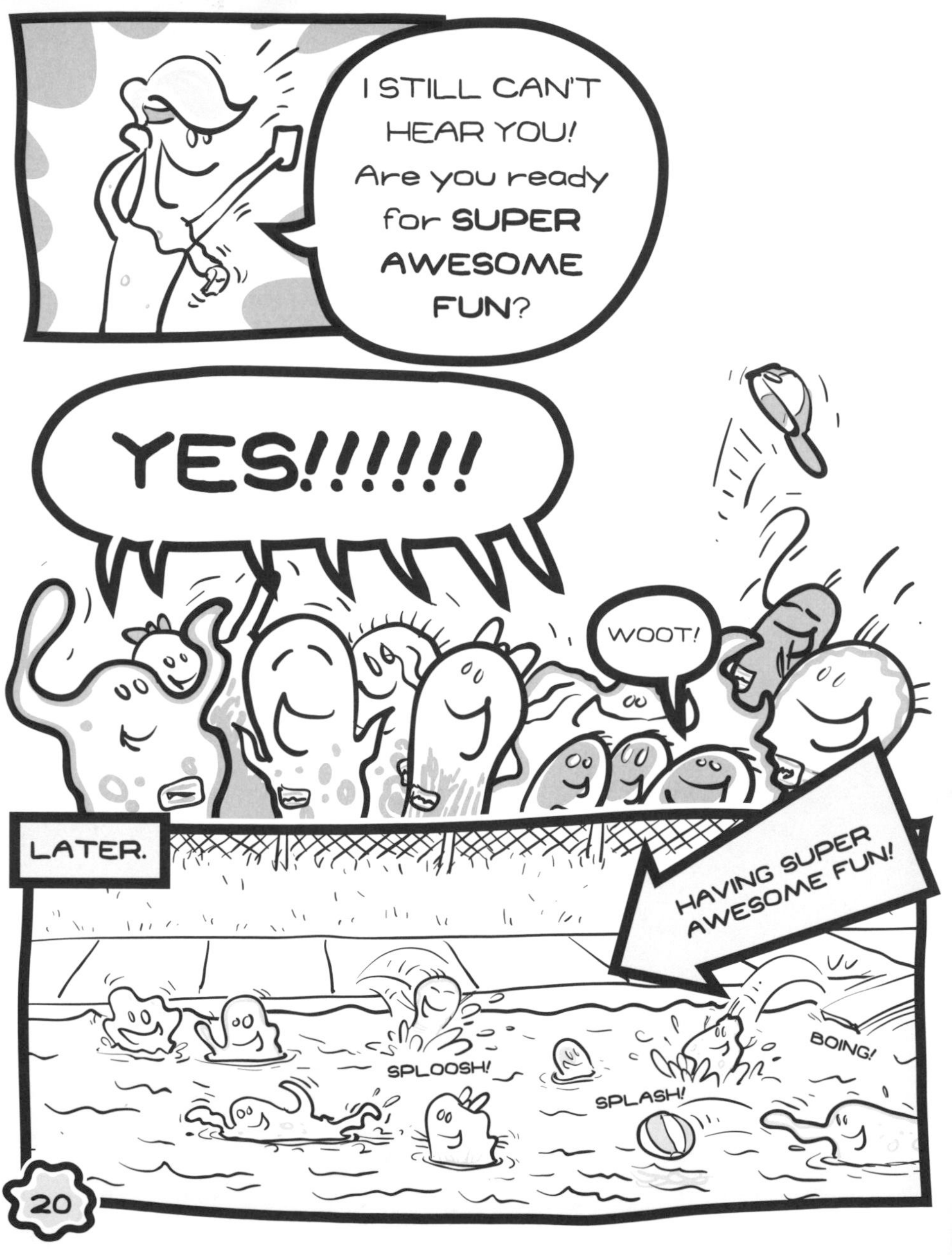
I STILL CAN'T HEAR YOU! Are you ready for SUPER AWESOME FUN?
YES!!!!!!!
WOOT!
LATER.
HAVING SUPER AWESOME FUN!
SPLOOSH!
SPLASH!
BOING!

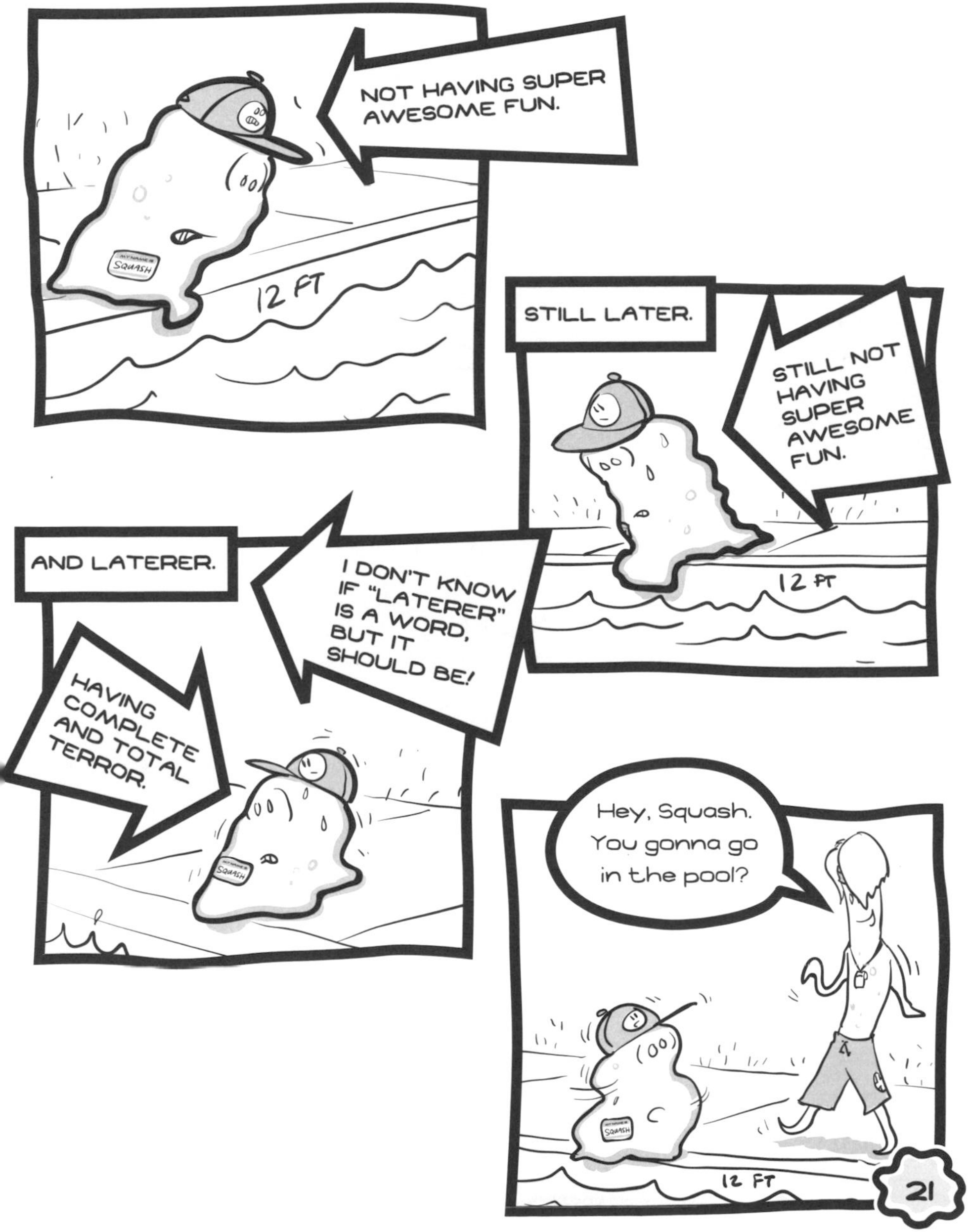
NOT HAVING SUPER AWESOME FUN.
12 FT
STILL LATER.
STILL NOT HAVING SUPER AWESOME FUN.
12 FT
AND LATERER.
I DON'T KNOW IF "LATERER" IS A WORD, BUT IT SHOULD BE!
HAVING COMPLETE AND TOTAL TERROR.
Hey, Squash. You gonna go in the pool?
12 FT

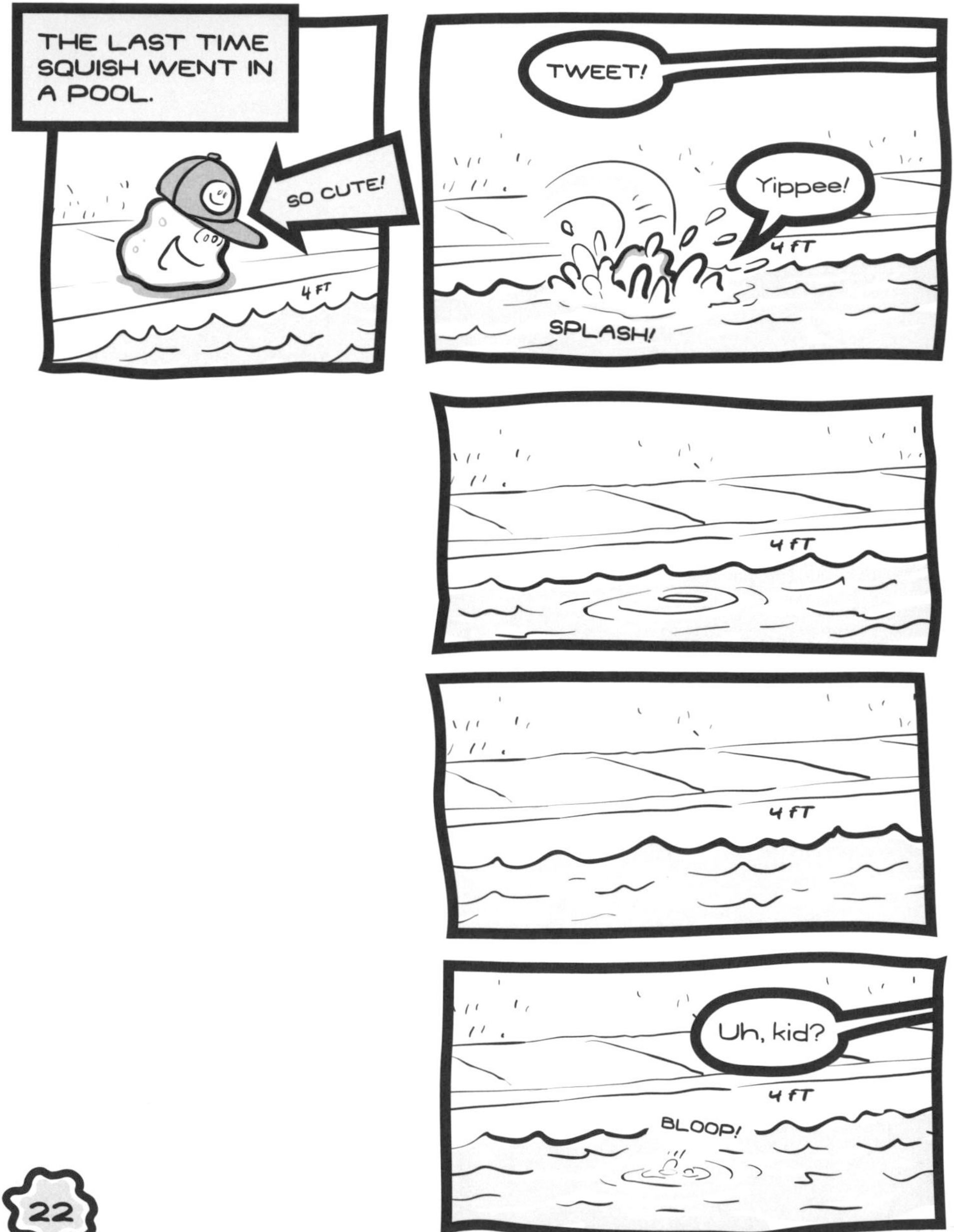
THE LAST TIME SQUISH WENT IN A POOL.
SO CUTE!
4 FT
TWEET!
Yippee!
4 FT
SPLASH!
4 FT
4 FT
Uh, kid?
4 FT
BLOOP!

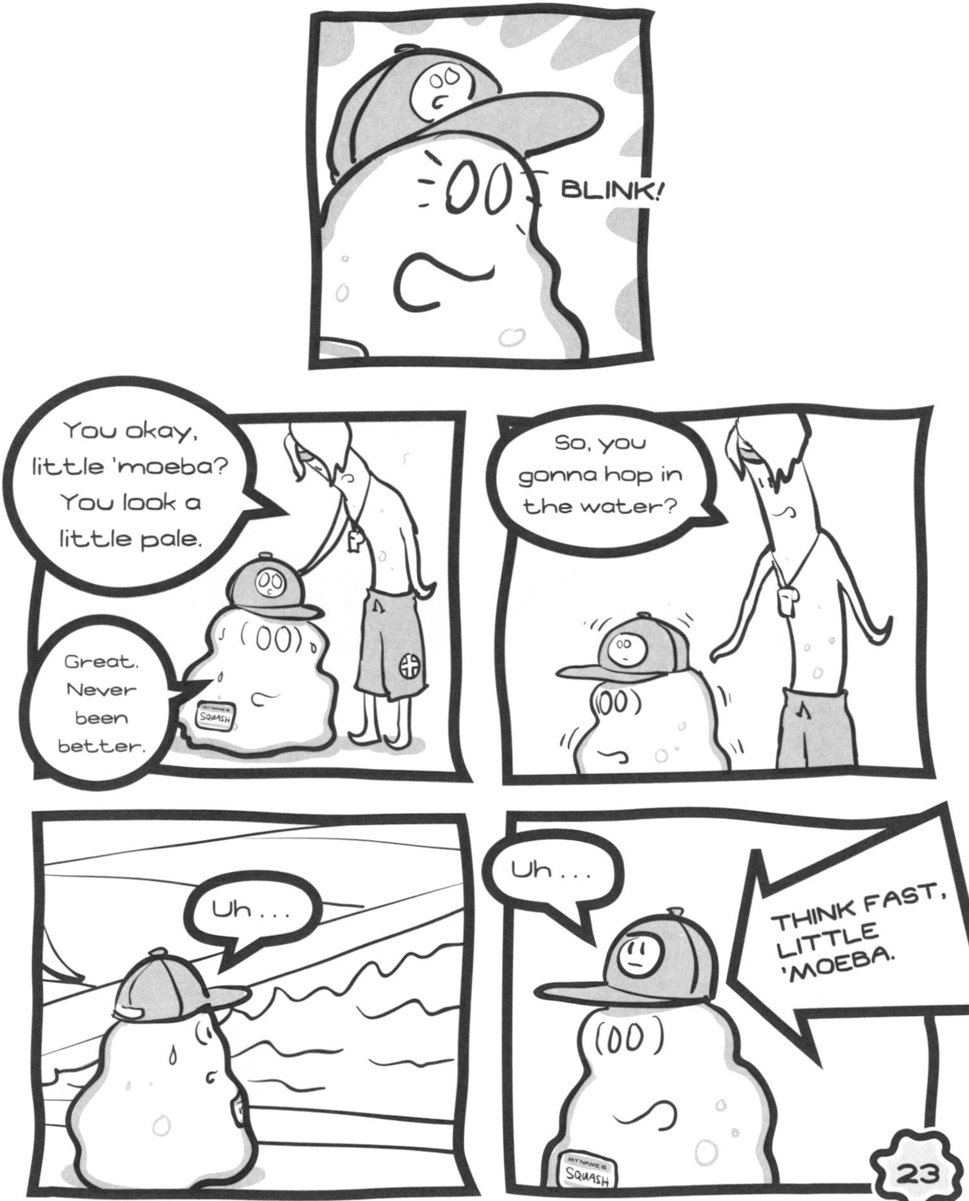
BLINK!
You okay, little 'moeba? You look a little pale.
Great. Never been better.
So, you gonna hop in the water?
Uh . . .
Uh . . .
THINK FAST, LITTLE 'MOEBA.
MY NAME IS SQUASH

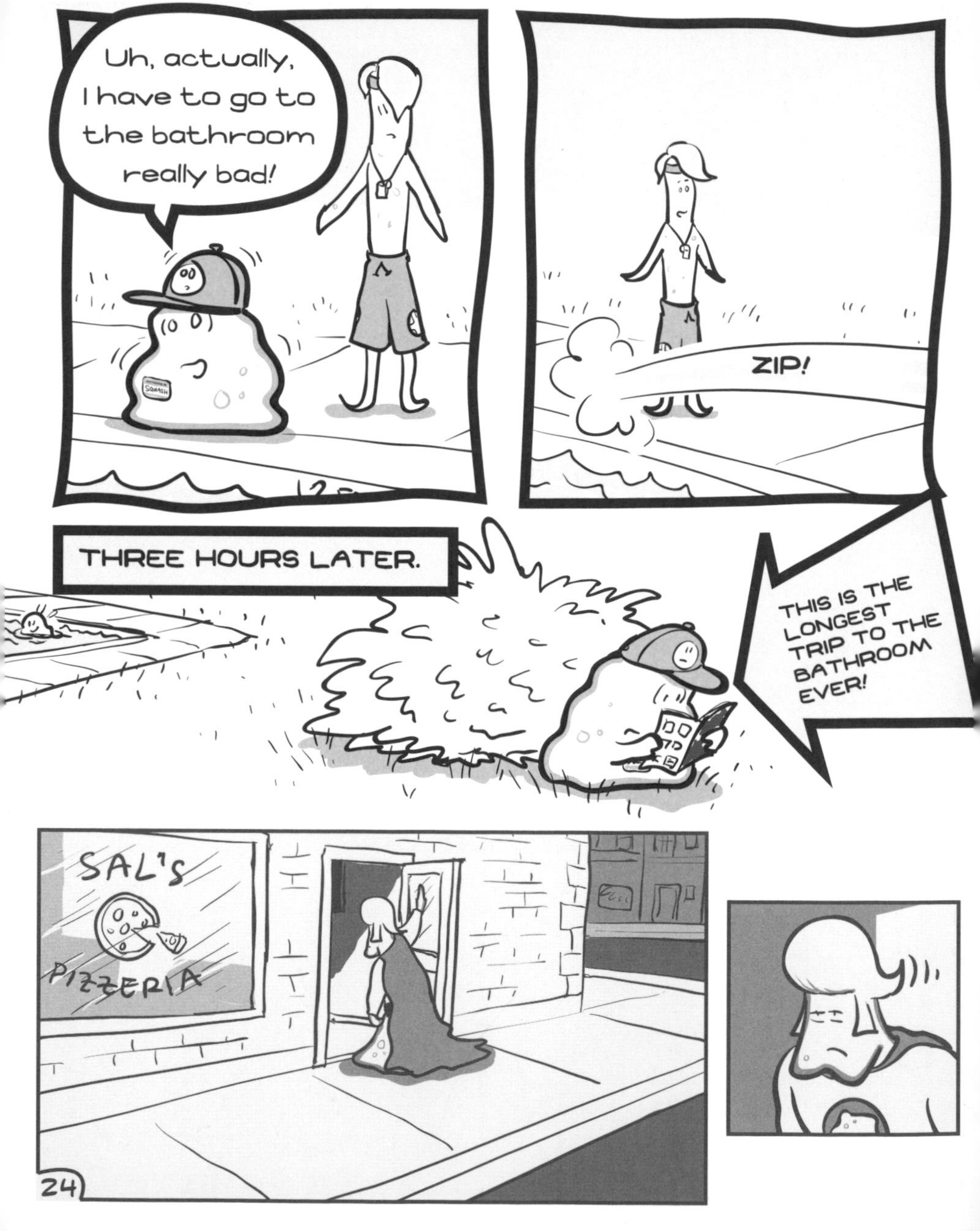
Uh, actually, I have to go to the bathroom really bad!
SQUASH
ZIP!
THREE HOURS LATER.
THIS IS THE LONGEST TRIP TO THE BATHROOM EVER!
SAL'S
PIZZERIA

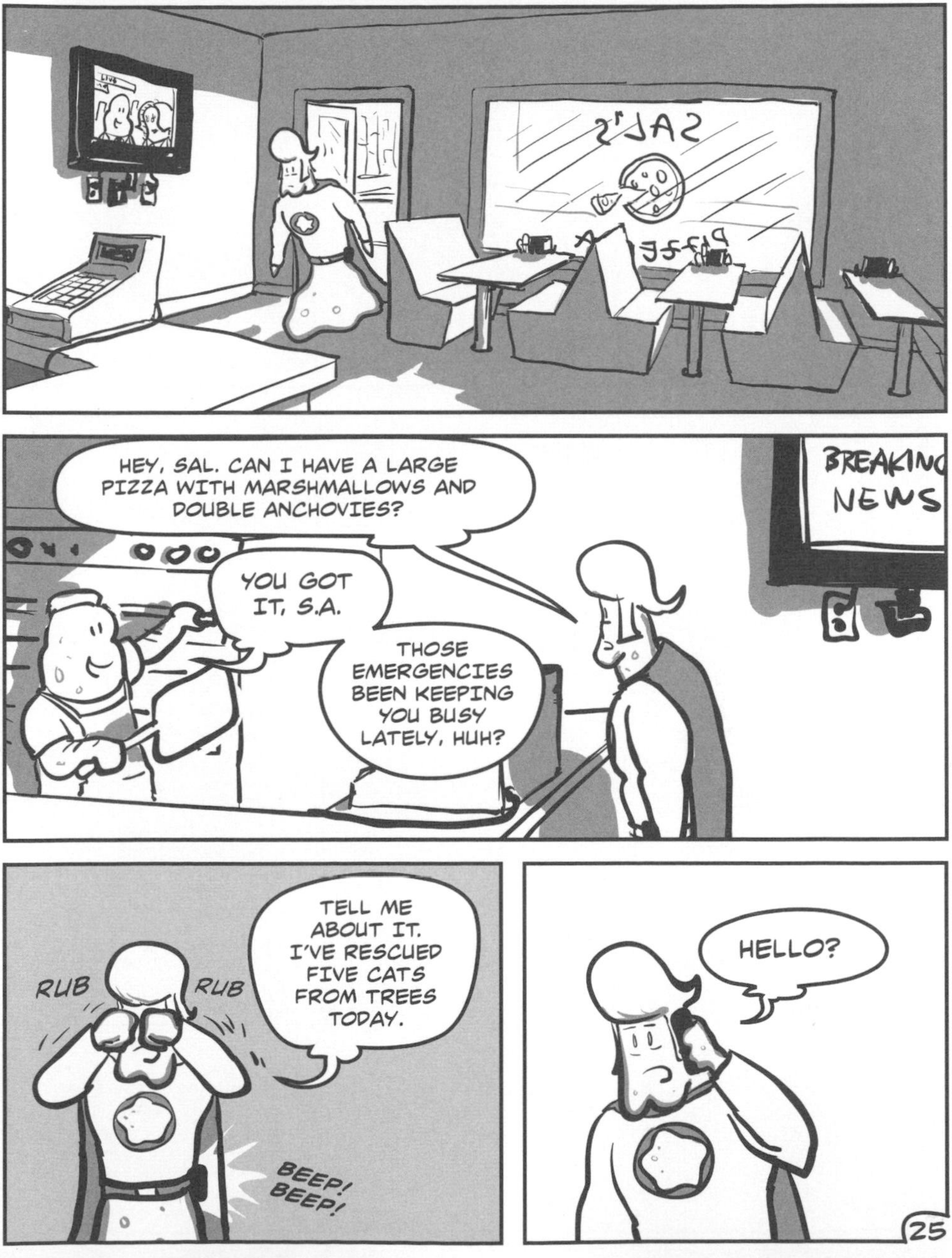
SAL'S
PIZZA
HEY, SAL. CAN I HAVE A LARGE PIZZA WITH MARSHMALLOWS AND DOUBLE ANCHOVIES?
BREAKING NEWS
YOU GOT IT, S.A.
THOSE EMERGENCIES BEEN KEEPING YOU BUSY LATELY, HUH?
RUB RUB
TELL ME ABOUT IT. I'VE RESCUED FIVE CATS FROM TREES TODAY.
BEEP! BEEP!
HELLO?

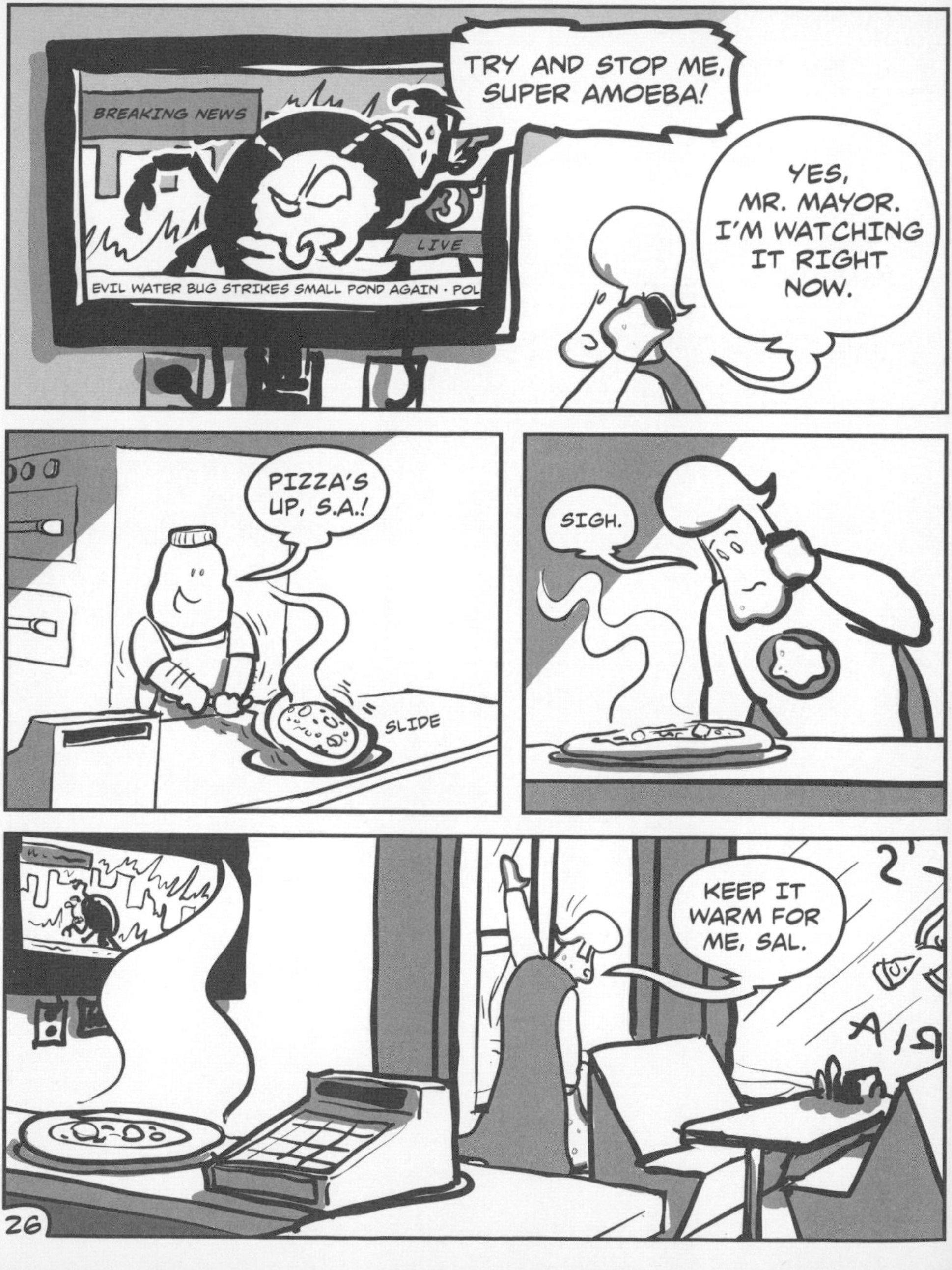
BREAKING NEWS
LIVE
EVIL WATER BUG STRIKES SMALL POND AGAIN • POL
TRY AND STOP ME, SUPER AMOEBA!
YES, MR. MAYOR. I'M WATCHING IT RIGHT NOW.
PIZZA'S UP, S.A.!
SLIDE
SIGH.
KEEP IT WARM FOR ME, SAL.

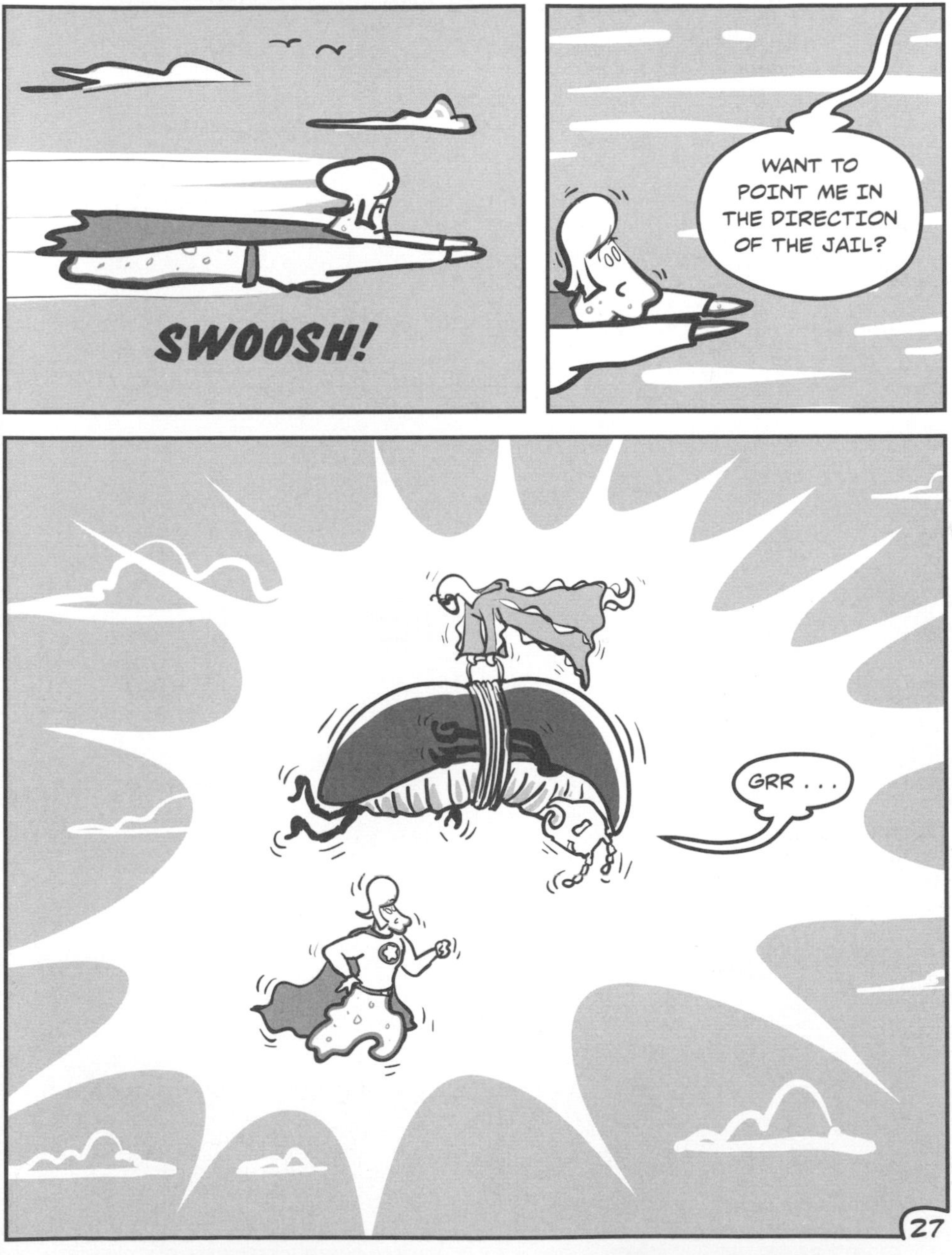
SWOOSH!
WANT TO POINT ME IN THE DIRECTION OF THE JAIL?
GRR . . .

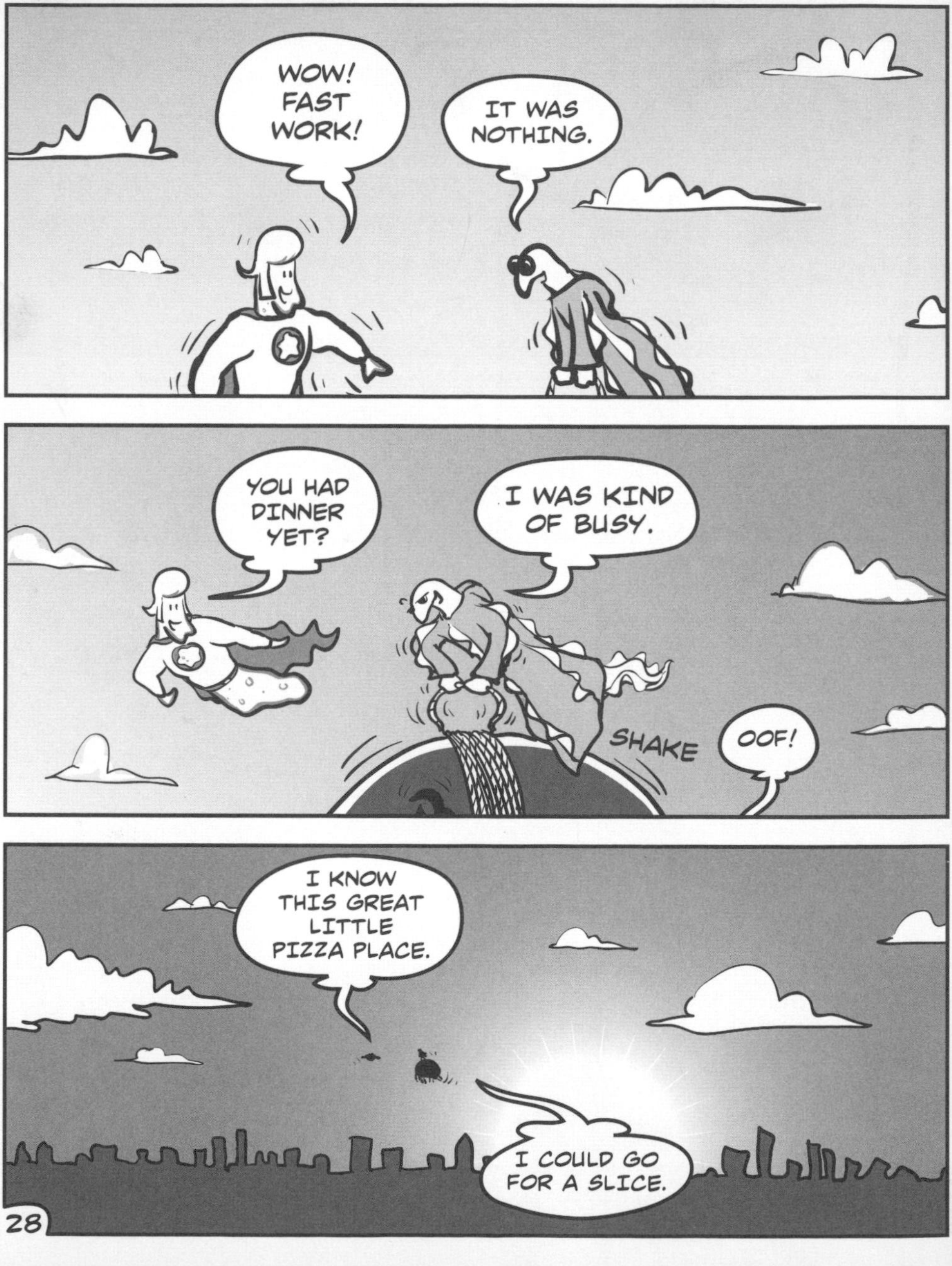
WOW! FAST WORK!
IT WAS NOTHING.
YOU HAD DINNER YET?
I WAS KIND OF BUSY.
SHAKE
OOF!
I KNOW THIS GREAT LITTLE PIZZA PLACE.
I COULD GO FOR A SLICE.

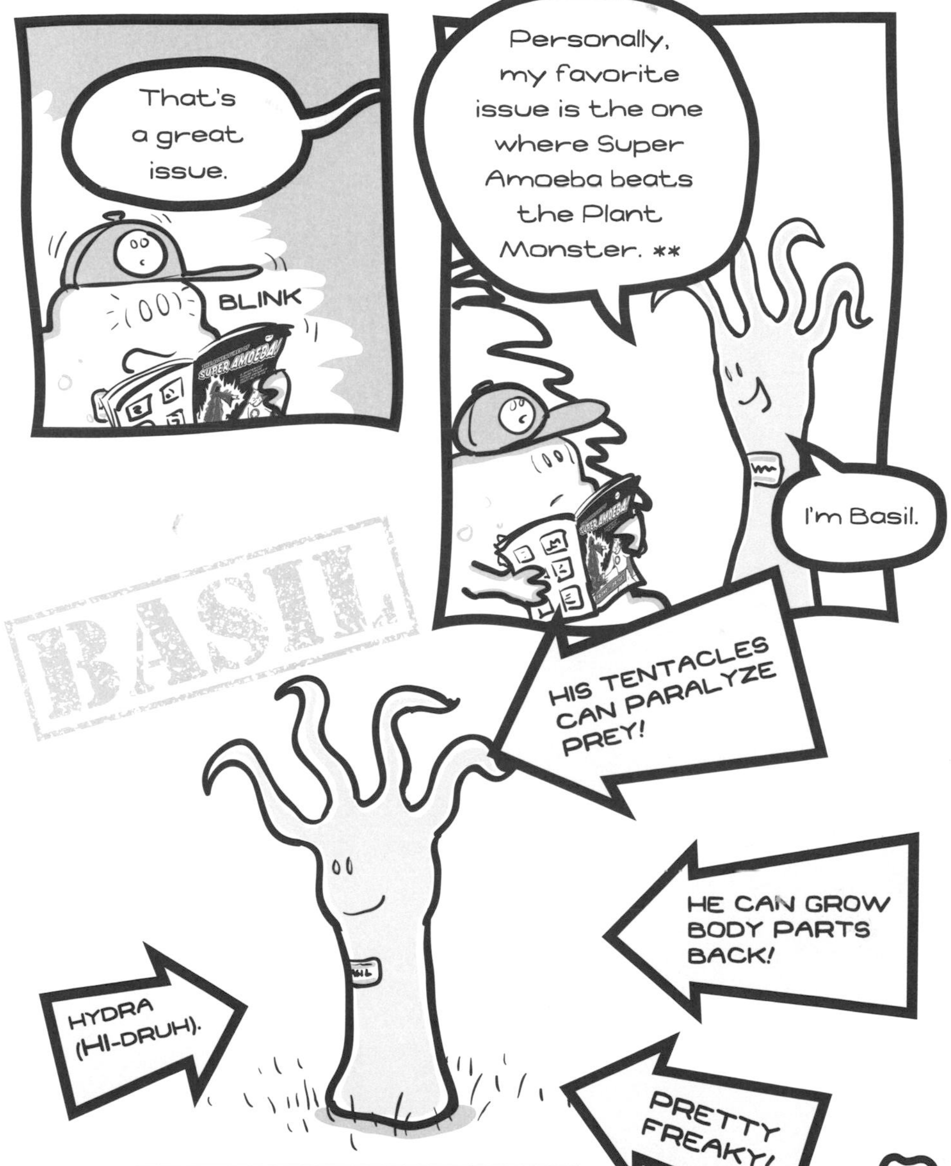
That's a great issue.
BLINK
Personally, my favorite issue is the one where Super Amoeba beats the Plant Monster. **
I'm Basil.
BASIL
HIS TENTACLES CAN PARALYZE PREY!
HE CAN GROW BODY PARTS BACK!
HYDRA (HI-DRUH).
PRETTY FREAKY!

** READ SQUISH #1: SUPER AMOEBA!

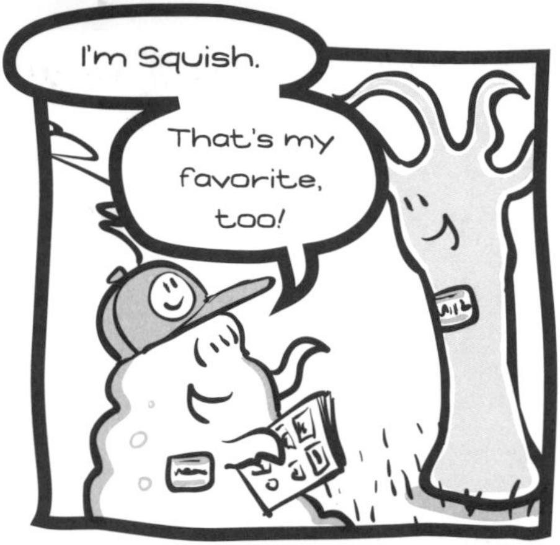
I'm Squish.
That's my favorite, too!

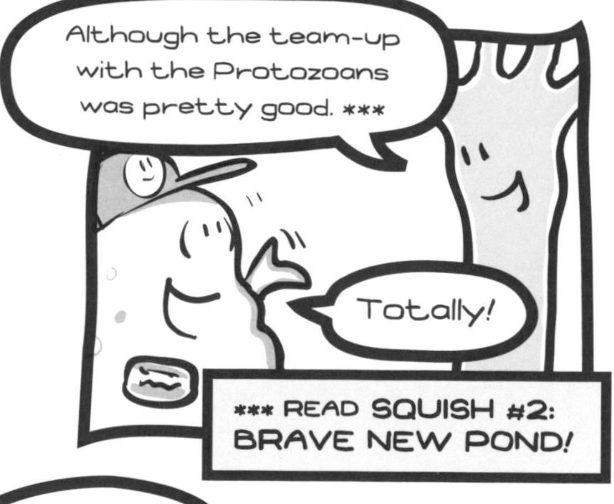
Although the team-up with the Protozoans was pretty good. ***
Totally!
*** READ SQUISH #2: BRAVE NEW POND!

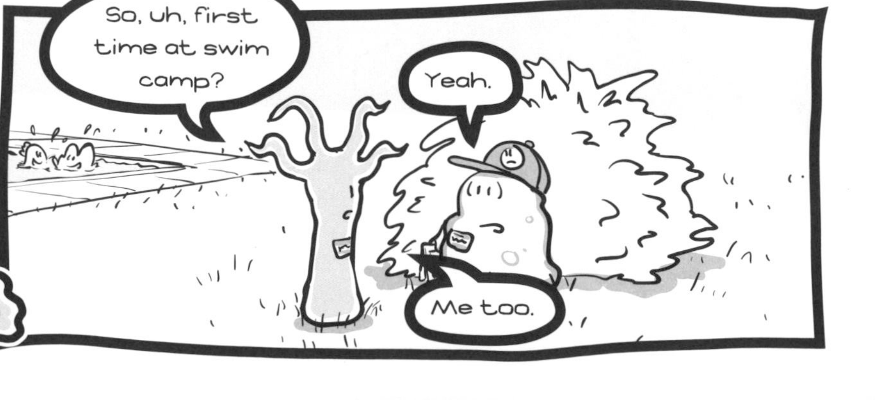
So, uh, first time at swim camp?
Yeah.
Me too.

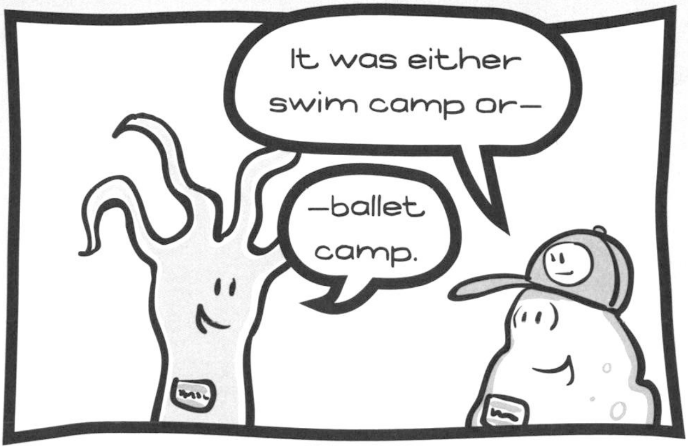
It was either swim camp or—
—ballet camp.

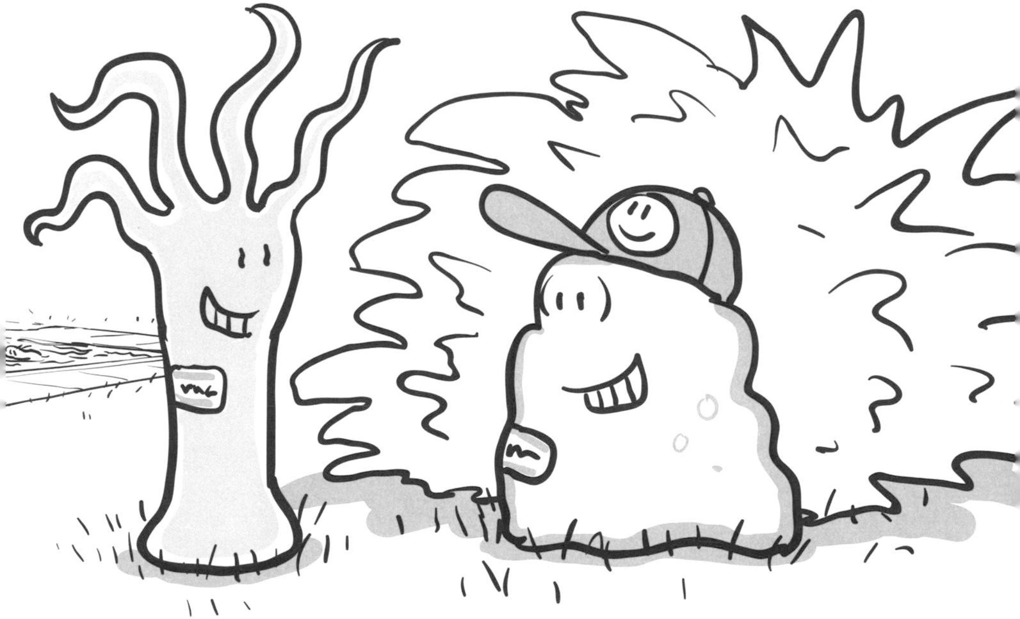

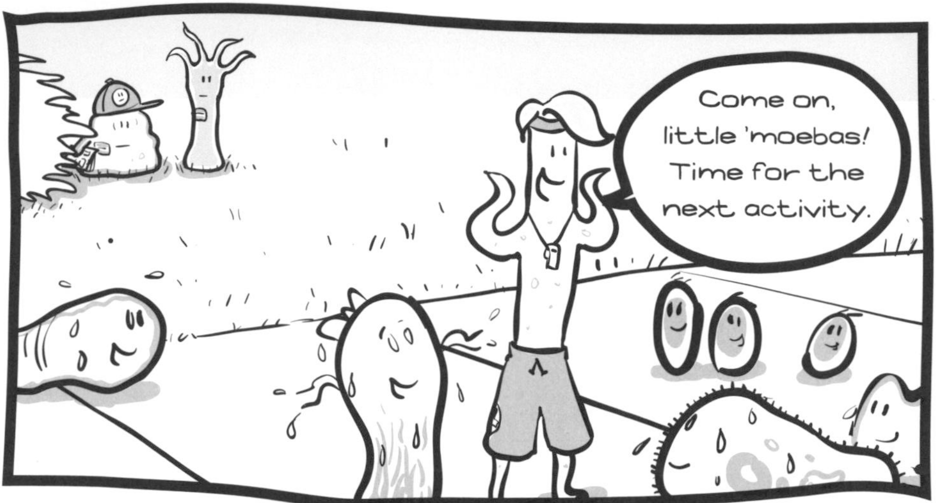
Come on, little 'moebas! Time for the next activity.

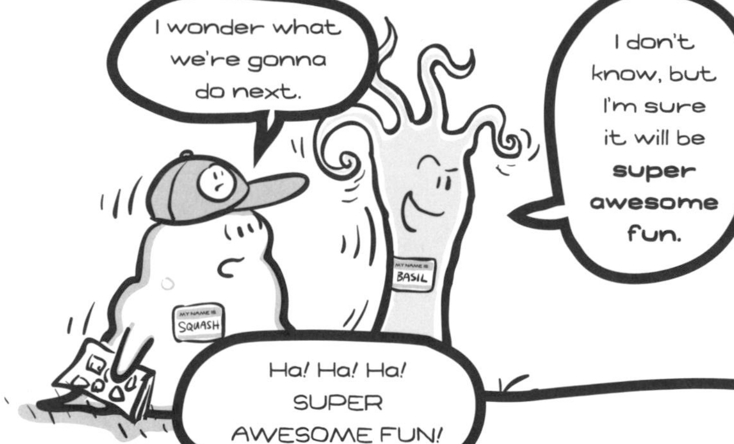
I wonder what we're gonna do next.
I don't know, but I'm sure it will be **super awesome fun.**
MY NAME IS
BASIL
MY NAME IS
SQUASH

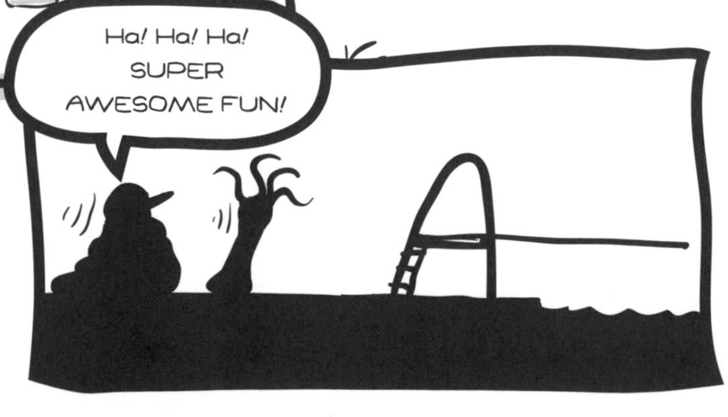
Ha! Ha! Ha! SUPER AWESOME FUN!

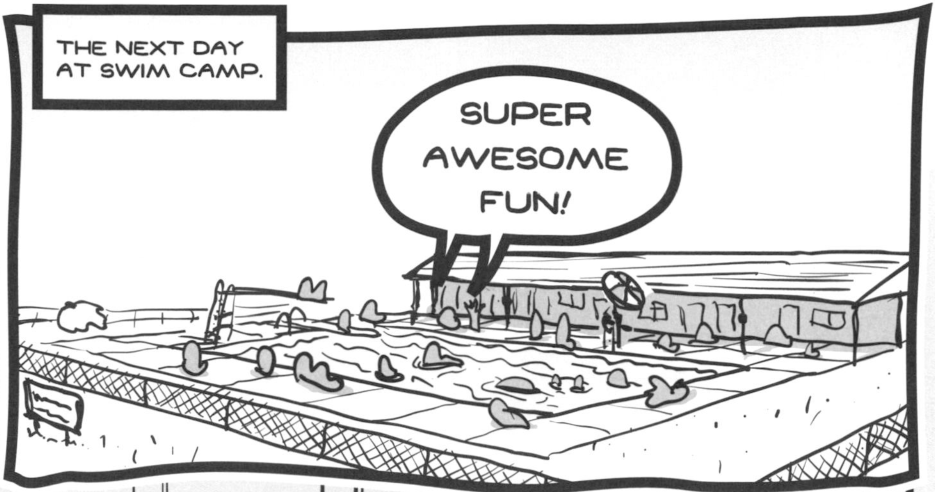
THE NEXT DAY AT SWIM CAMP.
SUPER AWESOME FUN!

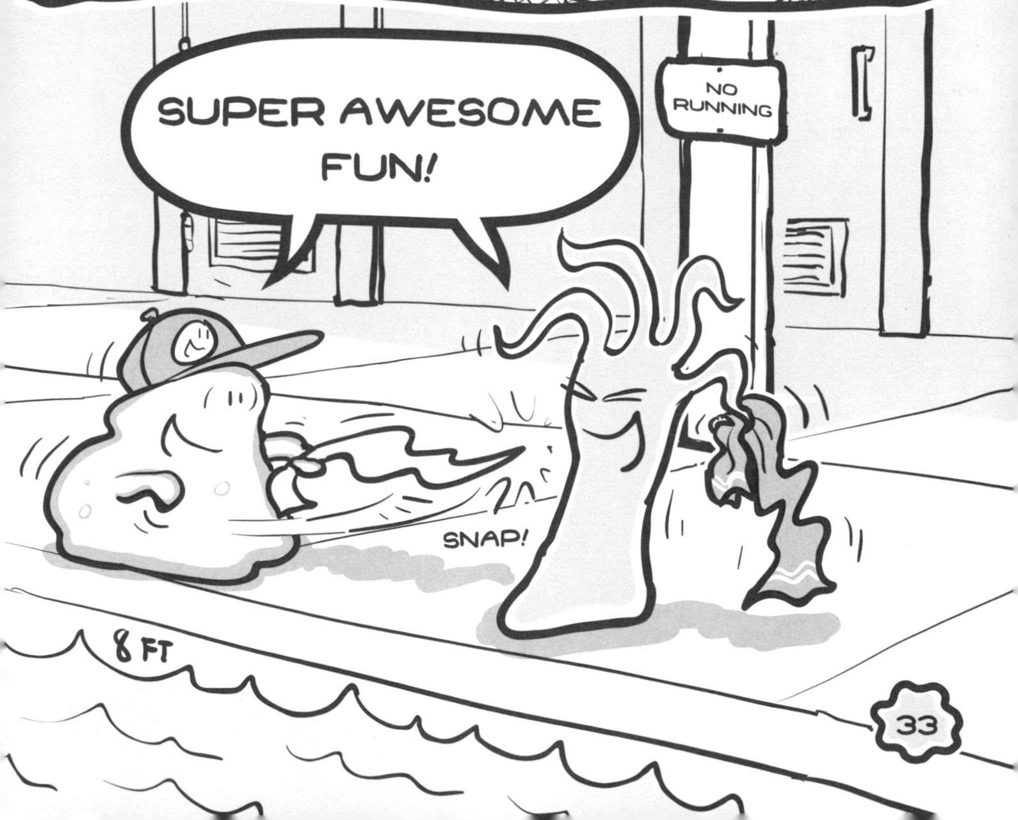
SUPER AWESOME FUN!
NO RUNNING
SNAP!
8 FT

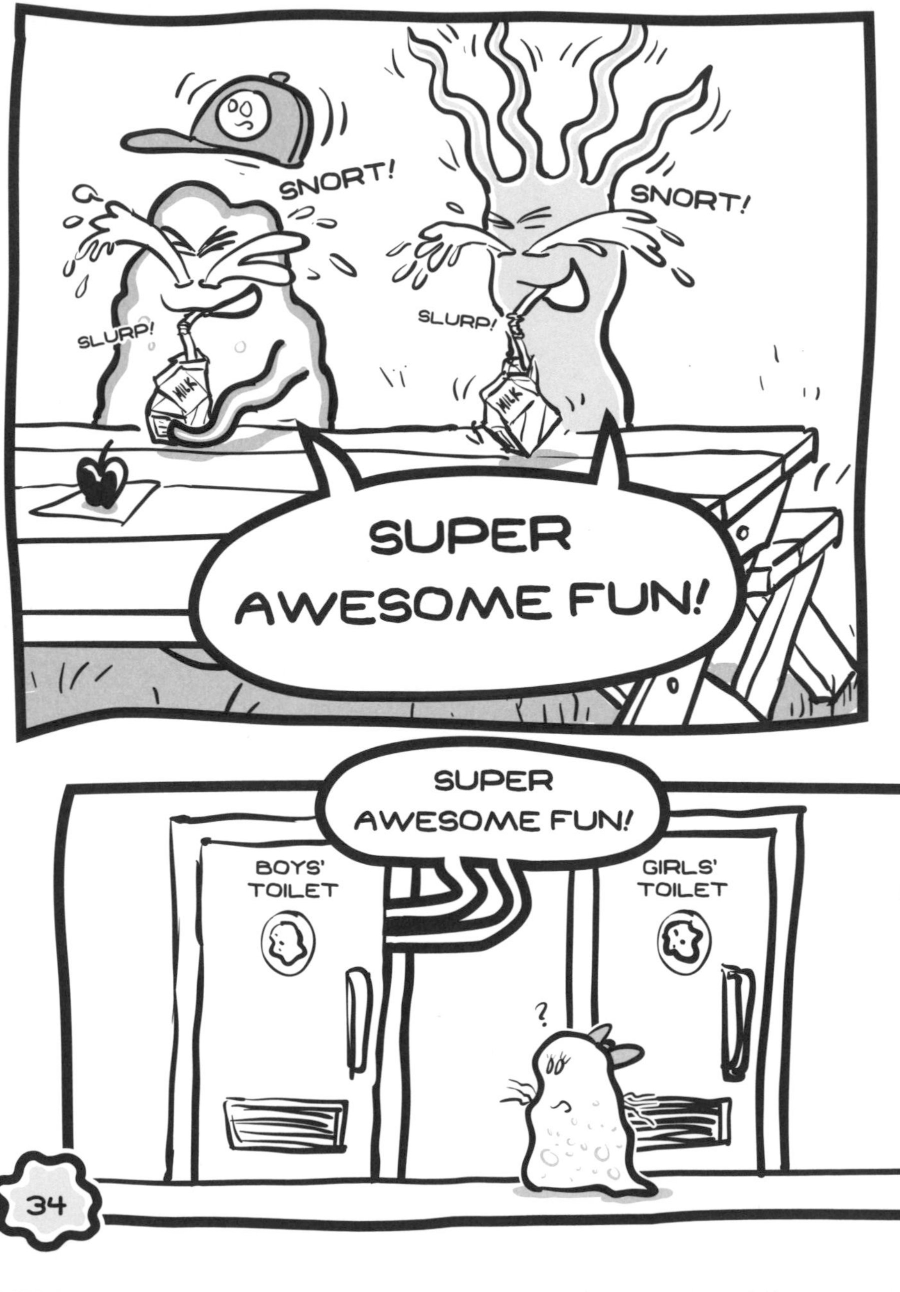
SNORT!
SNORT!
SLURP!
SLURP!
MILK
MILK
SUPER AWESOME FUN!
SUPER AWESOME FUN!
BOYS' TOILET
GIRLS' TOILET
?

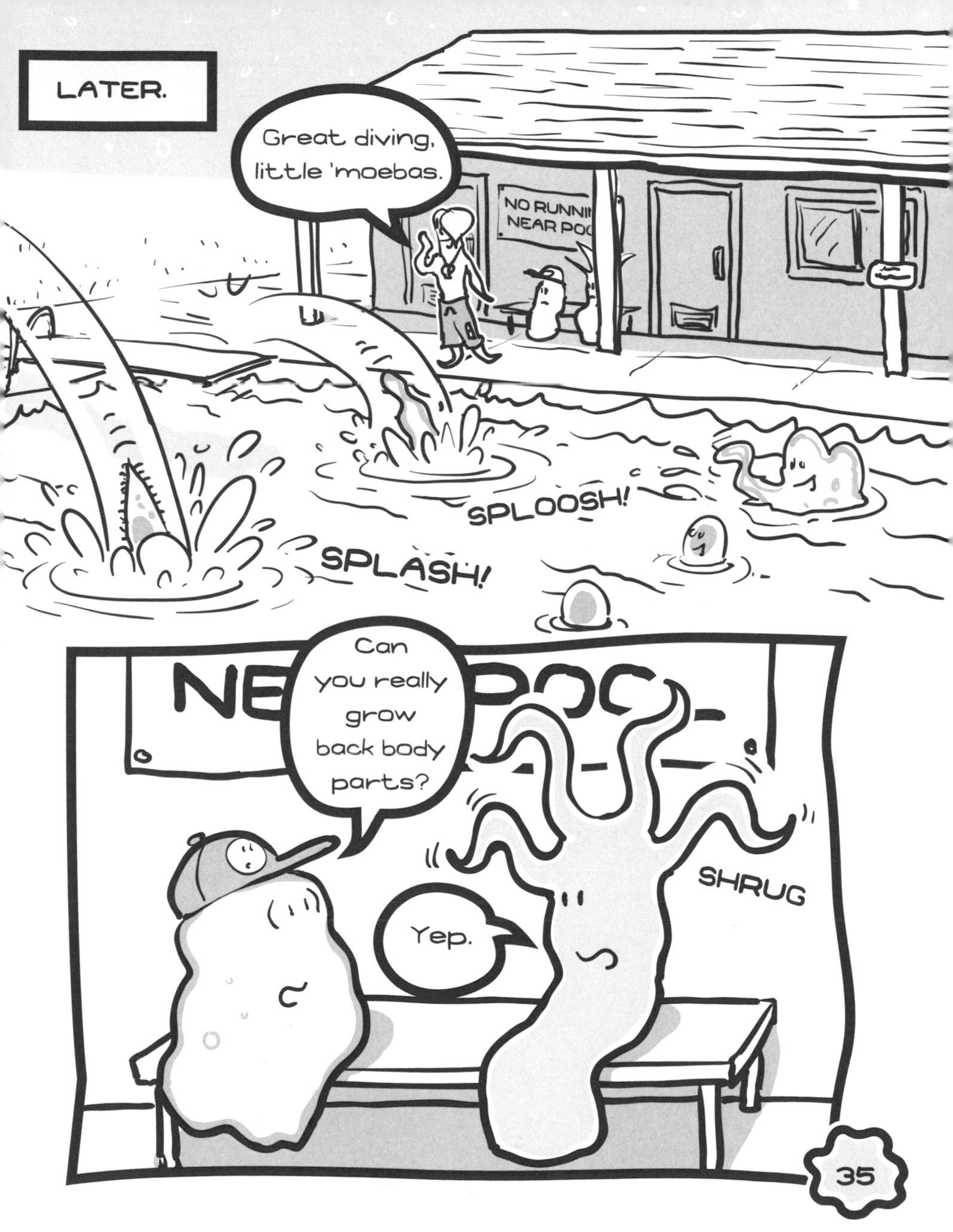
LATER.
Great diving, little 'moebas.
NO RUNNI
NEAR PO
SPLOOSH!
SPLASH!
Can you really grow back body parts?
Yep.
SHRUG

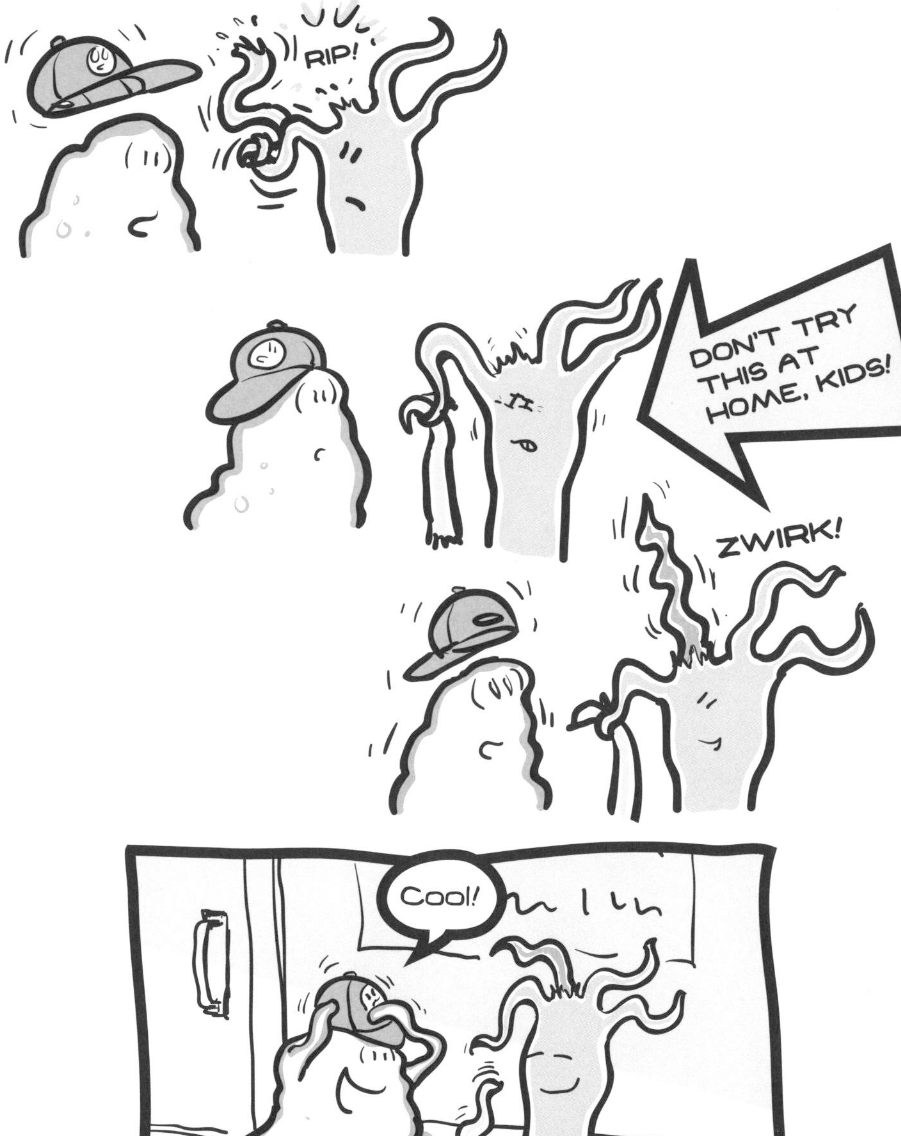
RIP!
DON'T TRY THIS AT HOME, KIDS!
ZWIRK!
Cool!

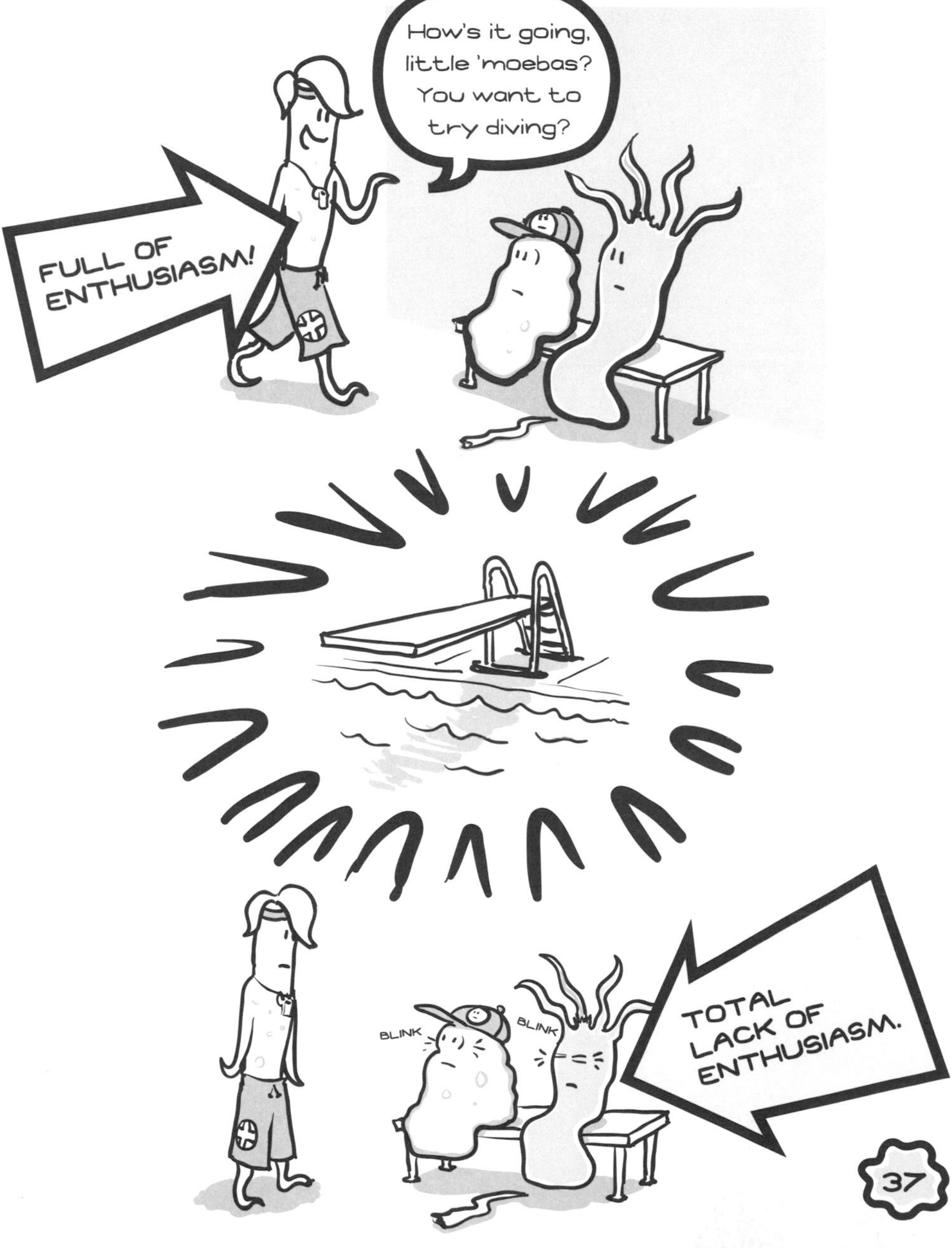
How's it going, little 'moebas? You want to try diving?
FULL OF ENTHUSIASM!
BLINK
BLINK
TOTAL LACK OF ENTHUSIASM.

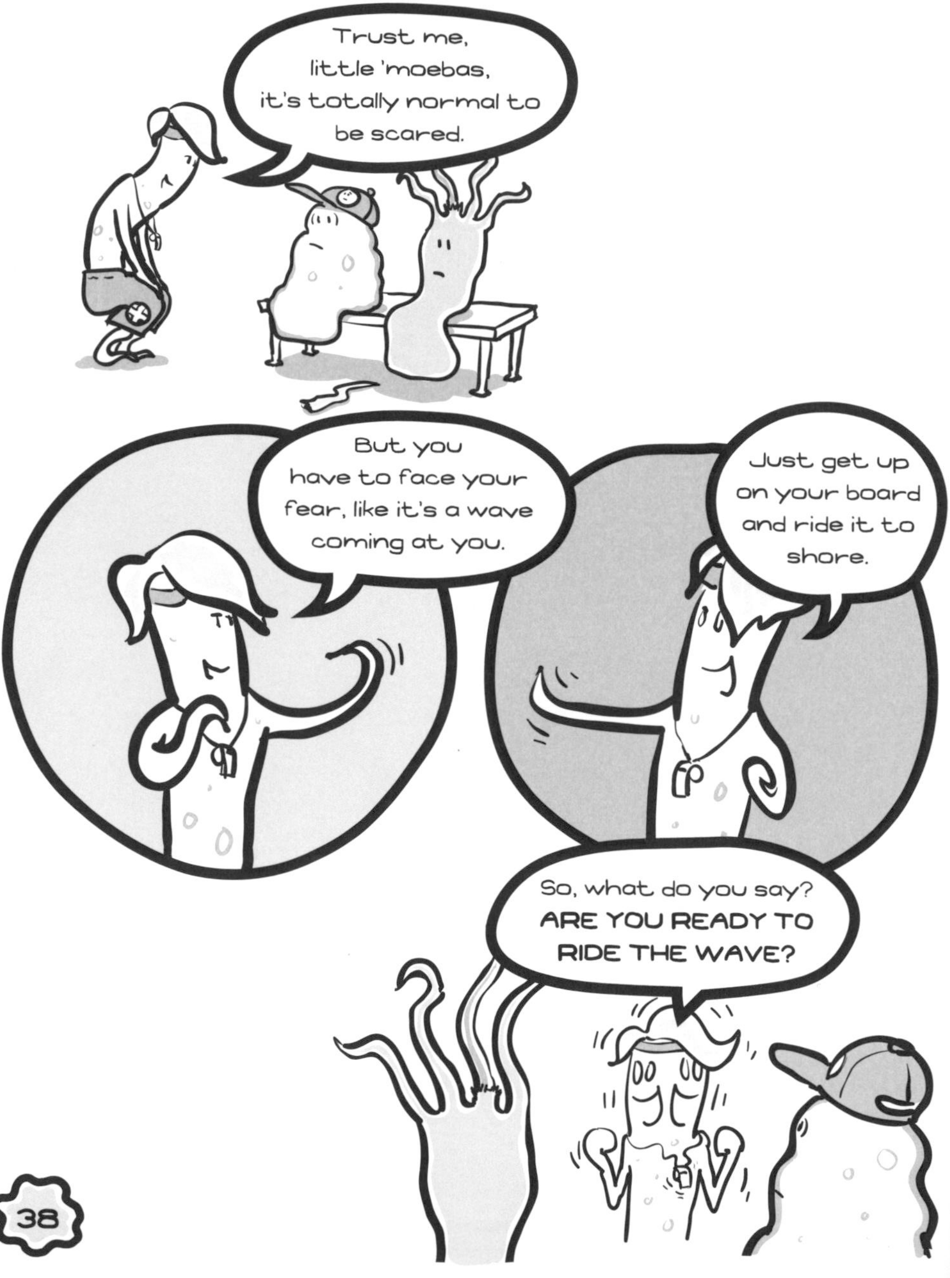
Trust me, little 'moebas, it's totally normal to be scared.
But you have to face your fear, like it's a wave coming at you.
Just get up on your board and ride it to shore.
So, what do you say? ARE YOU READY TO RIDE THE WAVE?

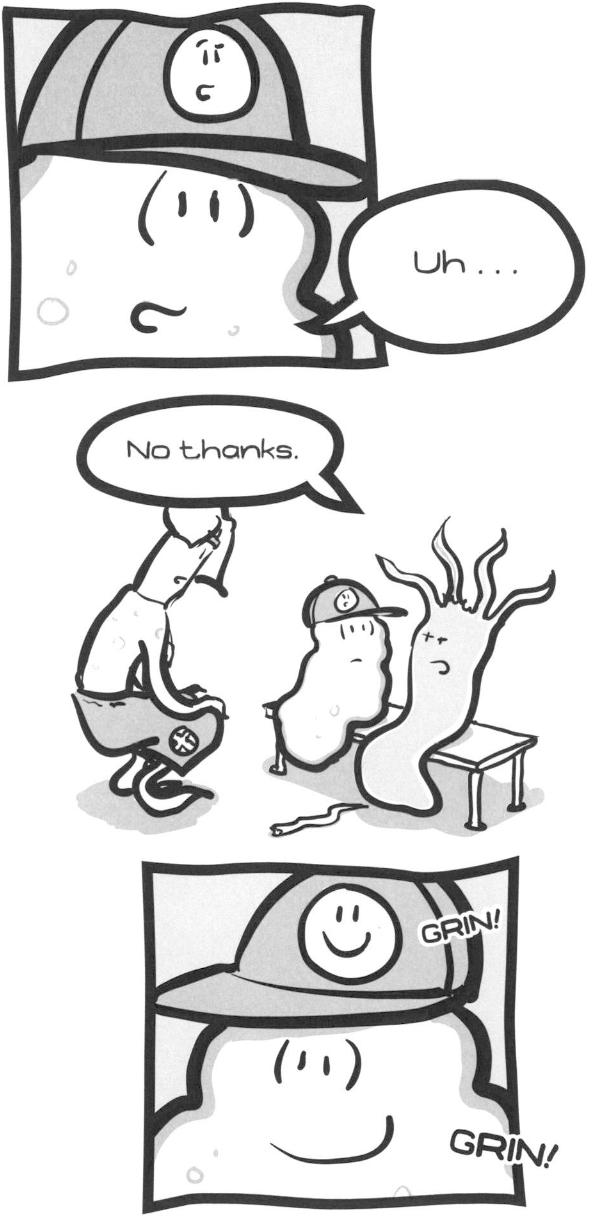
Uh . . .
No thanks.
GRIN!
GRIN!

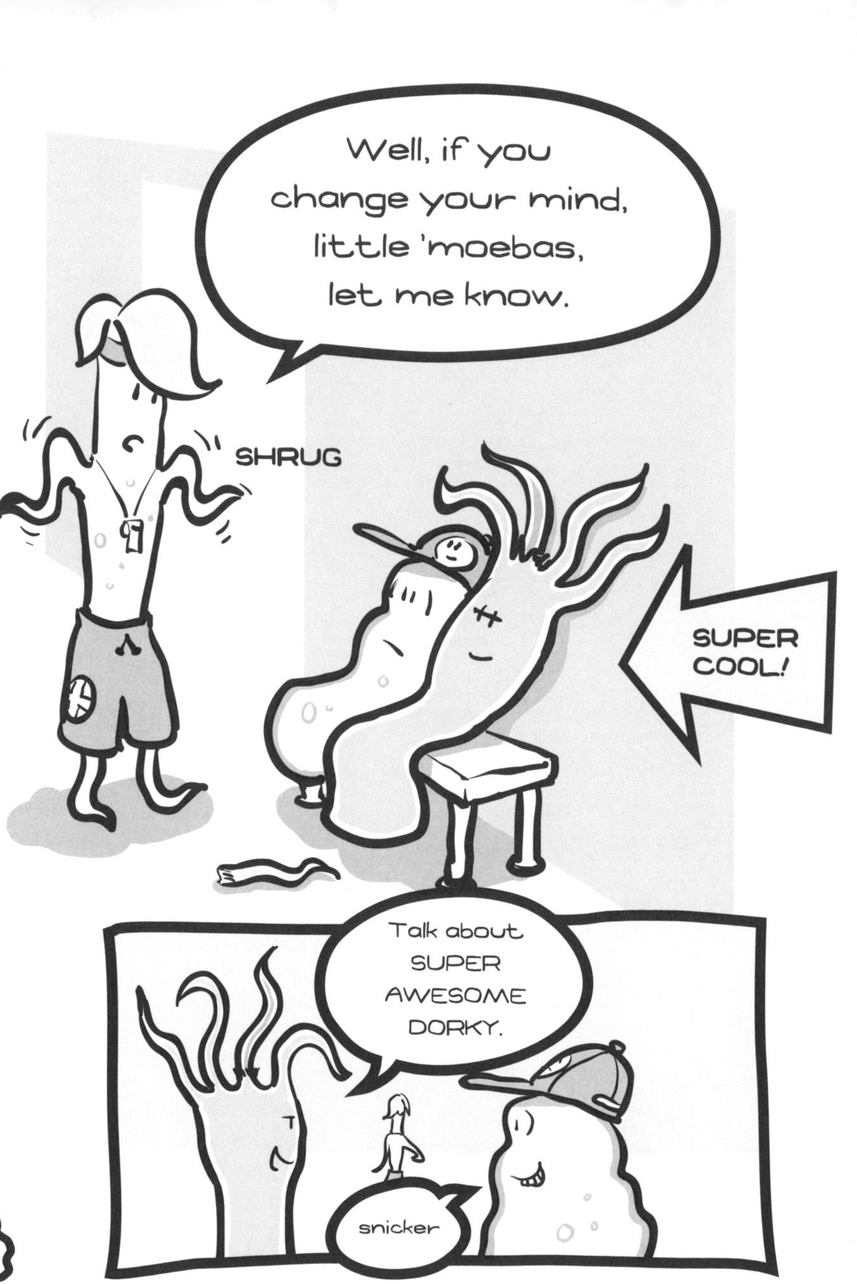
Well, if you change your mind, little 'moebas, let me know.
SHRUG
SUPER COOL!
Talk about SUPER AWESOME DORKY.
snicker

THAT NIGHT.

DUDE! CLEAN UP YOUR ROOM!

MUNCH MUNCH

THE ADVENTURES OF SUPER AM

A NYS FIGURE SUPER PAST! 6

THAT REALLY HIT THE SPOT. MARSHMALLOW AND DOUBLE ANCHOVIES IS MY FAVORITE.

REALLY?

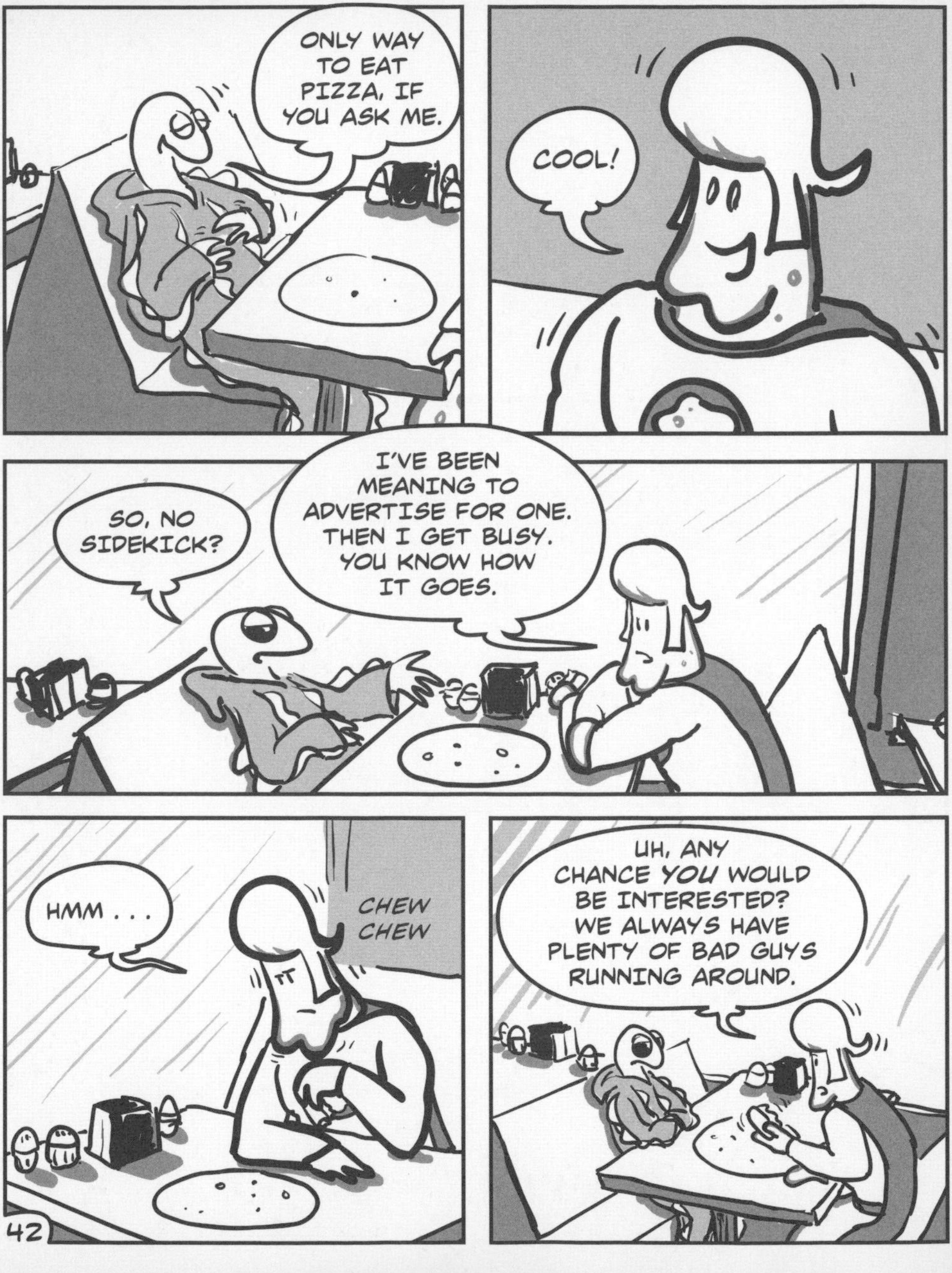
ONLY WAY TO EAT PIZZA, IF YOU ASK ME.
COOL!
SO, NO SIDEKICK?
I'VE BEEN MEANING TO ADVERTISE FOR ONE. THEN I GET BUSY. YOU KNOW HOW IT GOES.
HMM . . .
CHEW CHEW
UH, ANY CHANCE *YOU* WOULD BE INTERESTED? WE ALWAYS HAVE PLENTY OF BAD GUYS RUNNING AROUND.

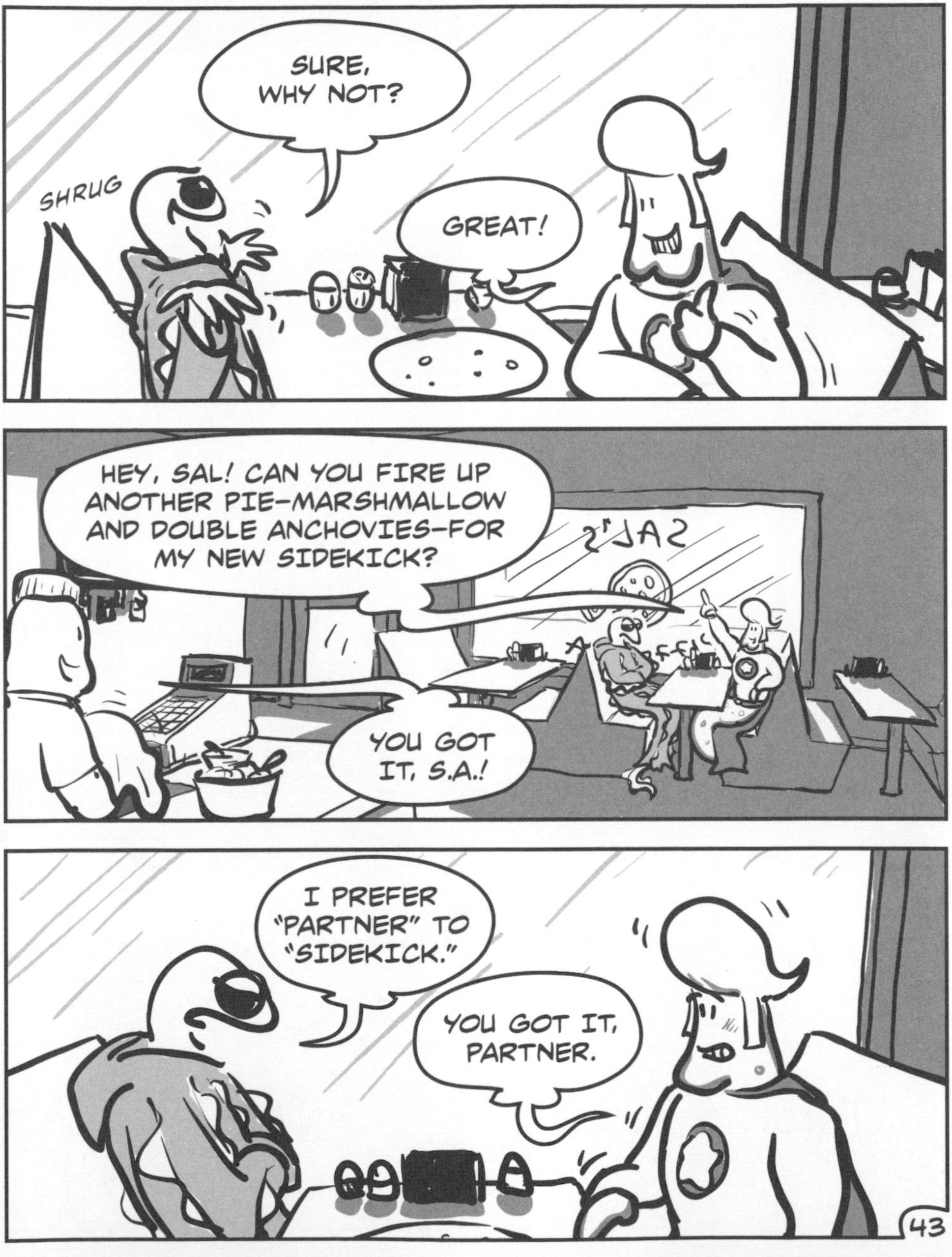
SURE, WHY NOT?
SHRUG
GREAT!
HEY, SAL! CAN YOU FIRE UP ANOTHER PIE–MARSHMALLOW AND DOUBLE ANCHOVIES–FOR MY NEW SIDEKICK?
YOU GOT IT, S.A.!
I PREFER "PARTNER" TO "SIDEKICK."
YOU GOT IT, PARTNER.

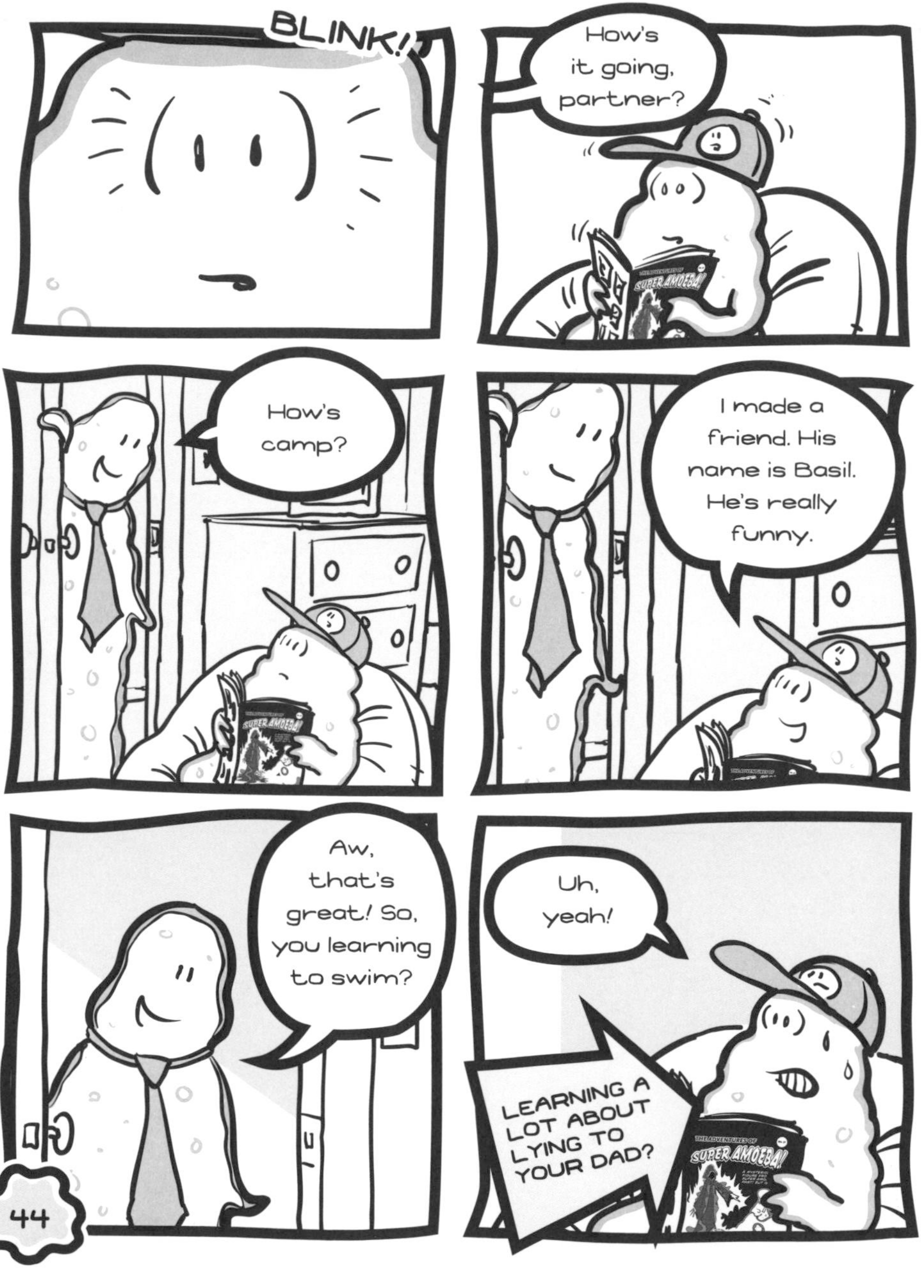
BLINK!
How's it going, partner?
How's camp?
I made a friend. His name is Basil. He's really funny.
Aw, that's great! So, you learning to swim?
Uh, yeah!
LEARNING A LOT ABOUT LYING TO YOUR DAD?
THE ADVENTURES OF SUPER AMOEBA!

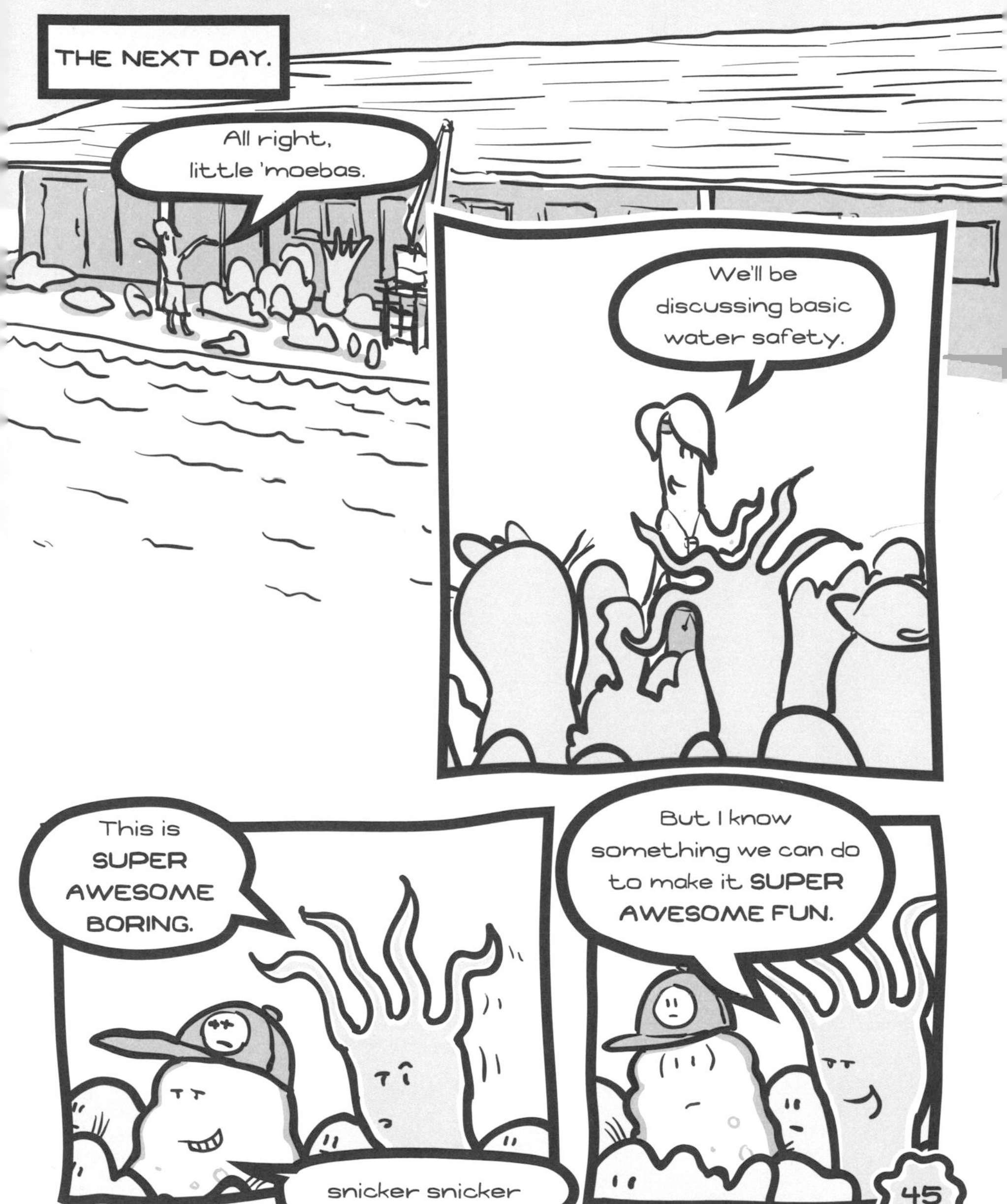
THE NEXT DAY.
All right, little 'moebas.
We'll be discussing basic water safety.
This is SUPER AWESOME BORING.
snicker snicker
But I know something we can do to make it SUPER AWESOME FUN.

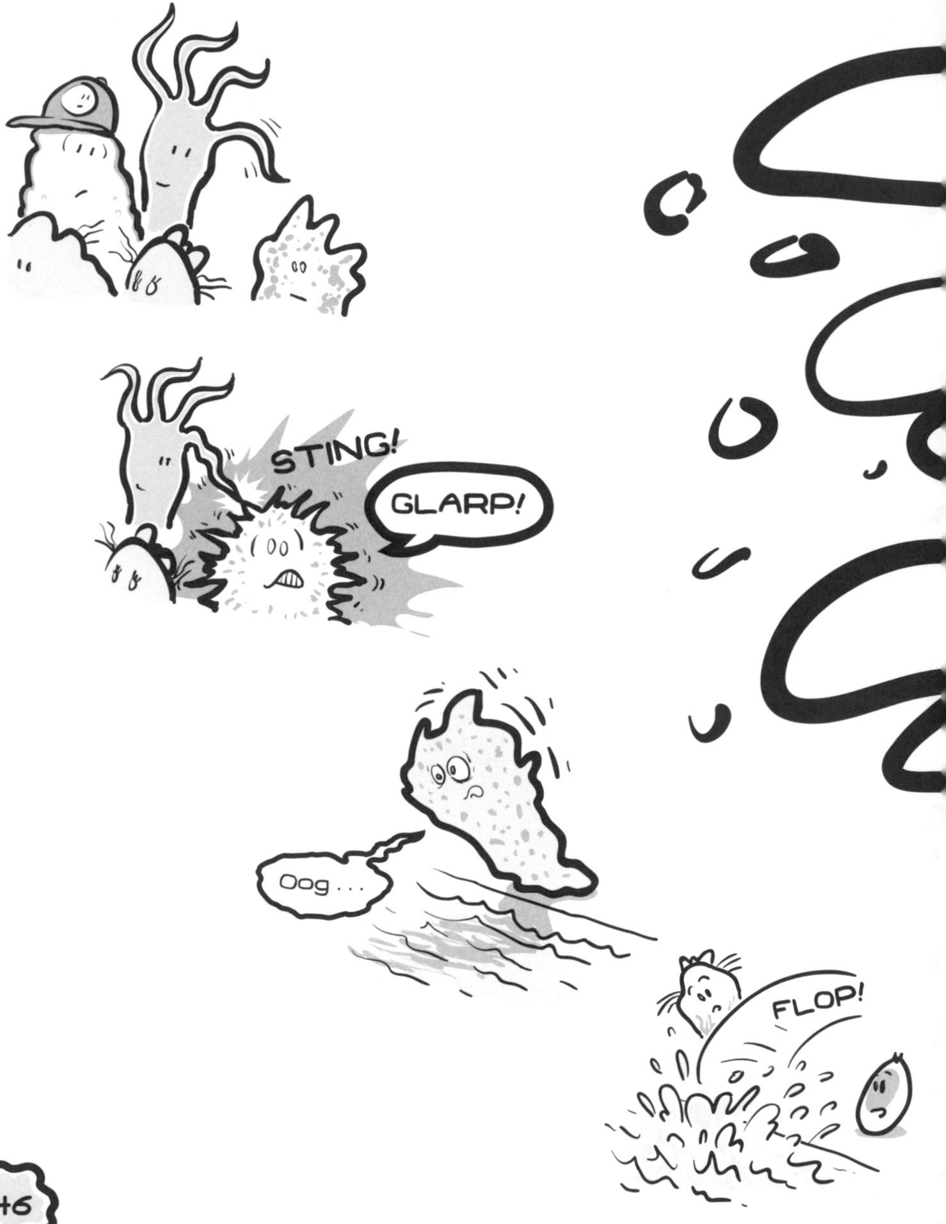
STING!
GLARP!
Oog . . .
FLOP!

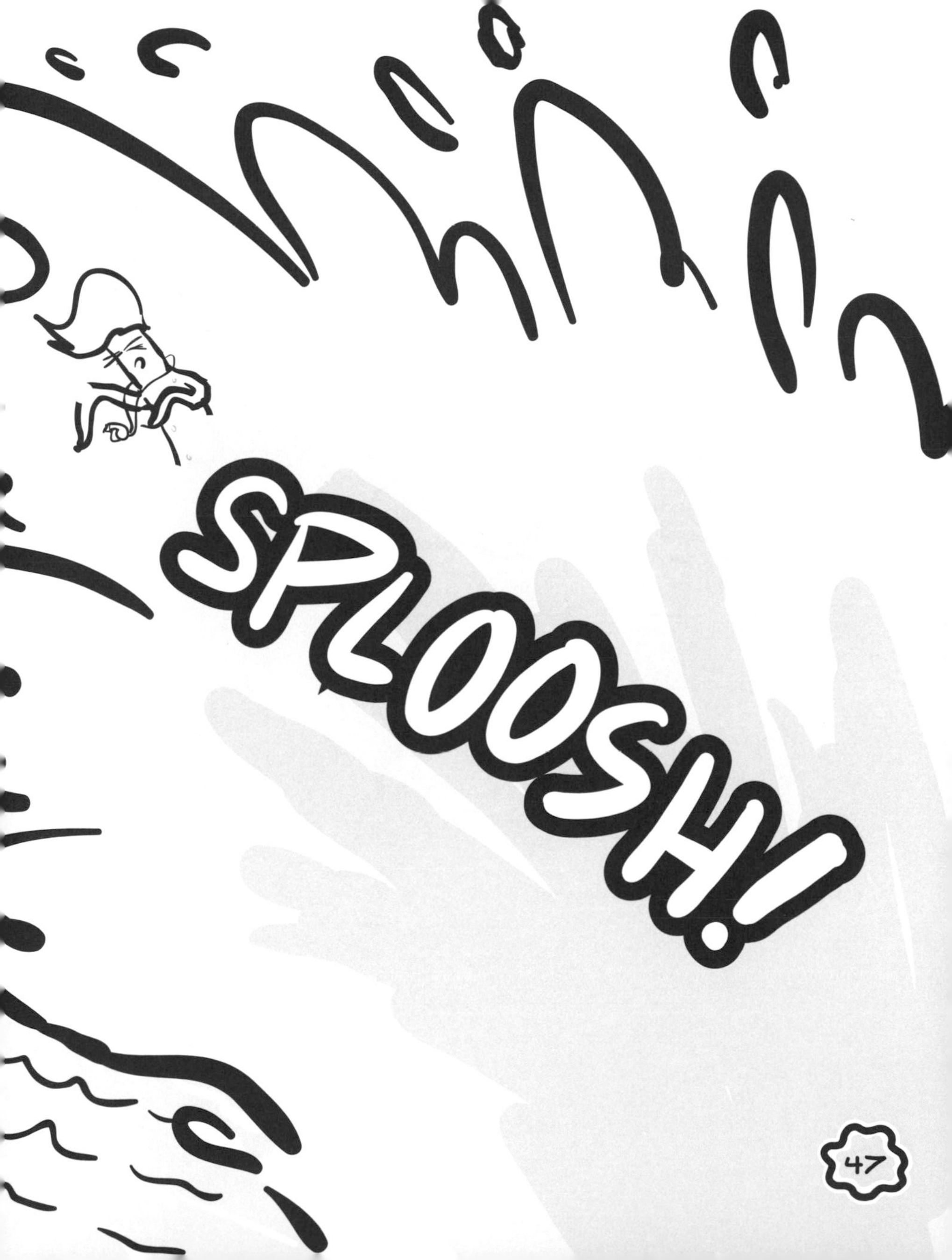
SPLOOSH!

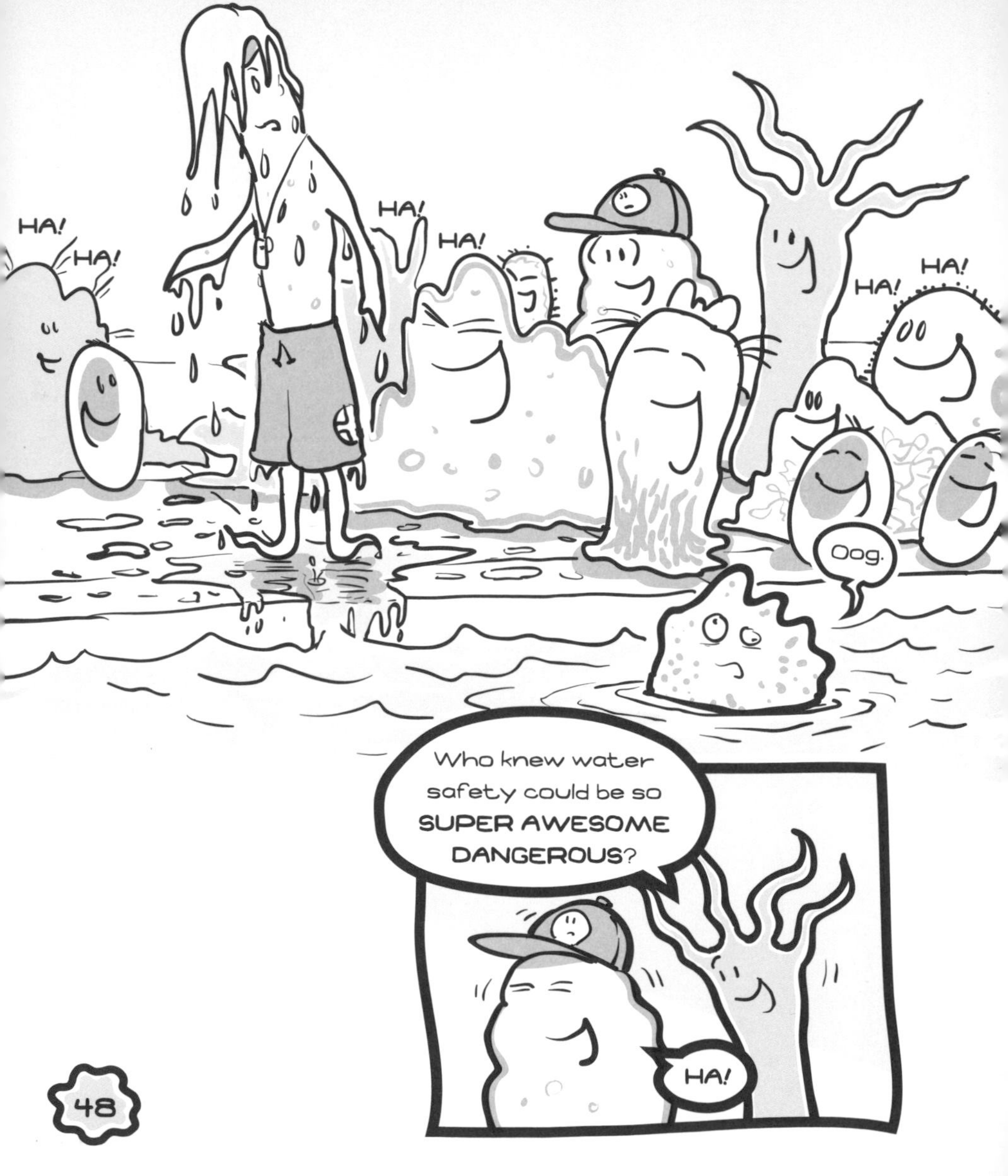
HA!
HA!
HA!
HA!
HA!
HA!
Oog.
Who knew water safety could be so SUPER AWESOME DANGEROUS?
HA!

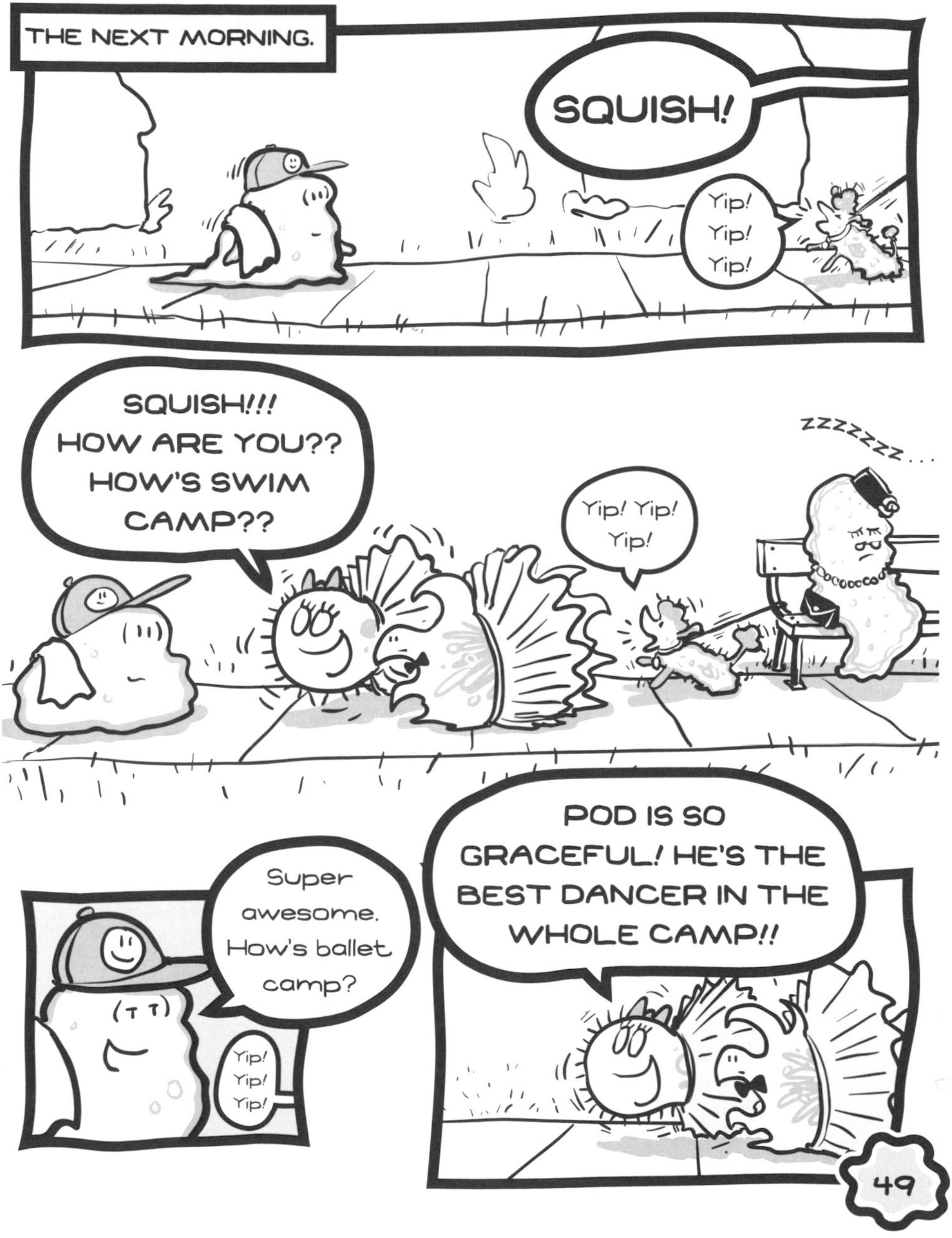
THE NEXT MORNING.
SQUISH!
Yip! Yip! Yip!
SQUISH!!! HOW ARE YOU?? HOW'S SWIM CAMP??
Yip! Yip! Yip!
ZZZZZZZ...
Super awesome. How's ballet camp?
Yip! Yip! Yip!
POD IS SO GRACEFUL! HE'S THE BEST DANCER IN THE WHOLE CAMP!!

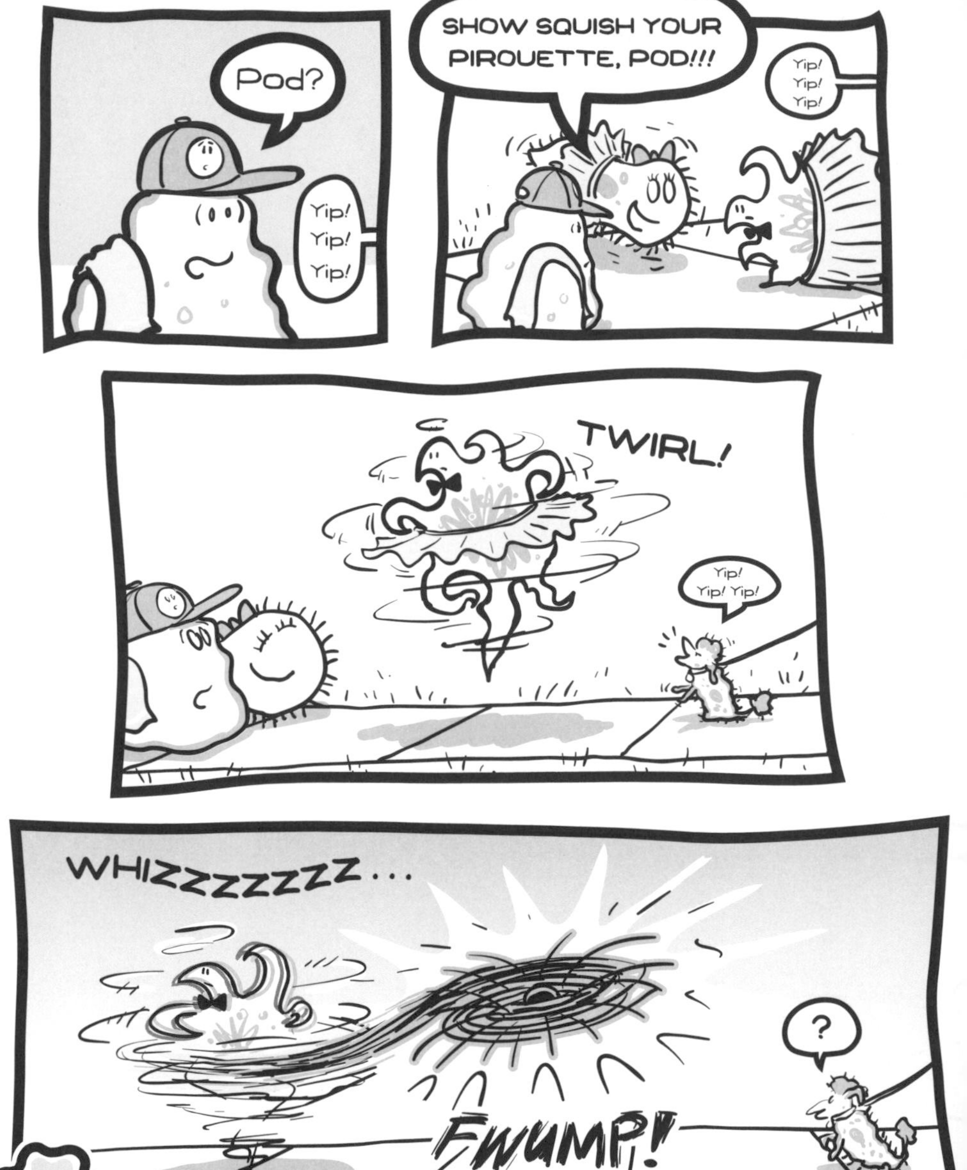
Pod?
Yip! Yip! Yip!
SHOW SQUISH YOUR PIROUETTE, POD!!!
Yip! Yip! Yip!
TWIRL!
Yip! Yip! Yip!
WHIZZZZZZZZ...
?
FWUMP!

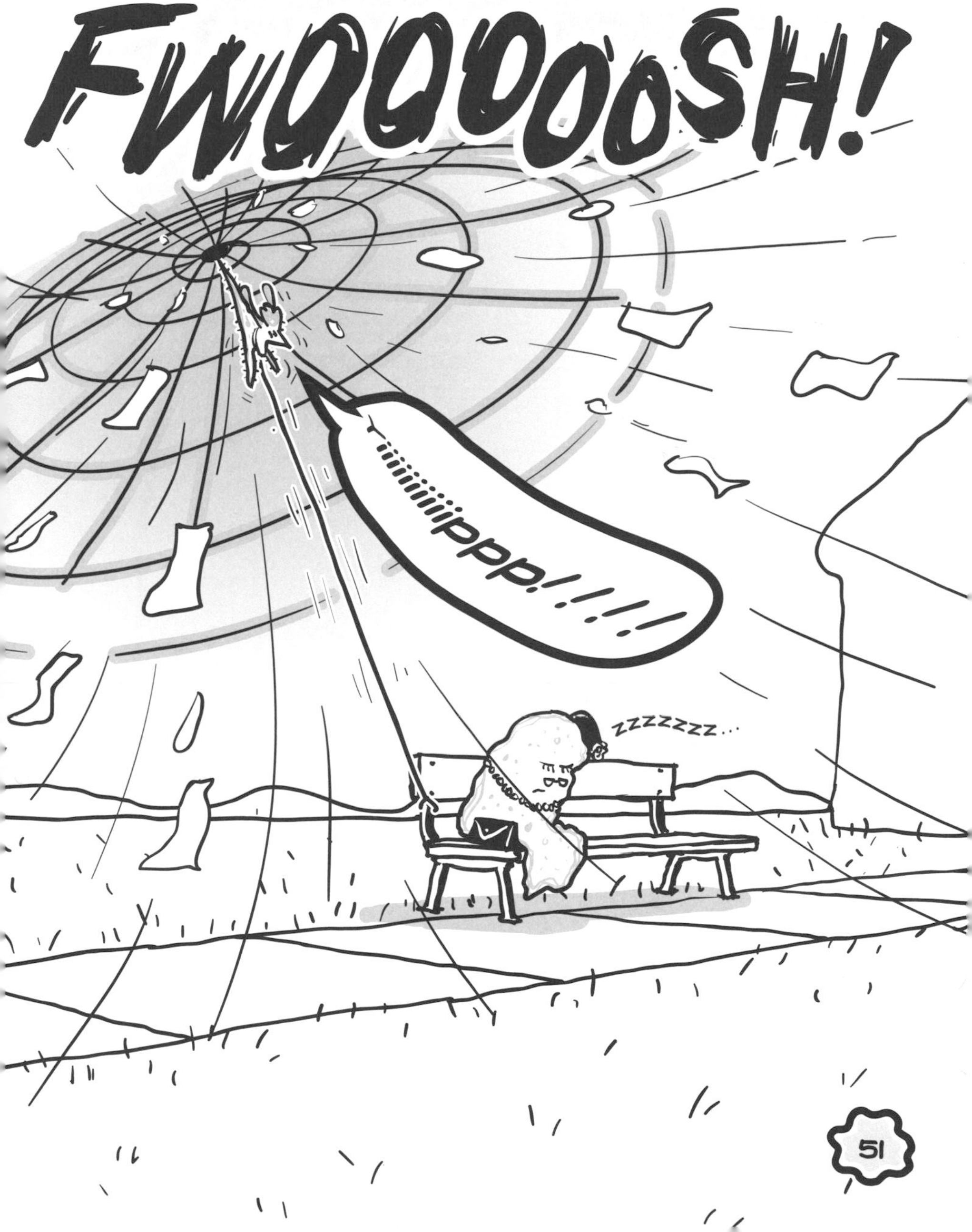
FWOOOOOSH!
riiiiiiiiiippp!!!!
ZZZZZZZ...

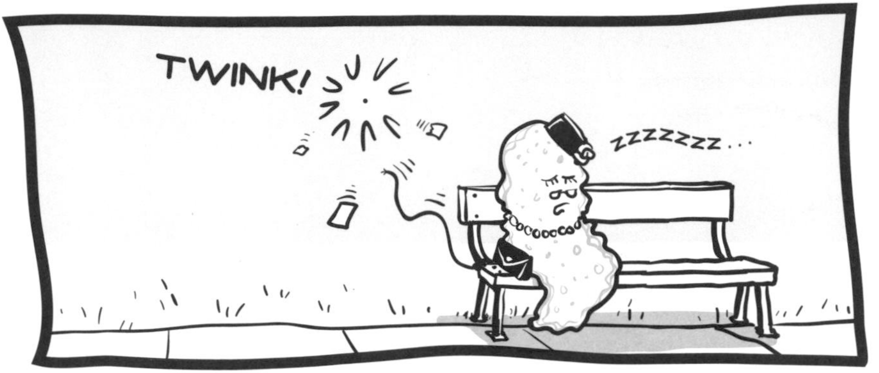
TWINK!
ZZZZZZZ...

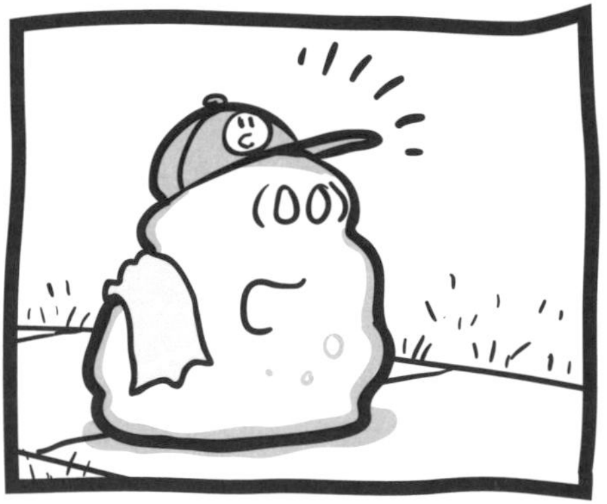

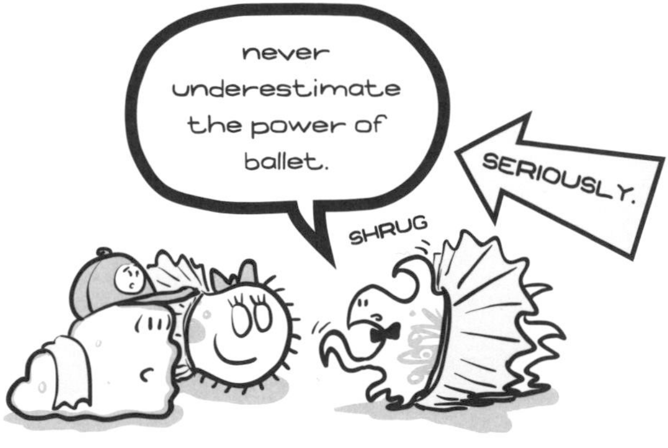
never underestimate the power of ballet.
SERIOUSLY.
SHRUG

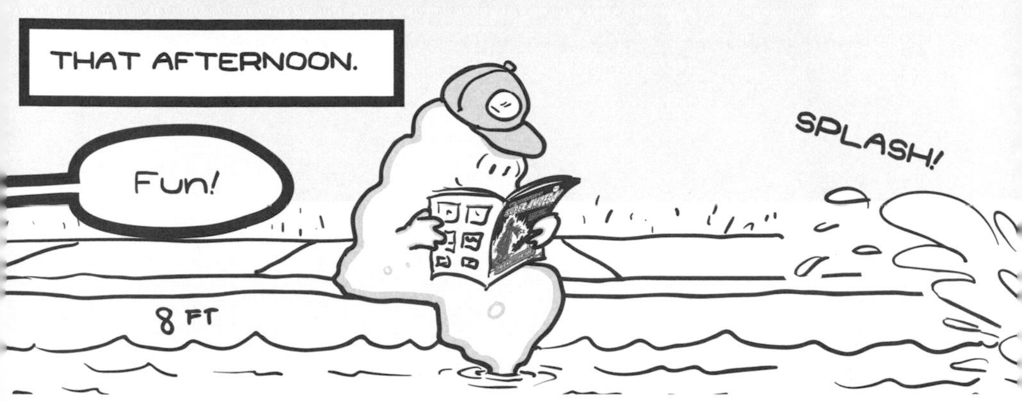
THAT AFTERNOON.
Fun!
SPLASH!
8 FT

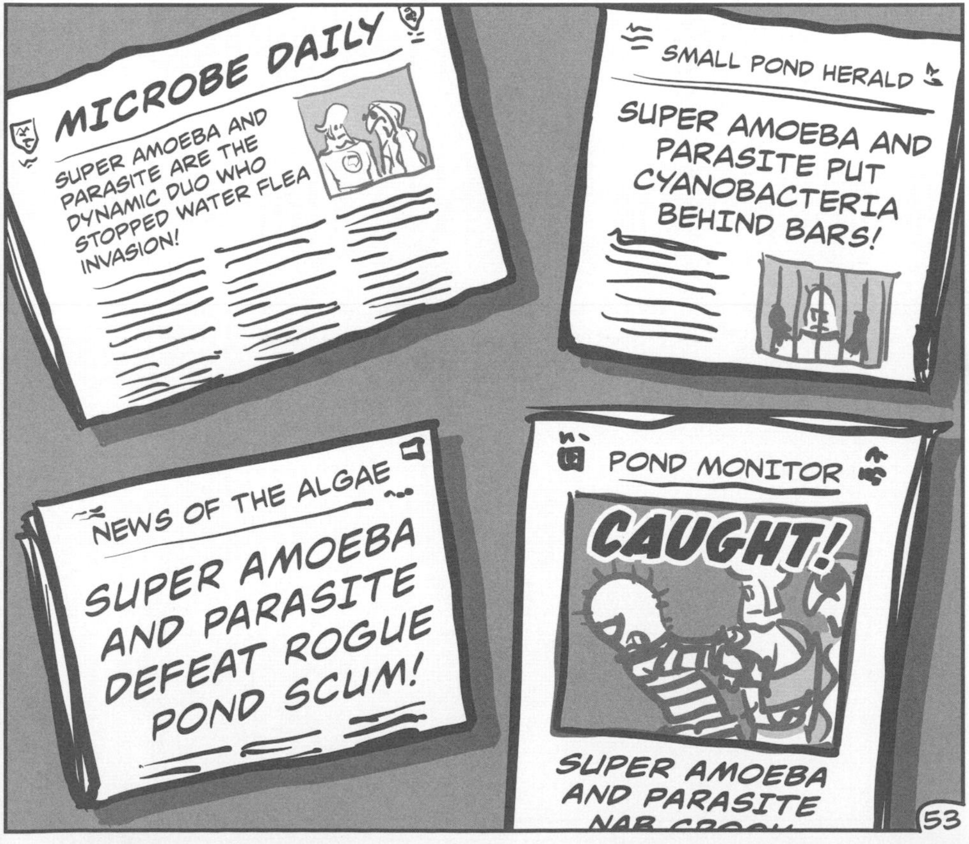
MICROBE DAILY
SUPER AMOEBA AND PARASITE ARE THE DYNAMIC DUO WHO STOPPED WATER FLEA INVASION!
SMALL POND HERALD
SUPER AMOEBA AND PARASITE PUT CYANOBACTERIA BEHIND BARS!
NEWS OF THE ALGAE
SUPER AMOEBA AND PARASITE DEFEAT ROGUE POND SCUM!
POND MONITOR
CAUGHT!
SUPER AMOEBA AND PARASITE

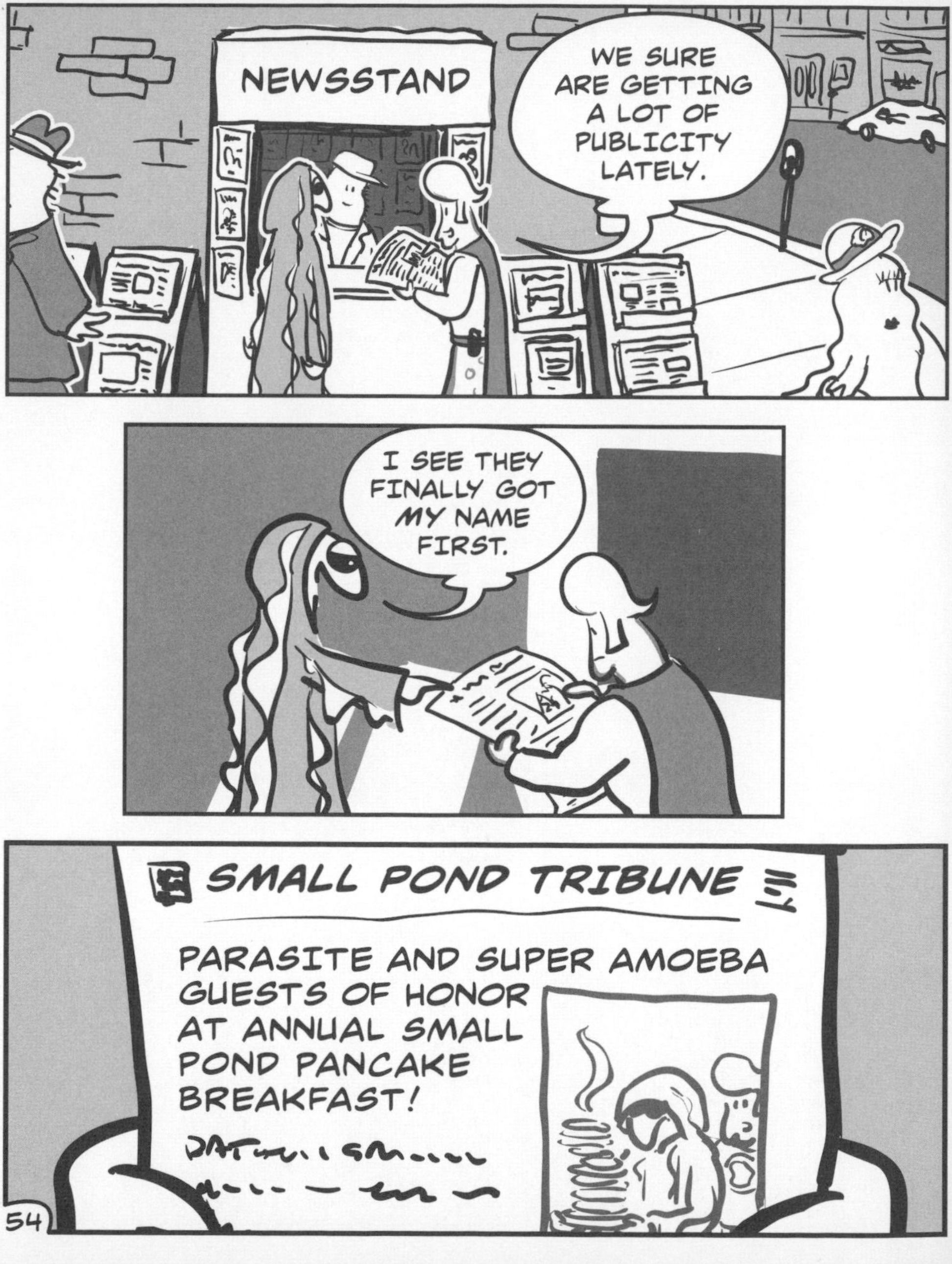
NEWSSTAND
WE SURE ARE GETTING A LOT OF PUBLICITY LATELY.
I SEE THEY FINALLY GOT *MY* NAME FIRST.
SMALL POND TRIBUNE
PARASITE AND SUPER AMOEBA GUESTS OF HONOR AT ANNUAL SMALL POND PANCAKE BREAKFAST!

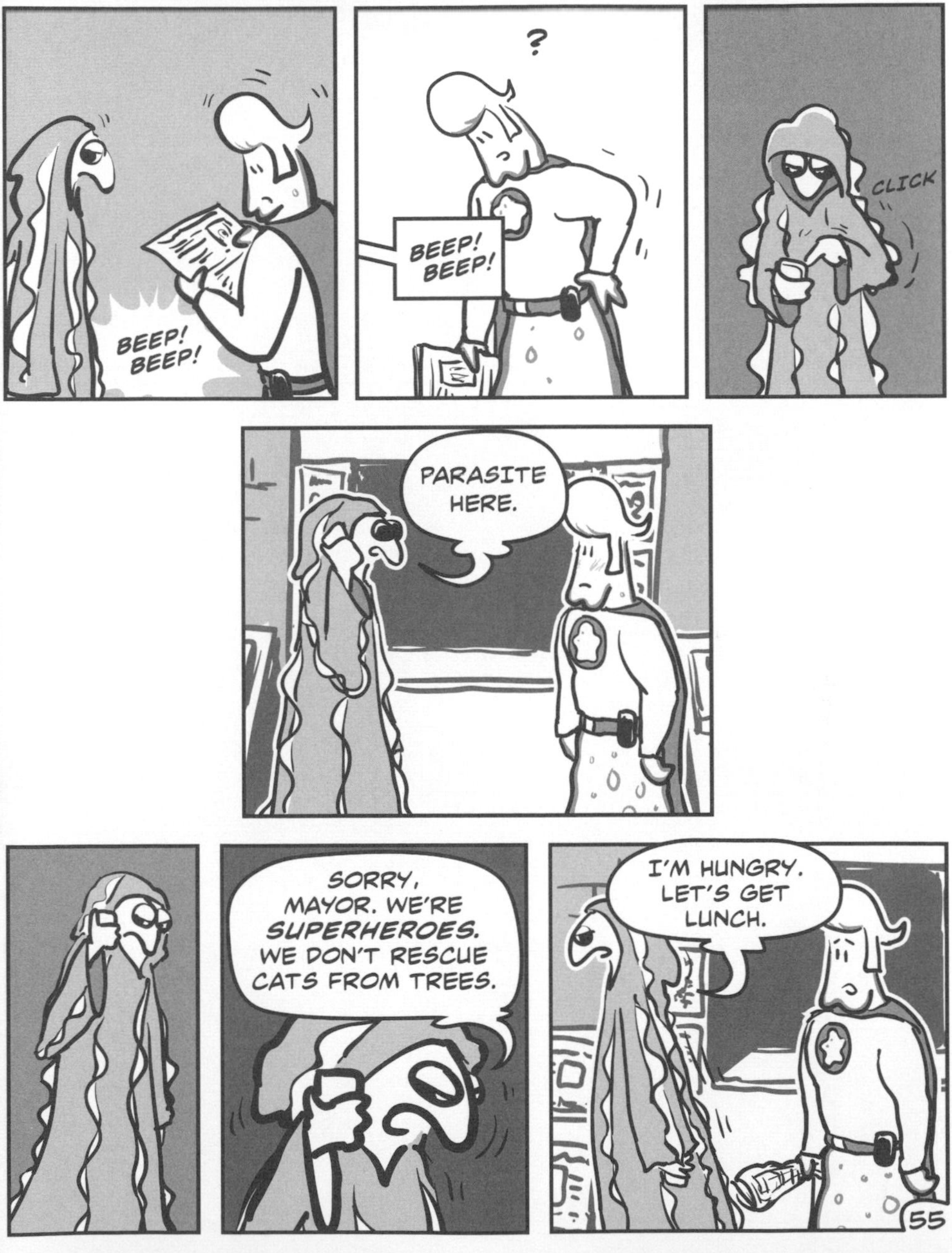

BEEP! BEEP!
?
BEEP! BEEP!
CLICK
PARASITE HERE.
SORRY, MAYOR. WE'RE SUPERHEROES. WE DON'T RESCUE CATS FROM TREES.
I'M HUNGRY. LET'S GET LUNCH.

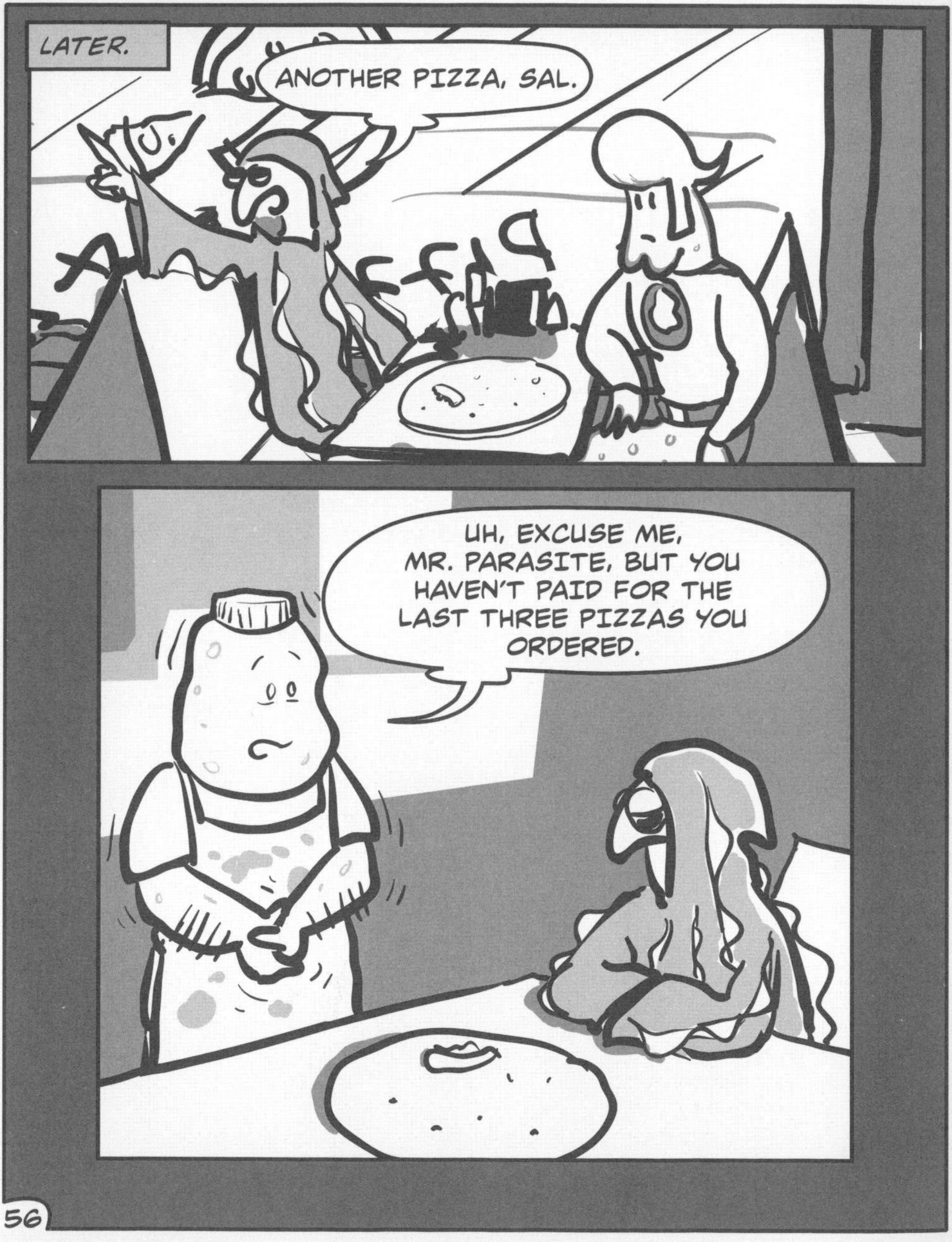
LATER.
ANOTHER PIZZA, SAL.
UH, EXCUSE ME, MR. PARASITE, BUT YOU HAVEN'T PAID FOR THE LAST THREE PIZZAS YOU ORDERED.

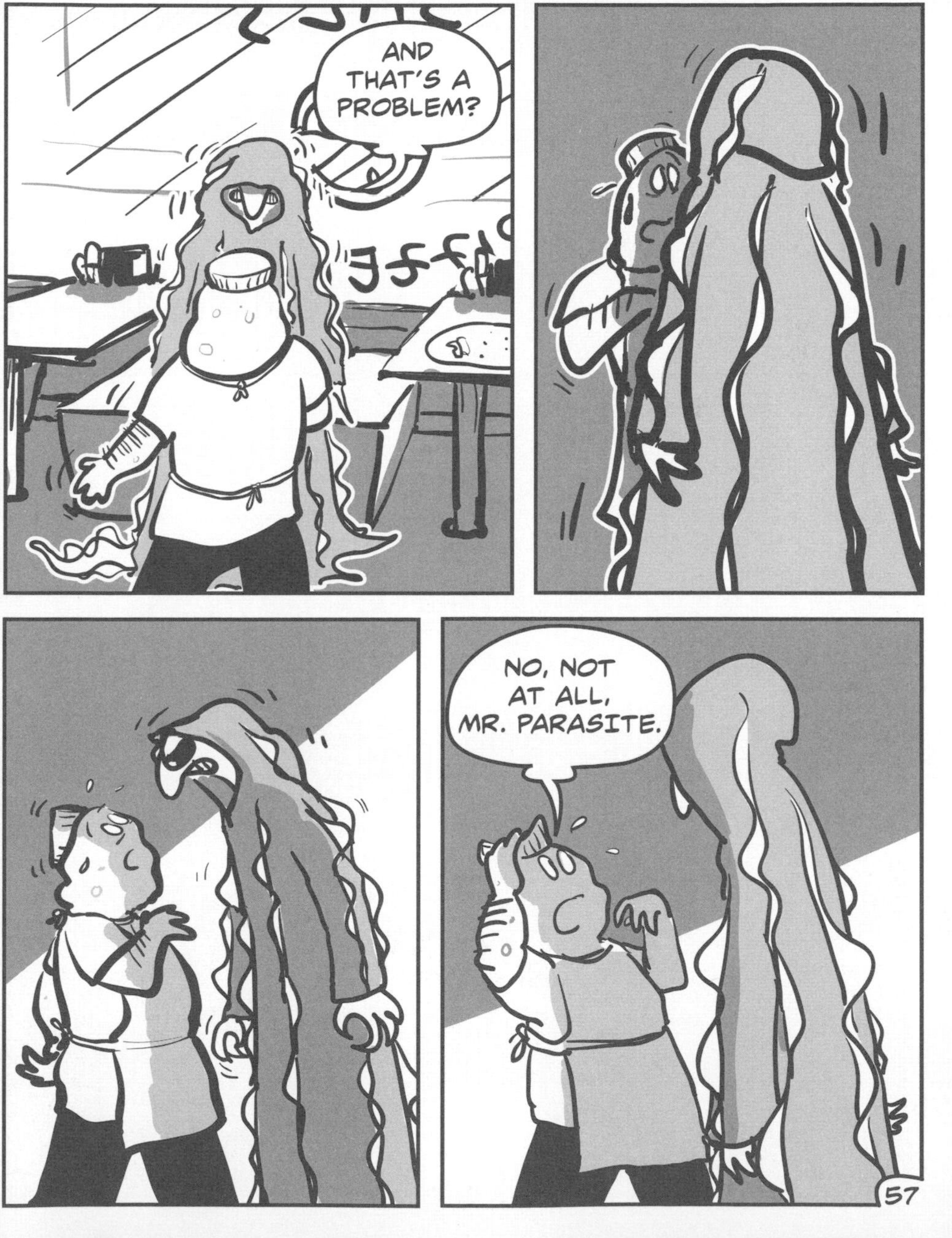
AND THAT'S A PROBLEM?
NO, NOT AT ALL, MR. PARASITE.

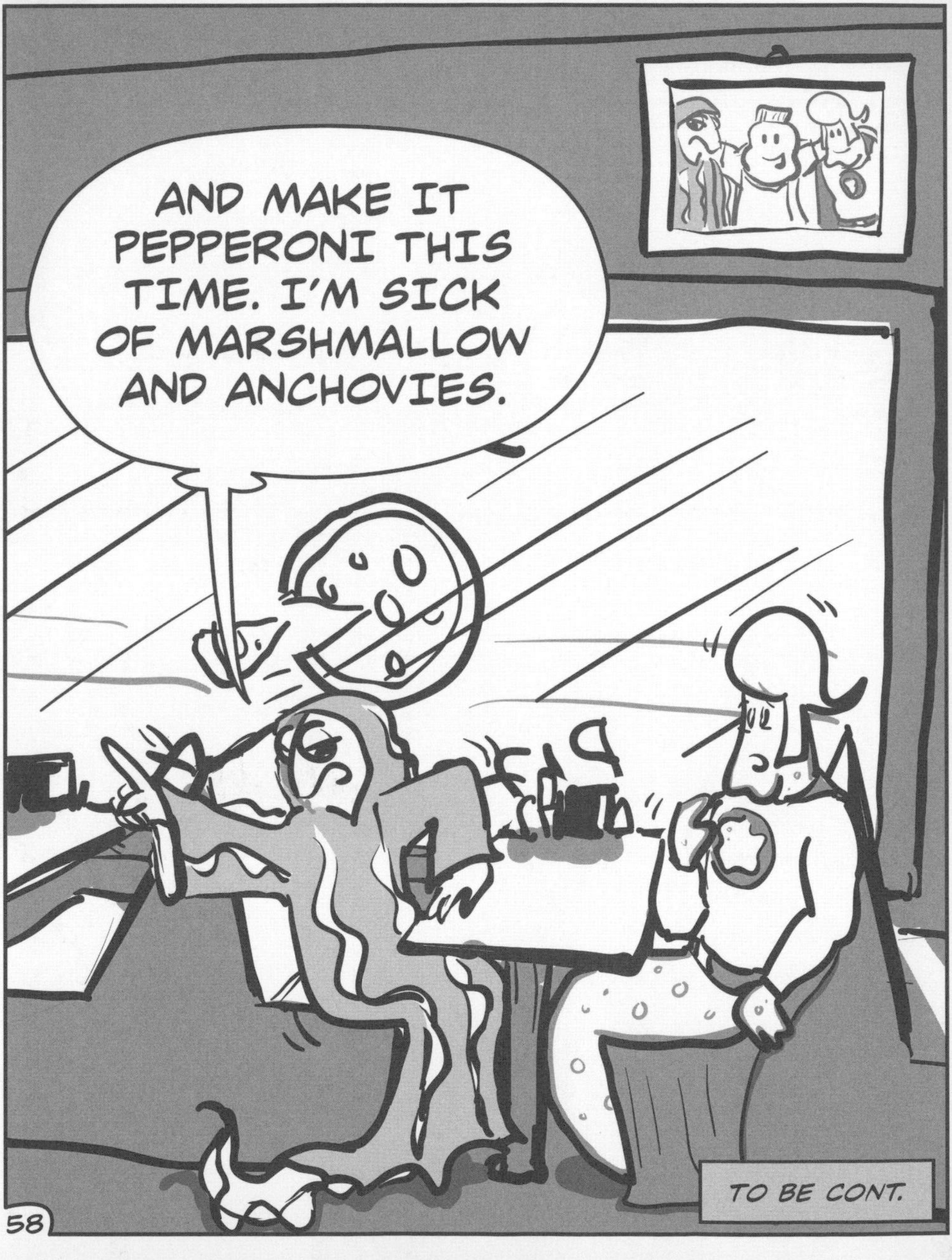
AND MAKE IT PEPPERONI THIS TIME. I'M SICK OF MARSHMALLOW AND ANCHOVIES.
TO BE CONT.

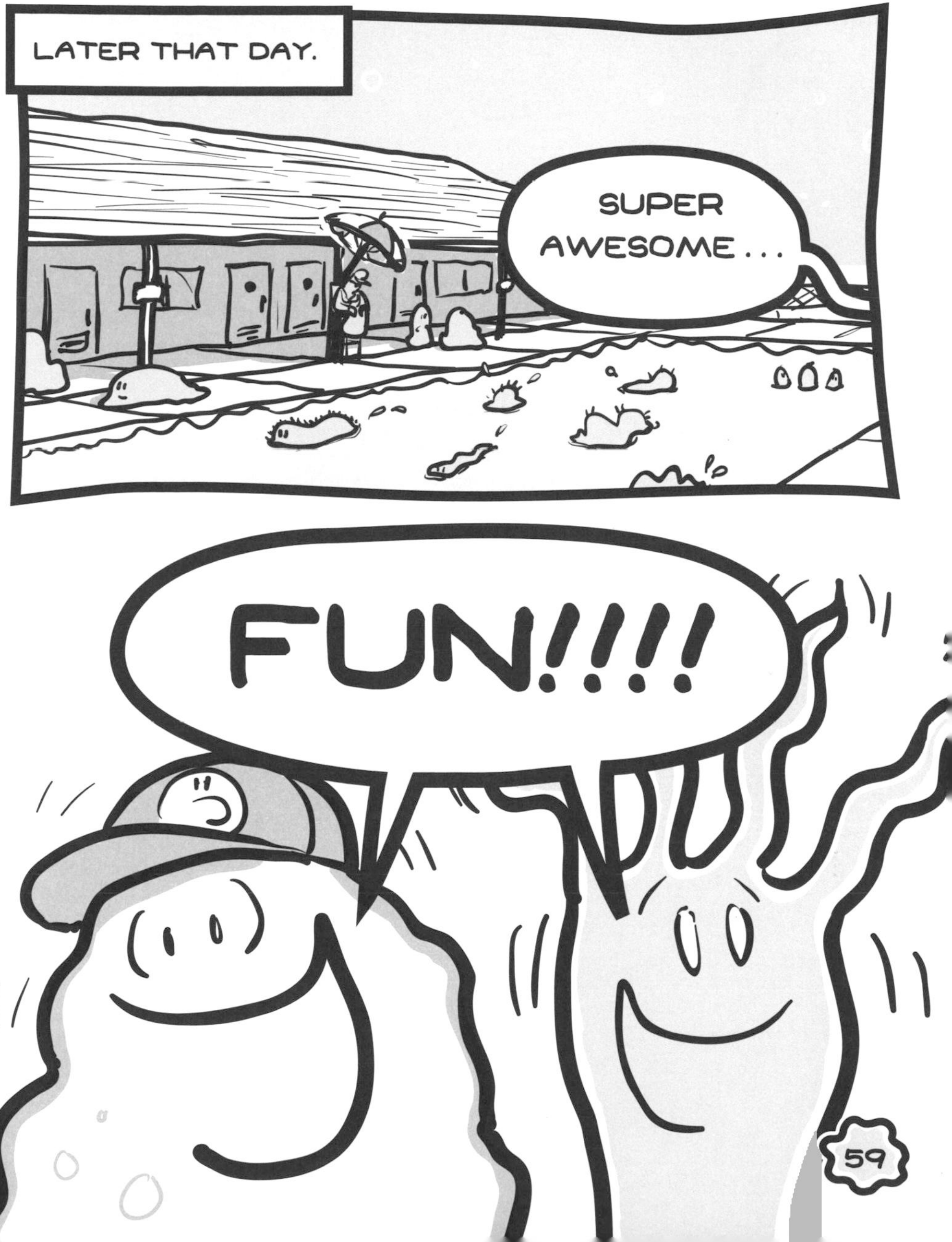
LATER THAT DAY.
SUPER AWESOME . . .
FUN!!!!

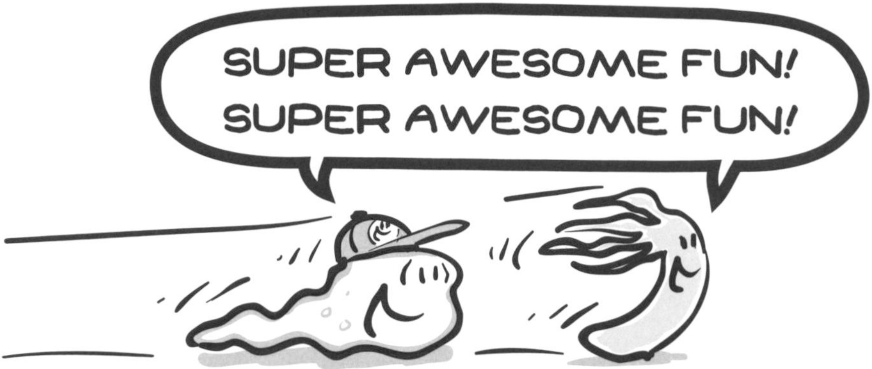
SUPER AWESOME FUN!
SUPER AWESOME FUN!

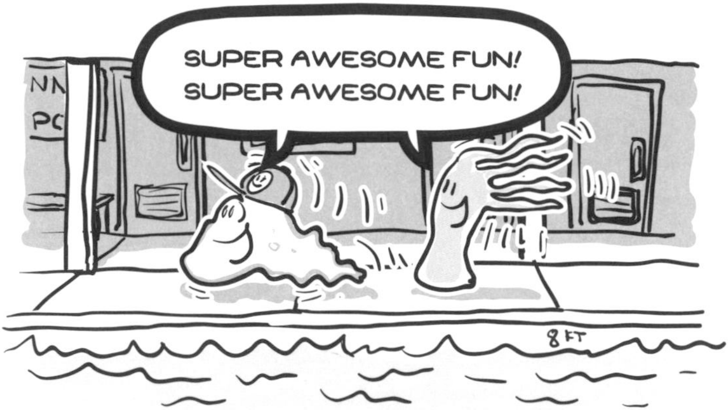
SUPER AWESOME FUN!
SUPER AWESOME FUN!
8 FT

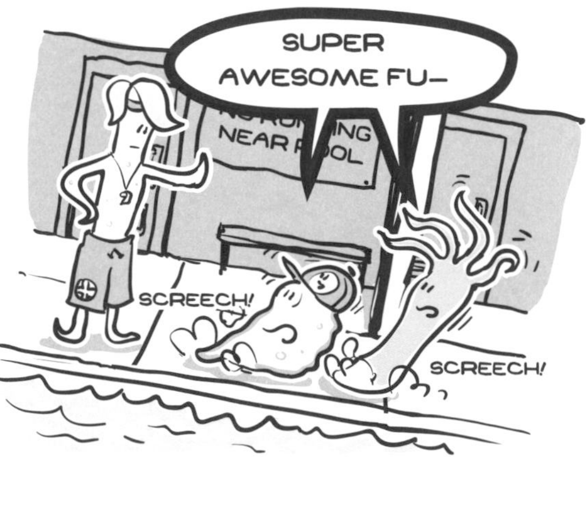
SUPER
AWESOME FU–
SCREECH!
SCREECH!

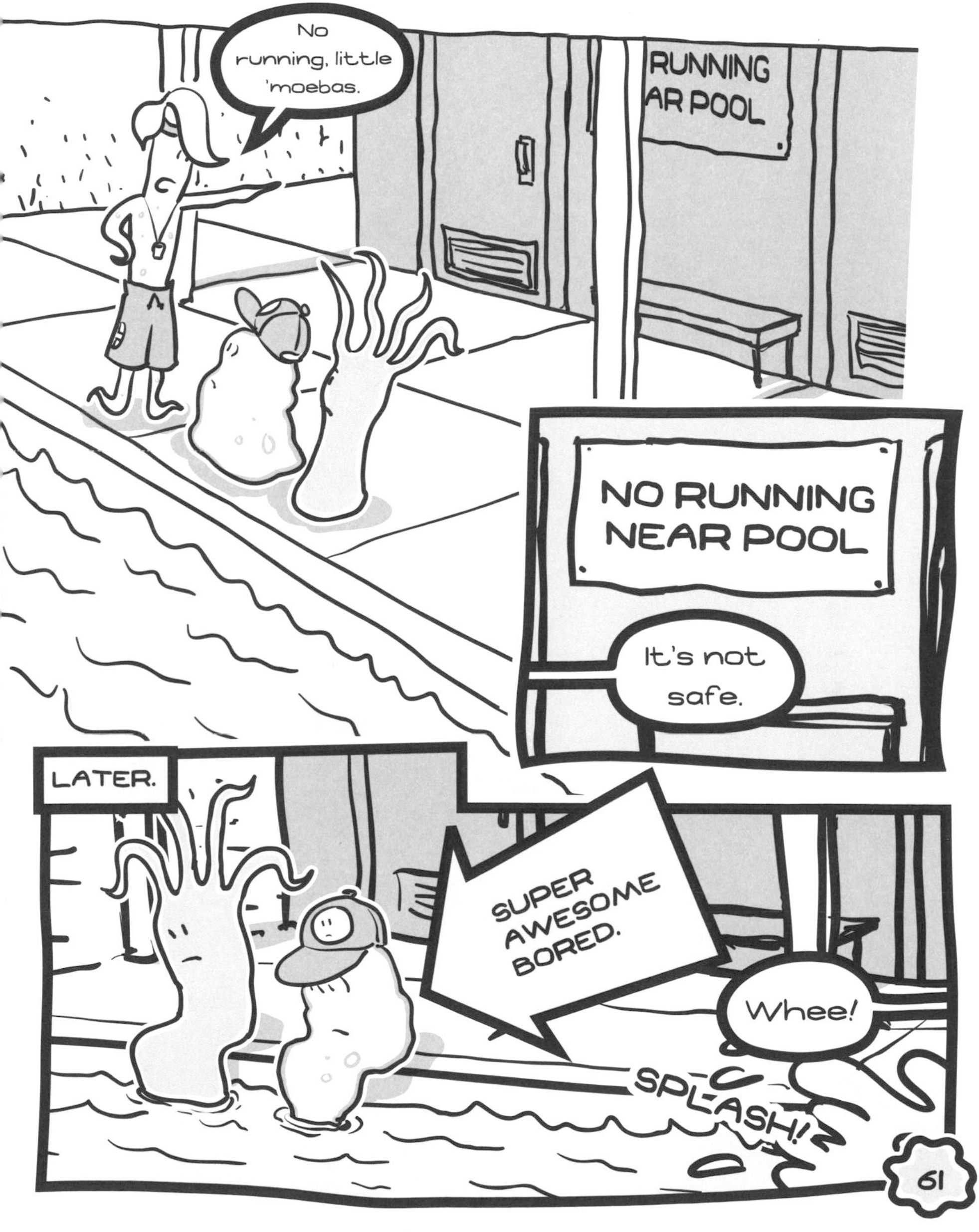
No running, little 'moebas.
RUNNING
AR POOL
NO RUNNING NEAR POOL
It's not safe.
LATER.
SUPER AWESOME BORED.
Whee!
SPLASH!

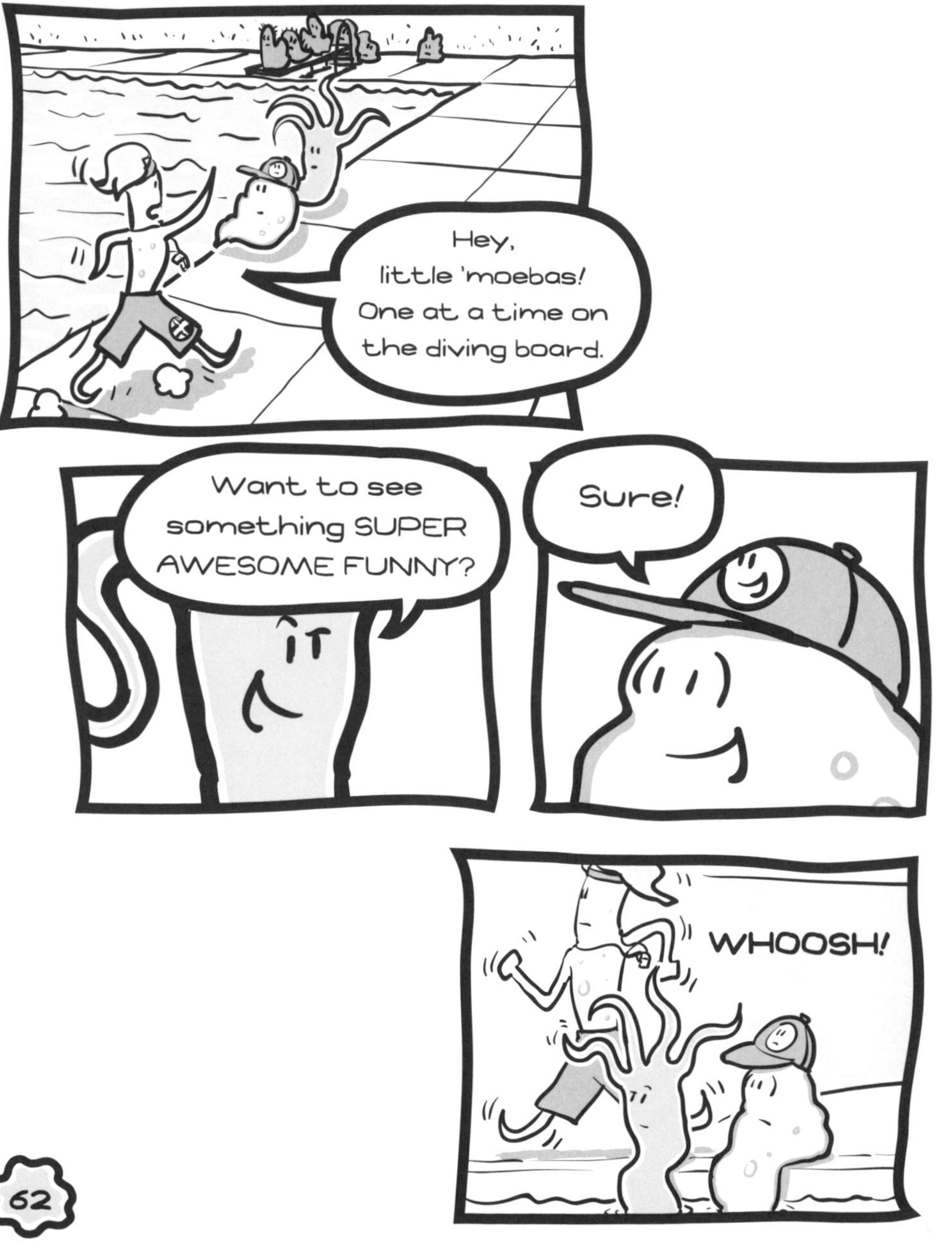
Hey, little 'moebas! One at a time on the diving board.
Want to see something SUPER AWESOME FUNNY?
Sure!
WHOOSH!

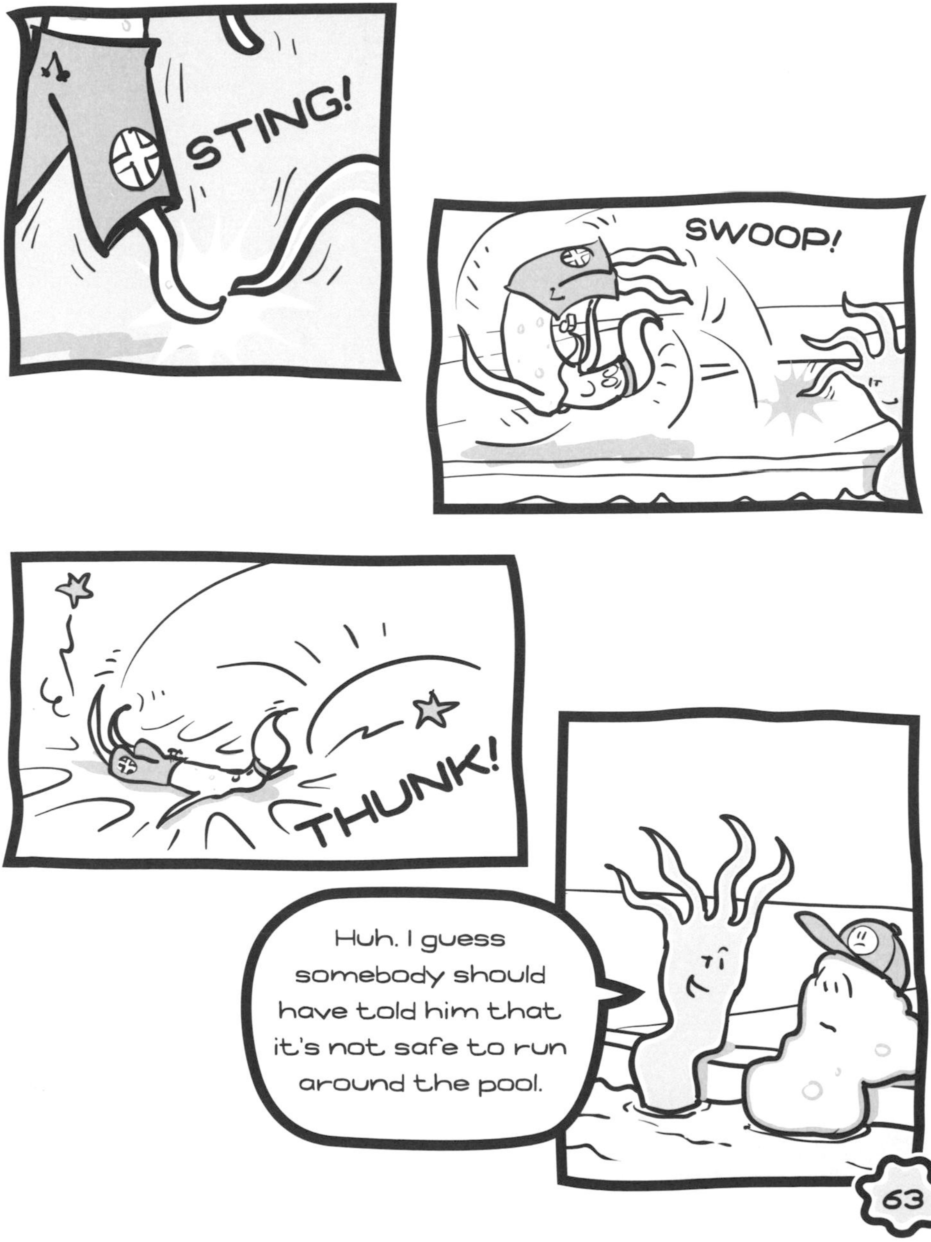
STING!
SWOOP!
THUNK!
Huh. I guess somebody should have told him that it's not safe to run around the pool.

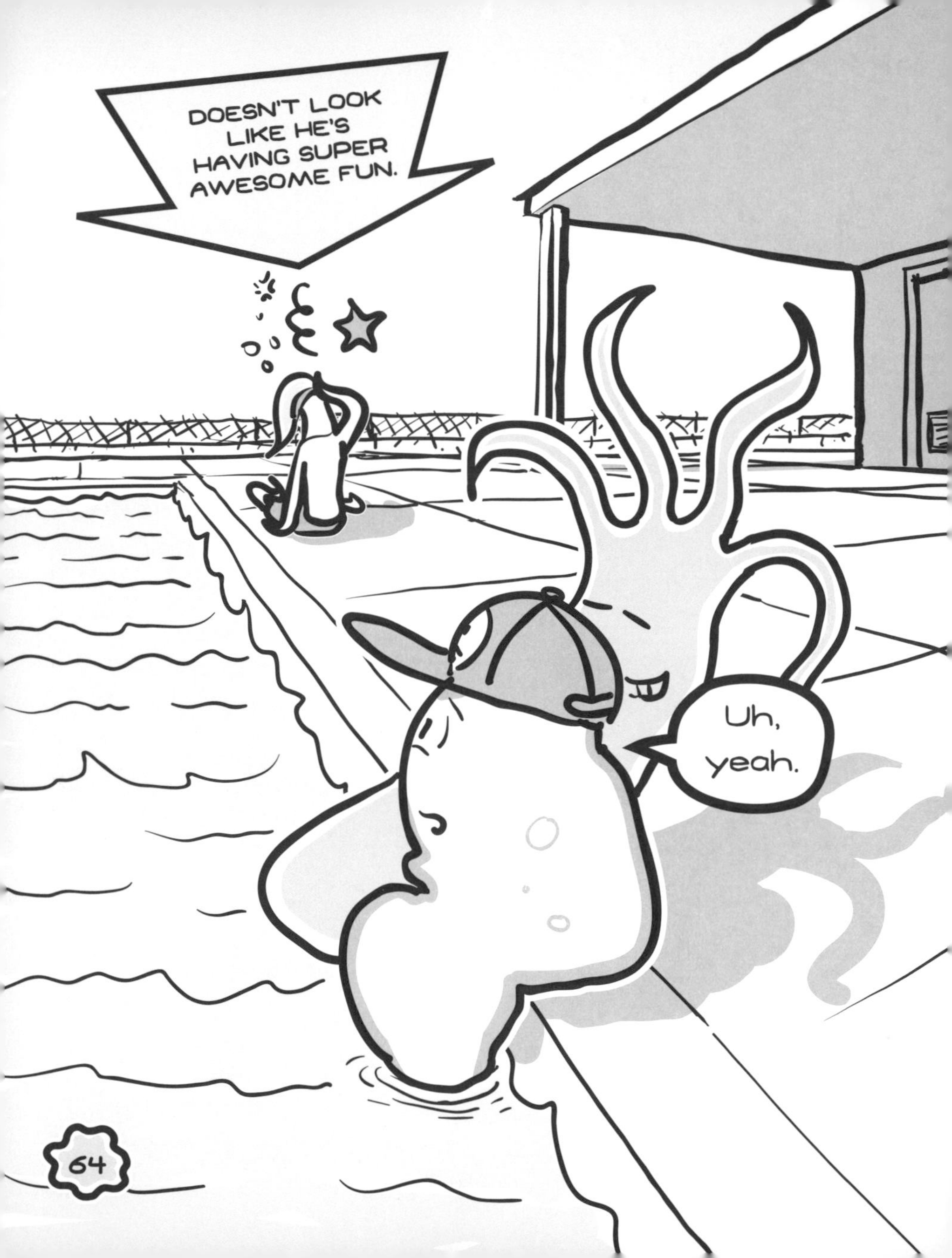
DOESN'T LOOK LIKE HE'S HAVING SUPER AWESOME FUN.
Uh, yeah.

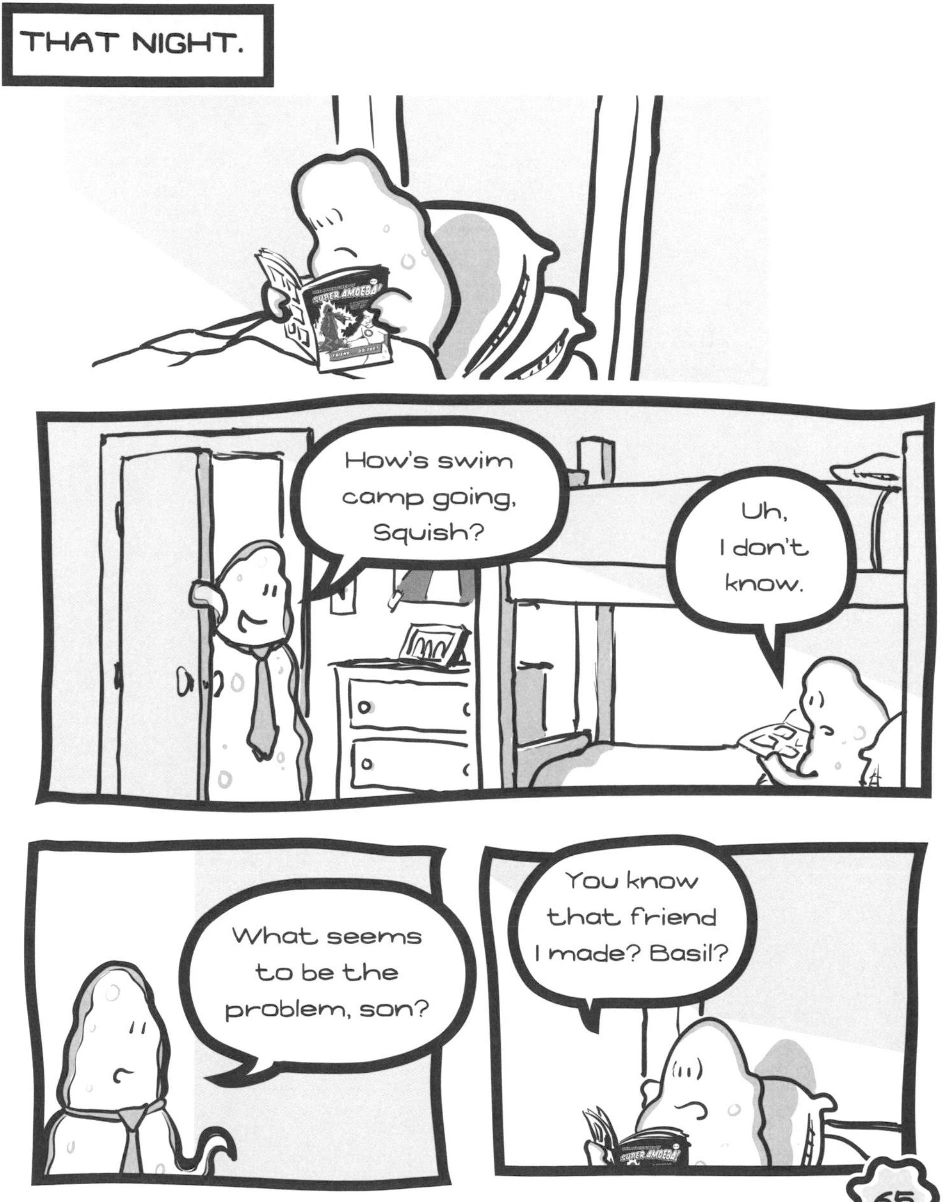
THAT NIGHT.
SUPER AMOEBA!
How's swim camp going, Squish?
Uh, I don't know.
What seems to be the problem, son?
You know that friend I made? Basil?
SUPER AMOEBA!

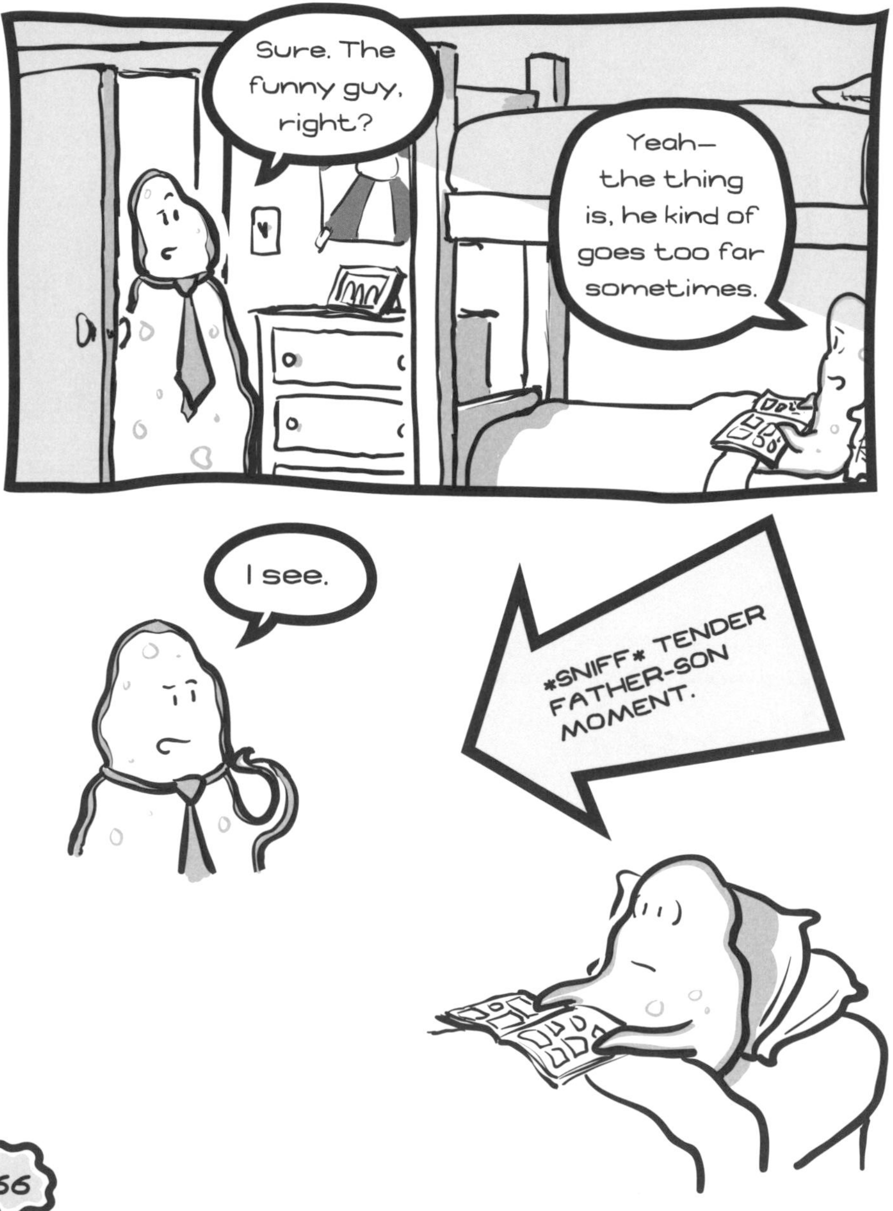
Sure. The funny guy, right?
Yeah— the thing is, he kind of goes too far sometimes.
I see.
SNIFF TENDER FATHER-SON MOMENT.

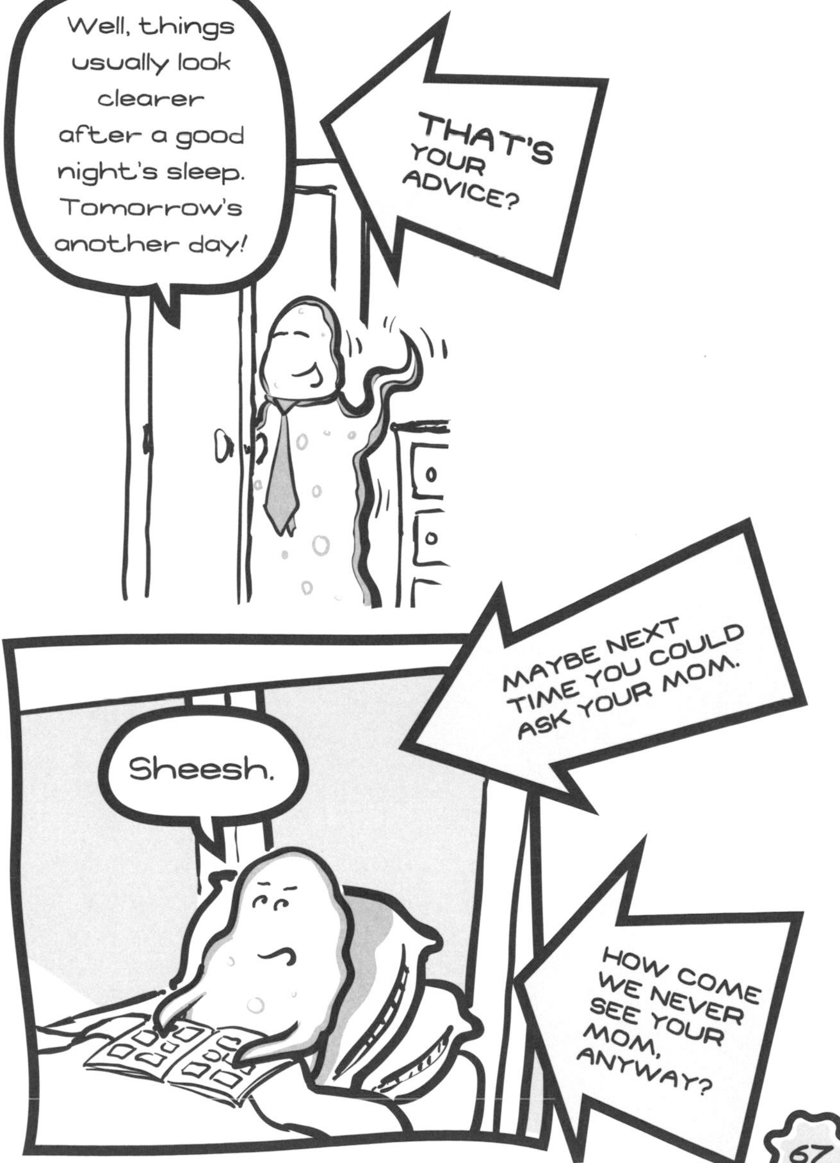

Well, things usually look clearer after a good night's sleep. Tomorrow's another day!
THAT'S YOUR ADVICE?
MAYBE NEXT TIME YOU COULD ASK YOUR MOM.
Sheesh.
HOW COME WE NEVER SEE YOUR MOM, ANYWAY?

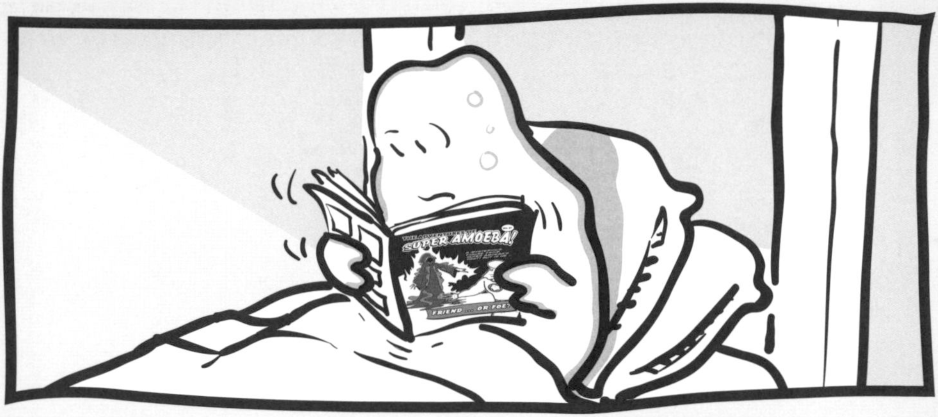
SUPER AMOEBA!
FRIEND ... OR FOE?

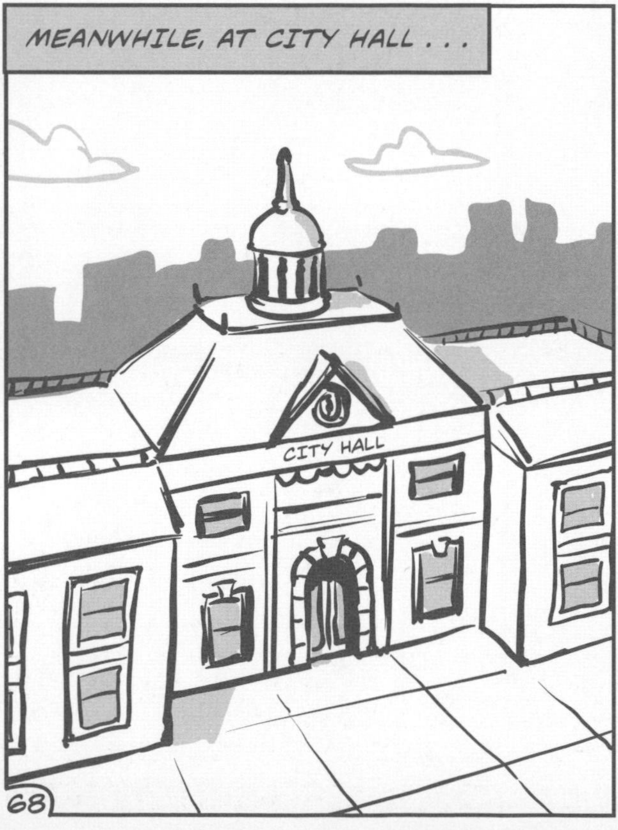
MEANWHILE, AT CITY HALL . . .
CITY HALL

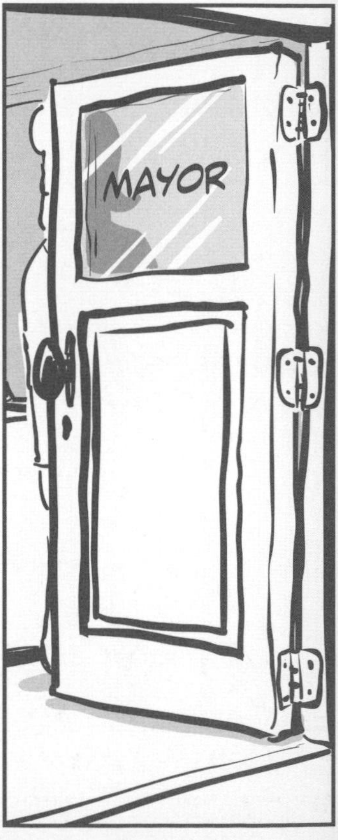
MAYOR

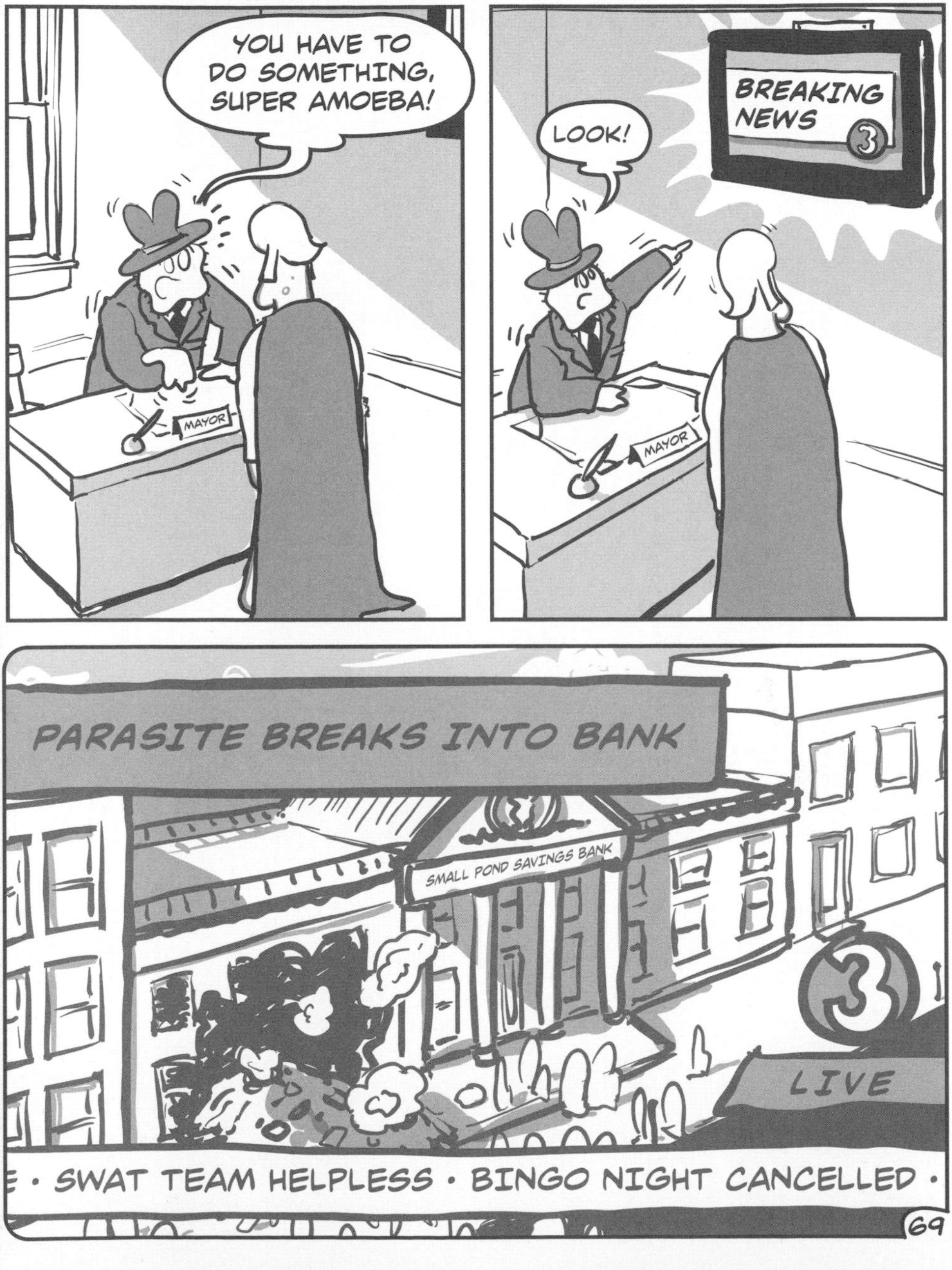
YOU HAVE TO DO SOMETHING, SUPER AMOEBA!
MAYOR
LOOK!
BREAKING NEWS
3
MAYOR
PARASITE BREAKS INTO BANK
SMALL POND SAVINGS BANK
3
LIVE
E • SWAT TEAM HELPLESS • BINGO NIGHT CANCELLED •

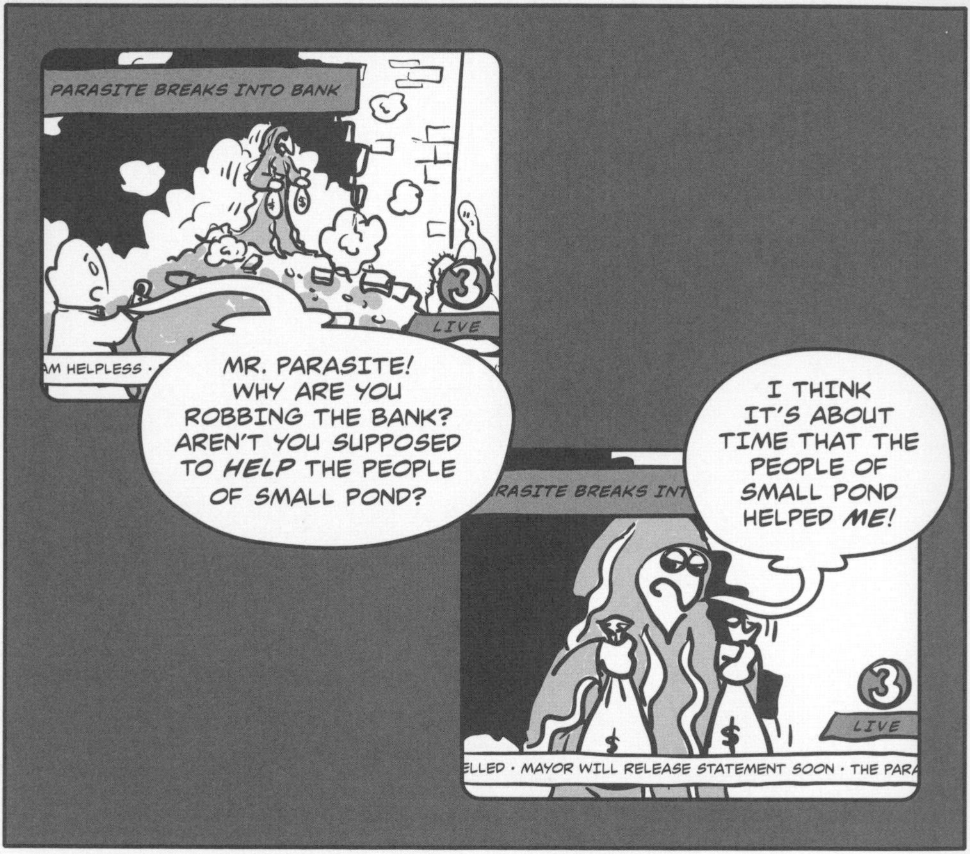
PARASITE BREAKS INTO BANK
LIVE
AM HELPLESS ·
MR. PARASITE! WHY ARE YOU ROBBING THE BANK? AREN'T YOU SUPPOSED TO *HELP* THE PEOPLE OF SMALL POND?
RASITE BREAKS INT
I THINK IT'S ABOUT TIME THAT THE PEOPLE OF SMALL POND HELPED *ME*!
LIVE
ELLED · MAYOR WILL RELEASE STATEMENT SOON · THE PARA

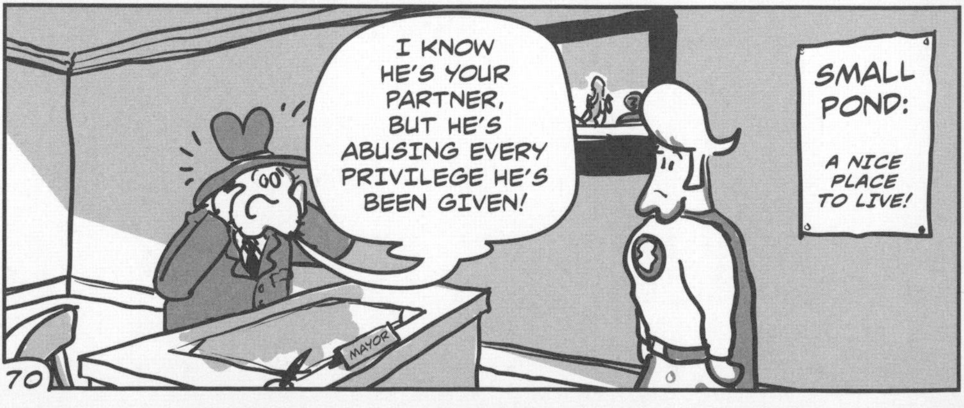
I KNOW HE'S YOUR PARTNER, BUT HE'S ABUSING EVERY PRIVILEGE HE'S BEEN GIVEN!
SMALL POND:
A NICE PLACE TO LIVE!
MAYOR

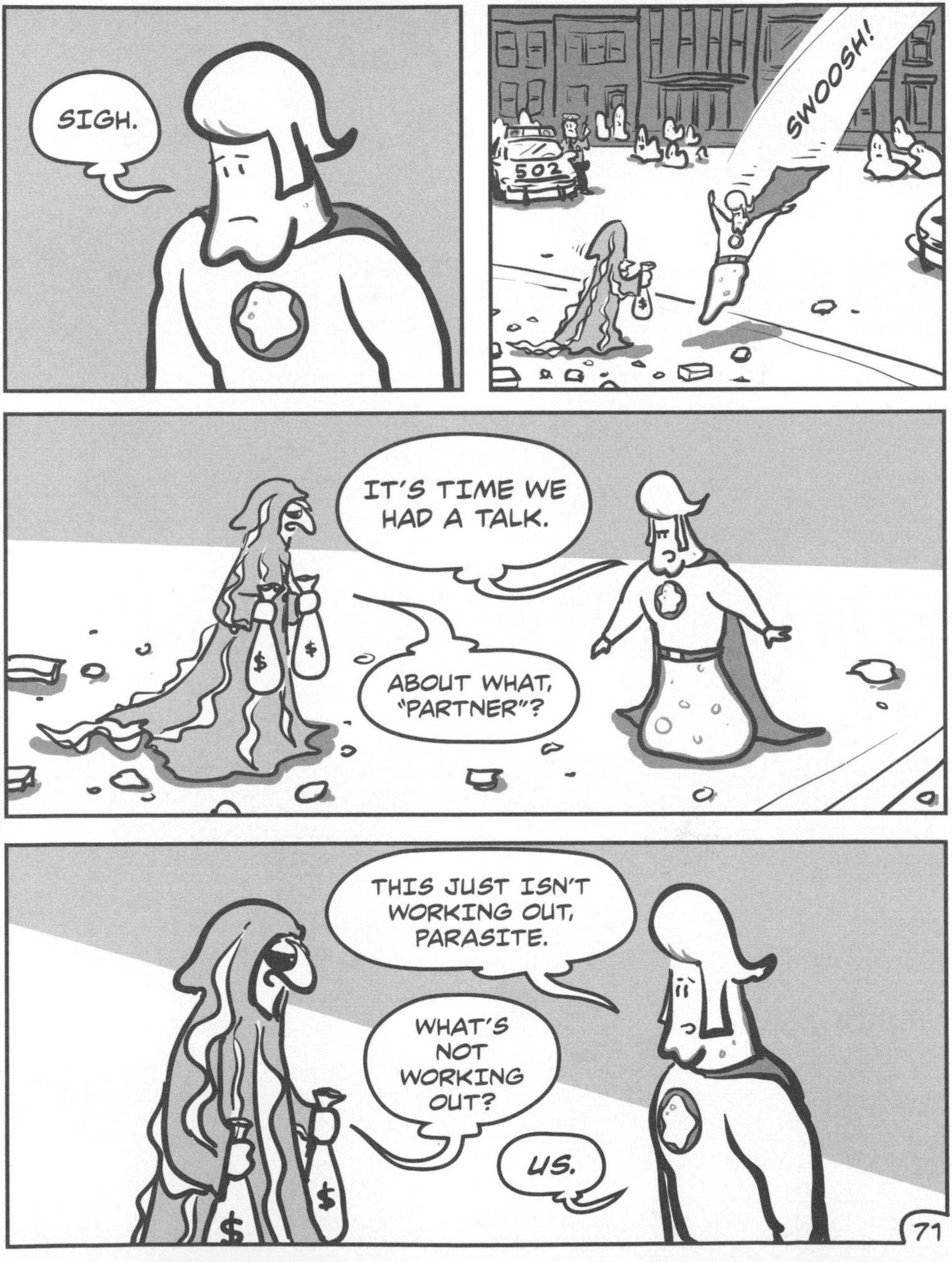

SIGH.
SWOOSH!
502
IT'S TIME WE HAD A TALK.
ABOUT WHAT, "PARTNER"?
THIS JUST ISN'T WORKING OUT, PARASITE.
WHAT'S NOT WORKING OUT?
US.

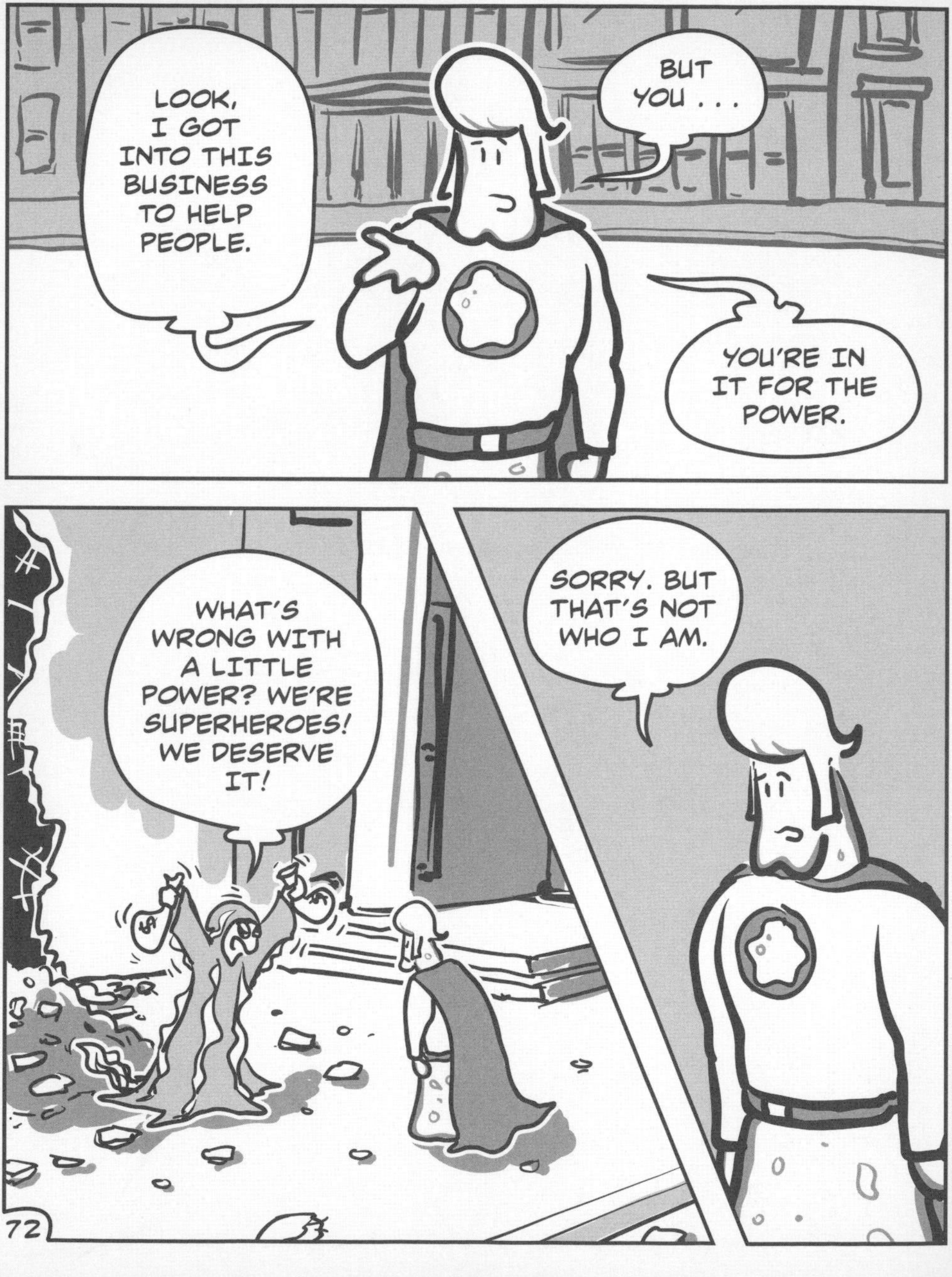
LOOK, I GOT INTO THIS BUSINESS TO HELP PEOPLE.
BUT YOU . . .
YOU'RE IN IT FOR THE POWER.
WHAT'S WRONG WITH A LITTLE POWER? WE'RE SUPERHEROES! WE DESERVE IT!
SORRY. BUT THAT'S NOT WHO I AM.

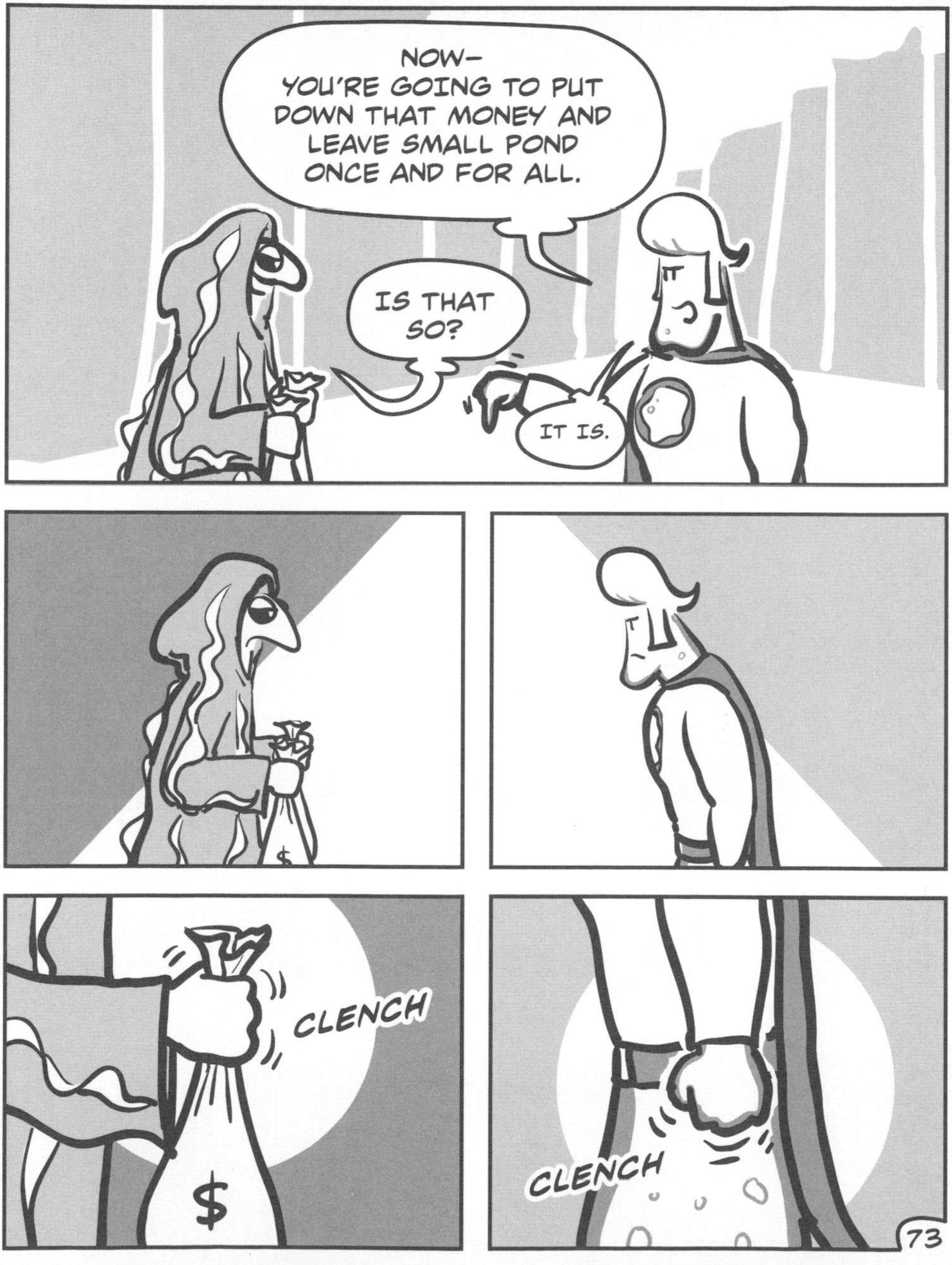
NOW-
YOU'RE GOING TO PUT DOWN THAT MONEY AND LEAVE SMALL POND ONCE AND FOR ALL.
IS THAT SO?
IT IS.
$
CLENCH
$
CLENCH

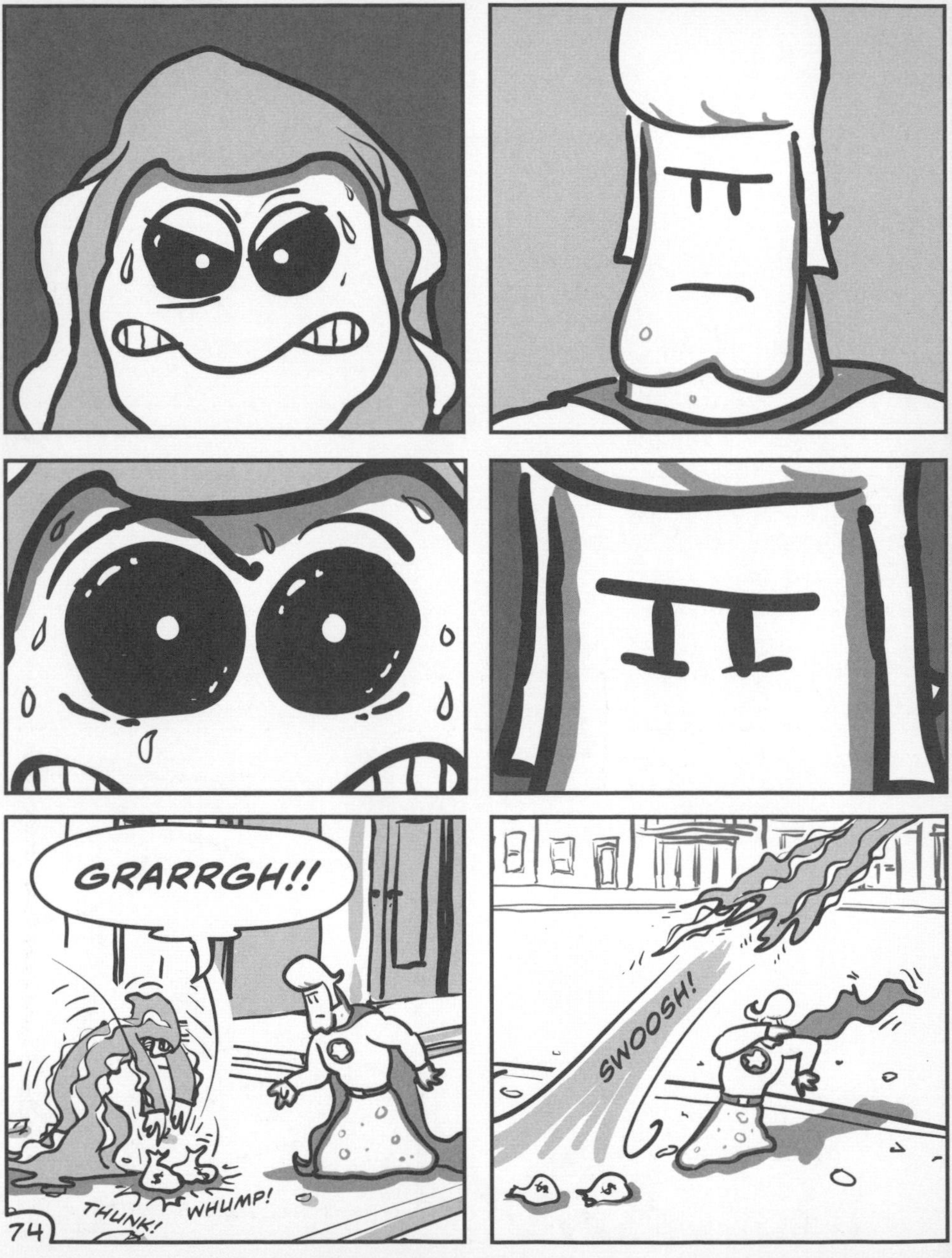
GRARRGH!!
THUNK!
WHUMP!
SWOOSH!

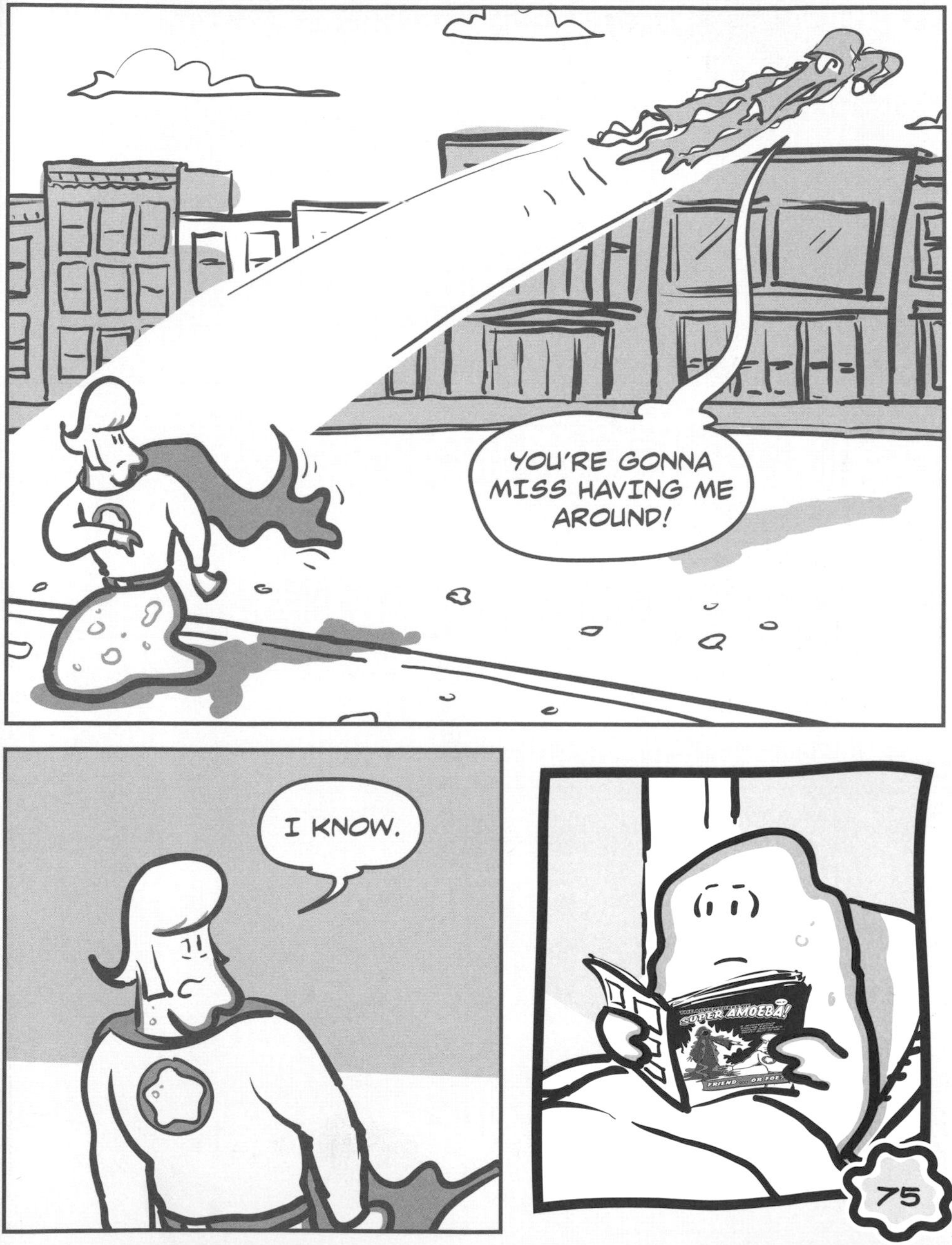
YOU'RE GONNA MISS HAVING ME AROUND!
I KNOW.
SUPER AMOEBA!
FRIEND . . . OR FOE?

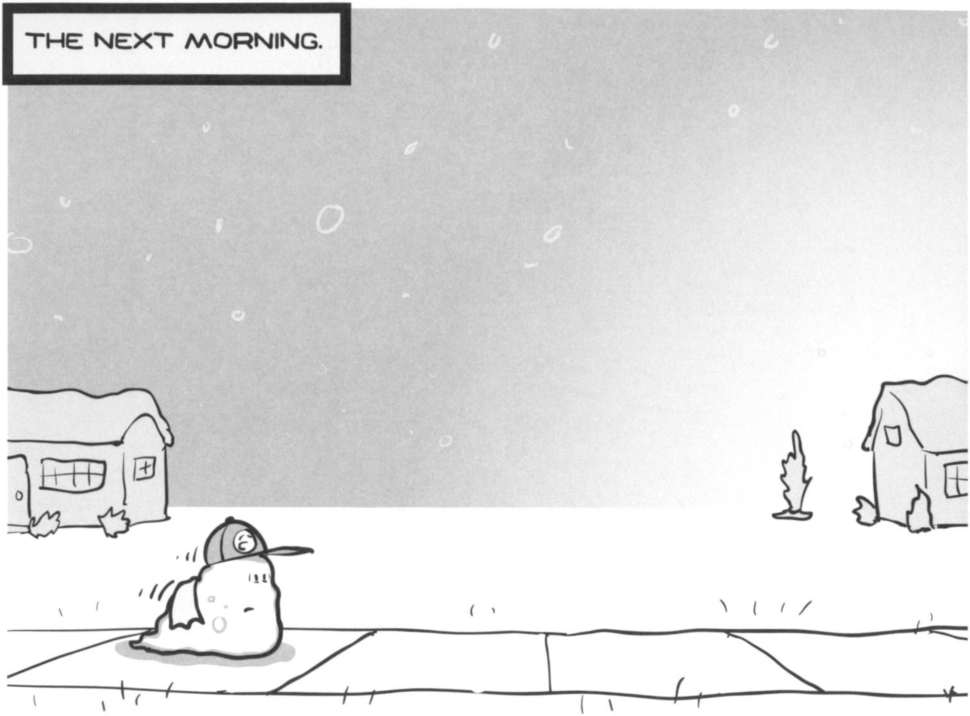
THE NEXT MORNING.

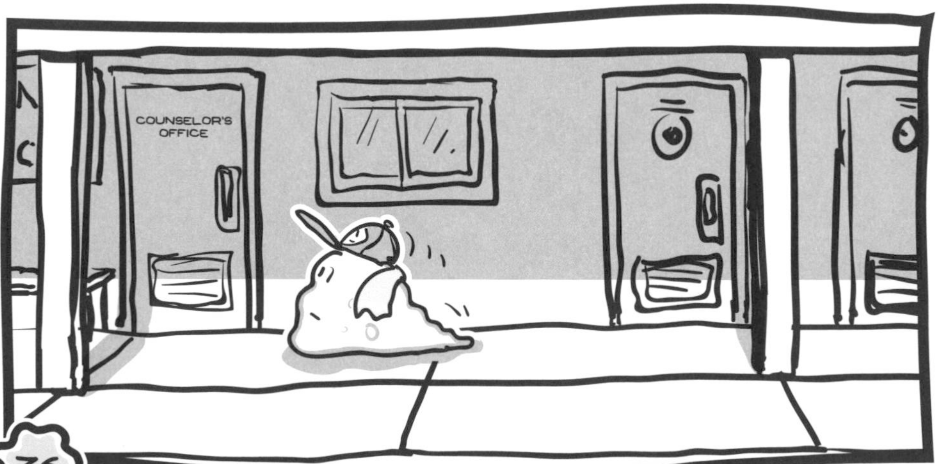
COUNSELOR'S OFFICE

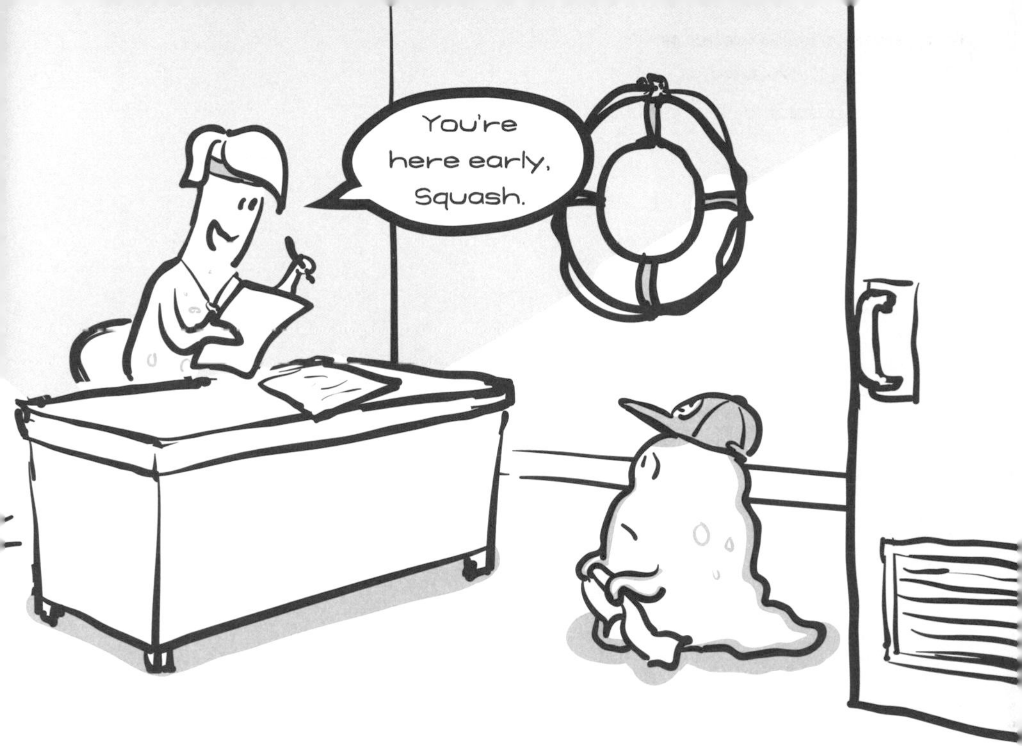
You're here early, Squash.

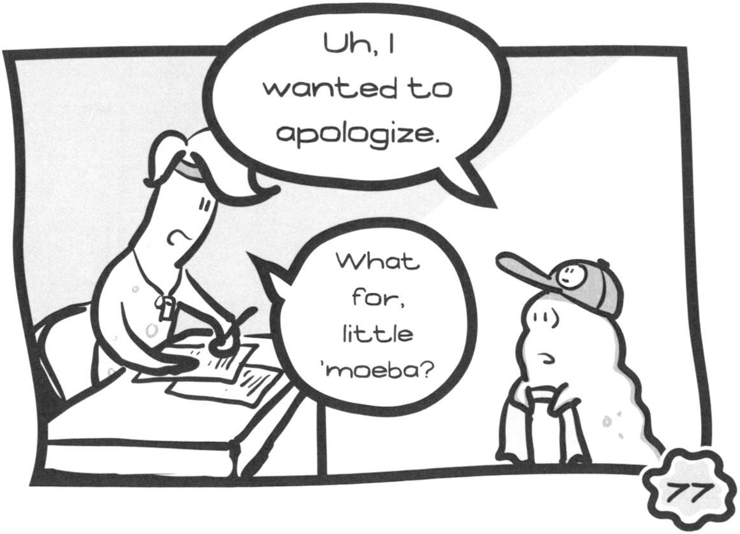
Uh, I wanted to apologize.
What for, little 'moeba?

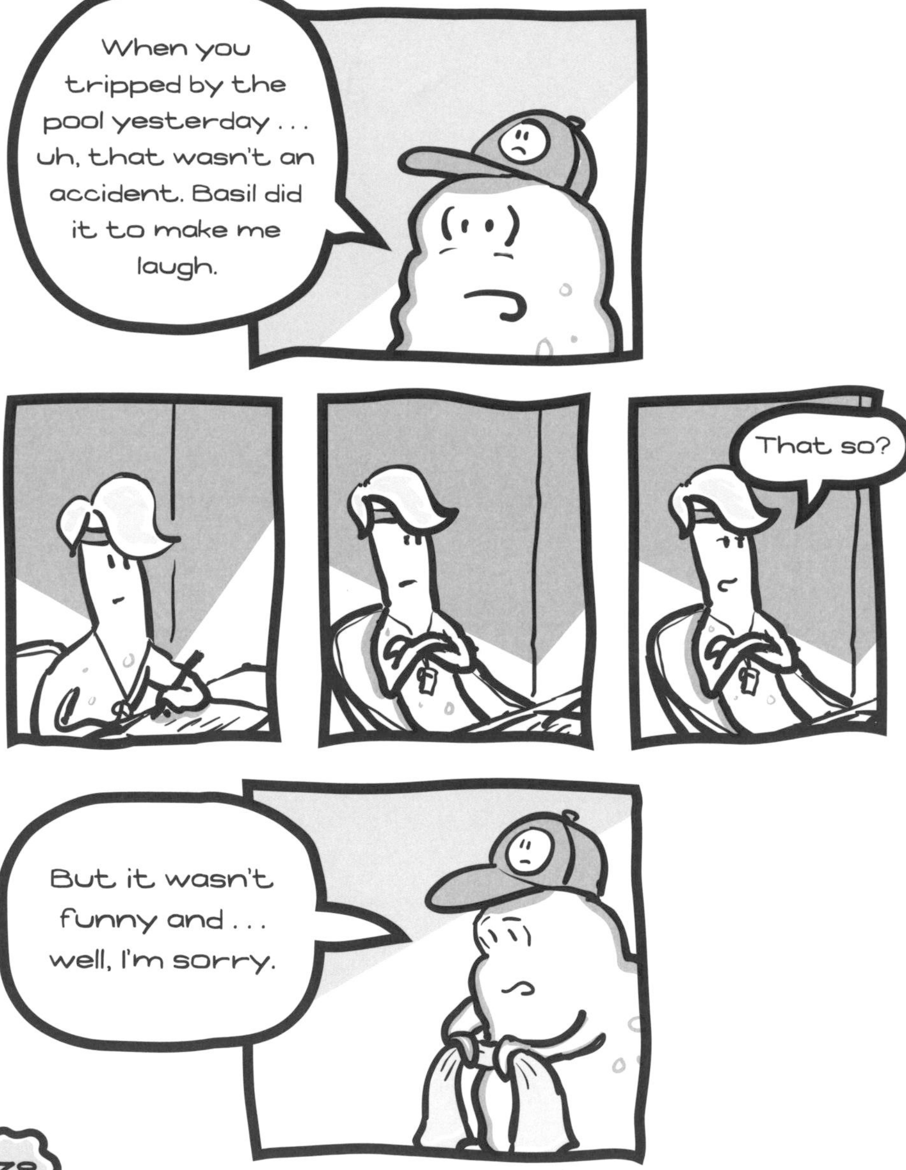
When you tripped by the pool yesterday . . . uh, that wasn't an accident. Basil did it to make me laugh.
That so?
But it wasn't funny and . . . well, I'm sorry.

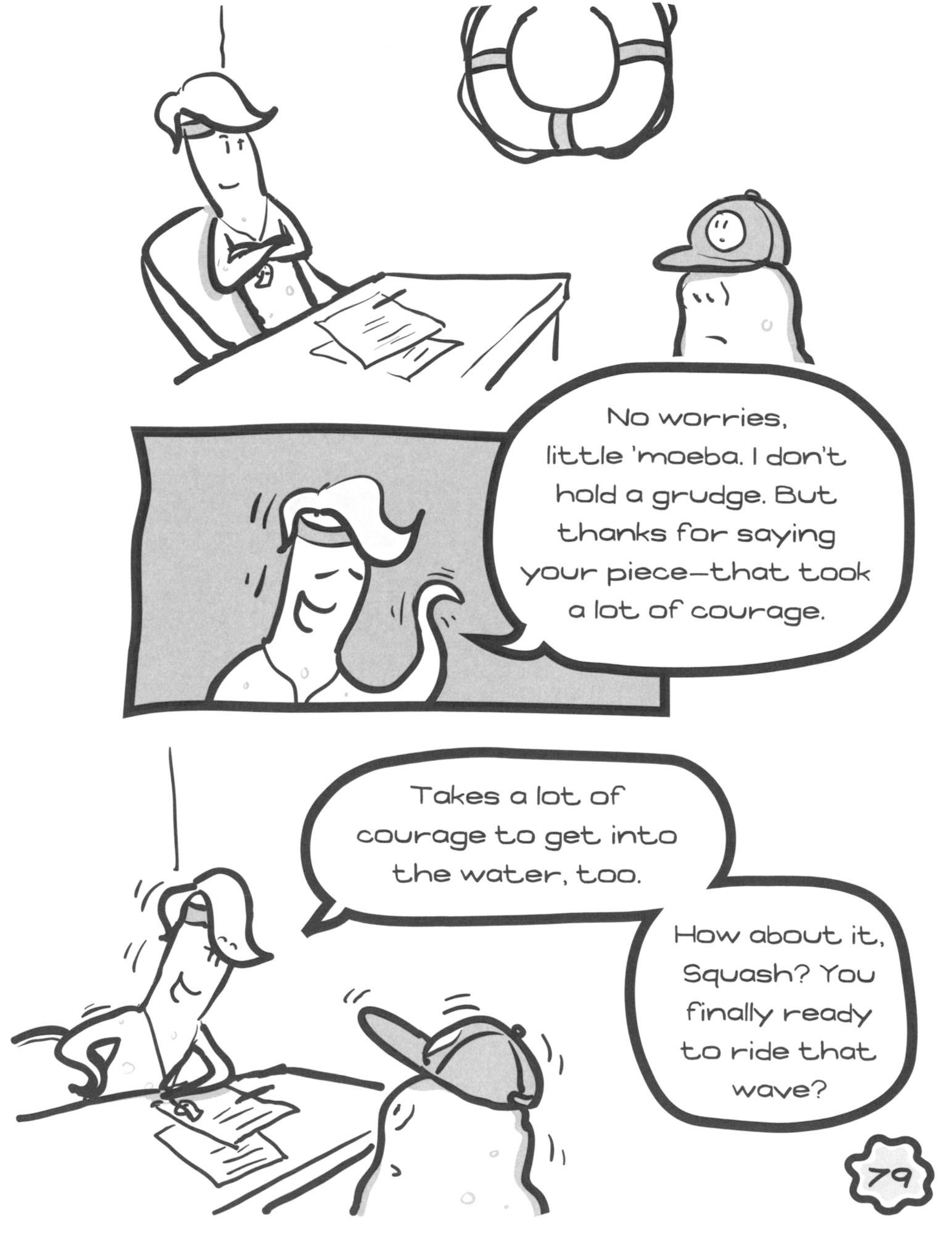
No worries, little 'moeba. I don't hold a grudge. But thanks for saying your piece—that took a lot of courage.
Takes a lot of courage to get into the water, too.
How about it, Squash? You finally ready to ride that wave?
79

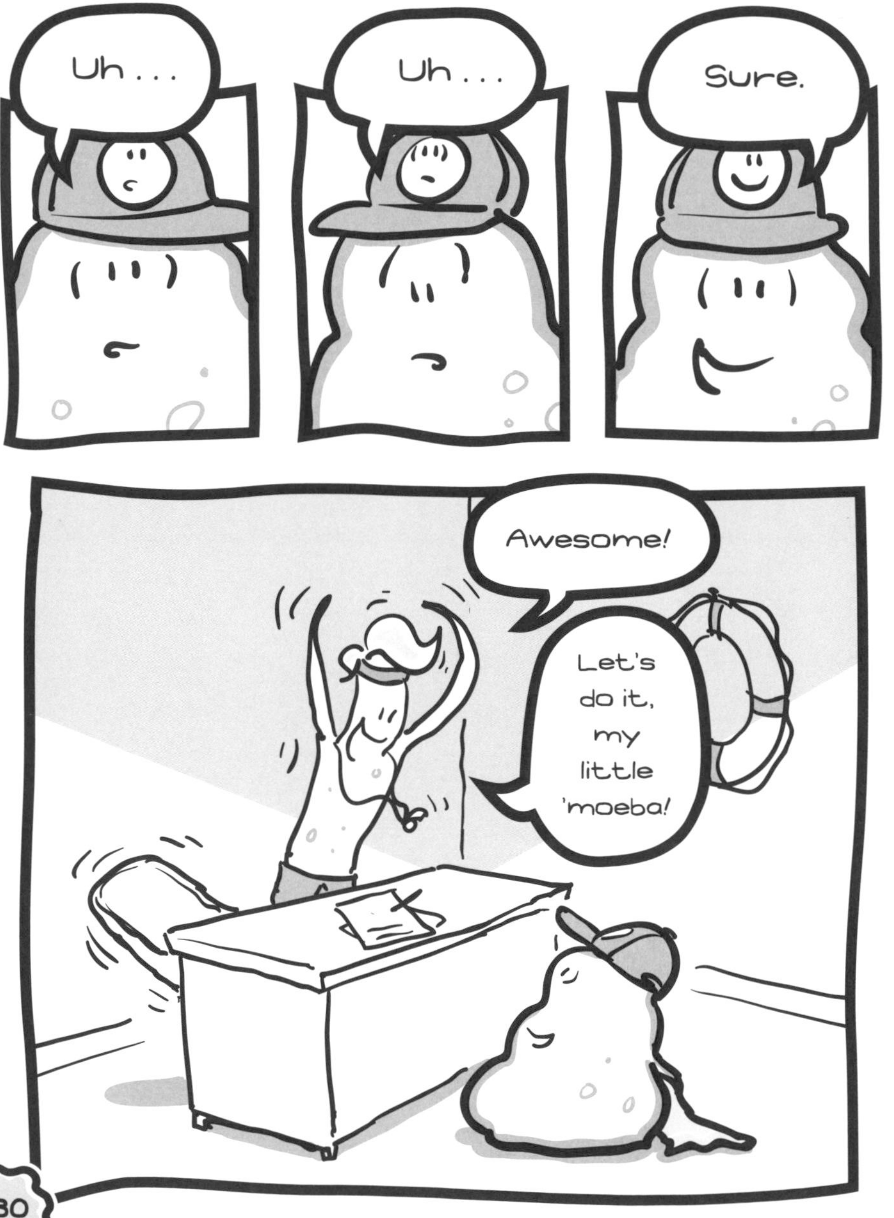
Uh . . .
Uh . . .
Sure.
Awesome!
Let's do it, my little 'moeba!

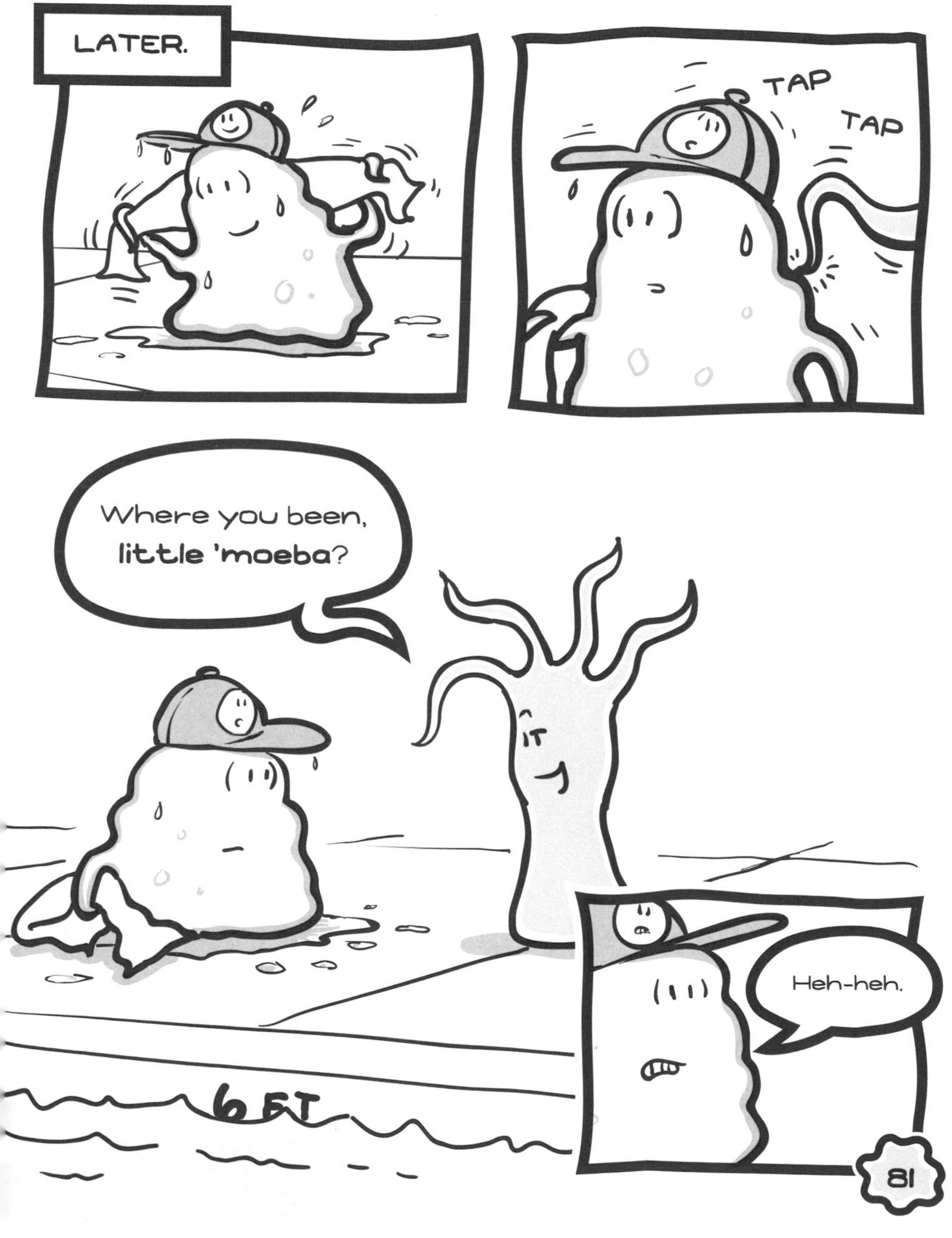
LATER.
TAP
TAP
Where you been, **little 'moeba**?
6 FT
Heh-heh.

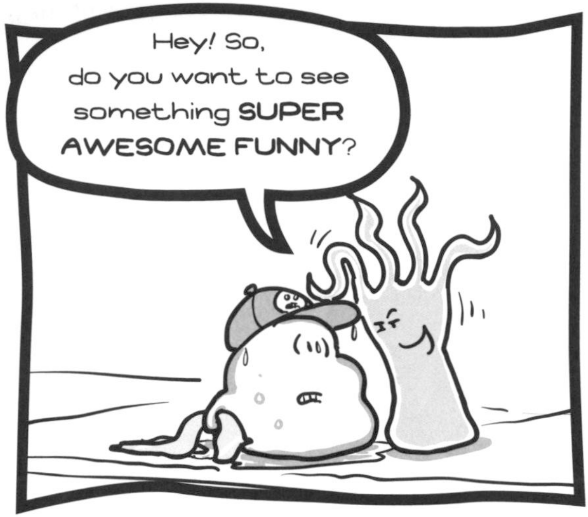
Hey! So, do you want to see something **SUPER AWESOME FUNNY**?
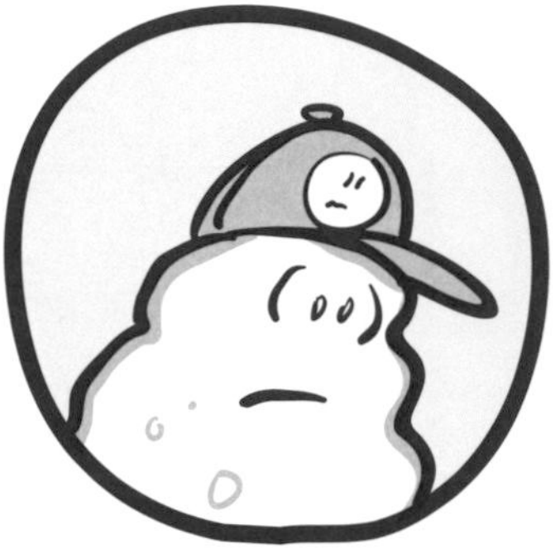
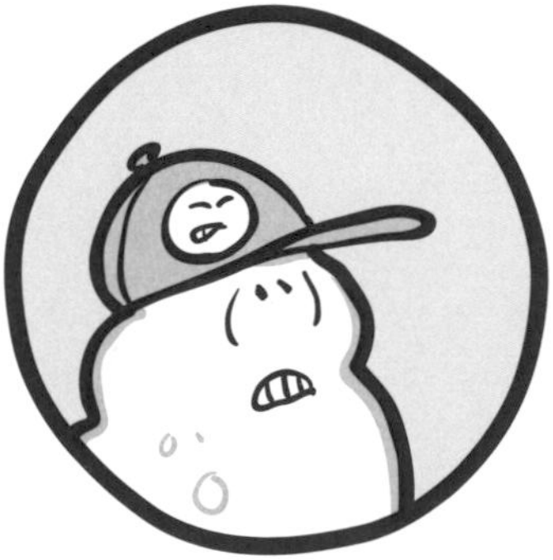
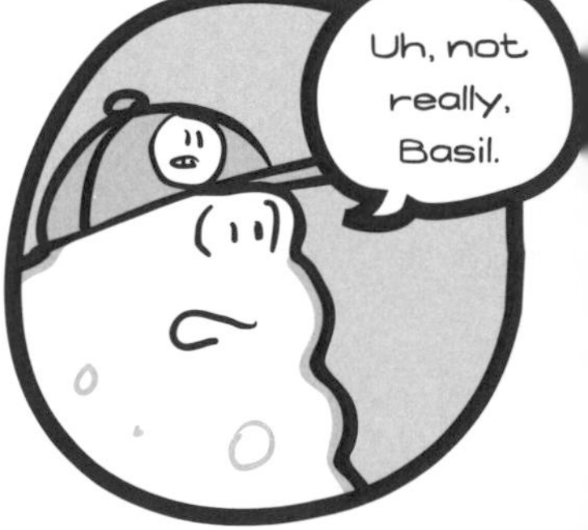
Uh, not really, Basil.

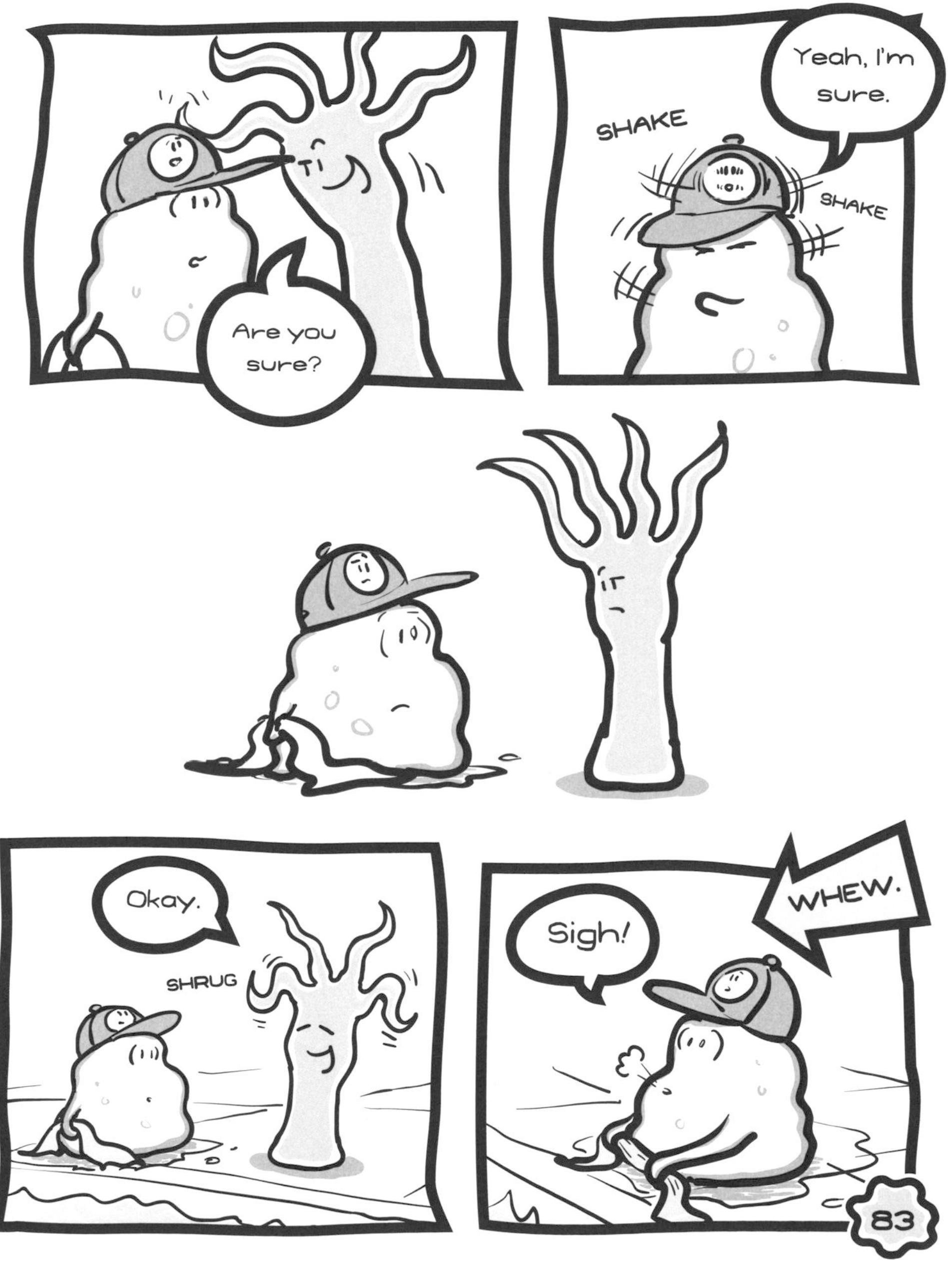
Are you sure?
SHAKE
Yeah, I'm sure.
SHAKE
Okay.
SHRUG
WHEW.
Sigh!

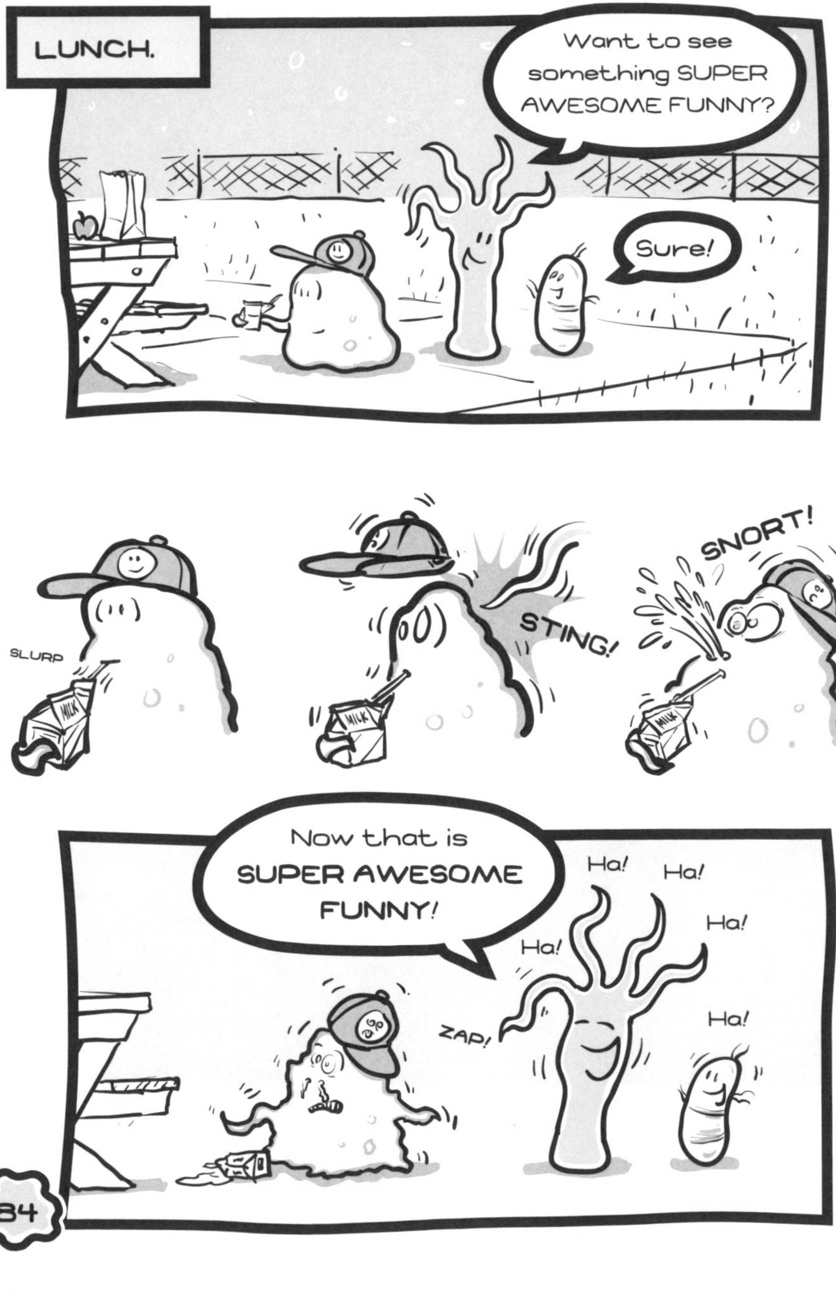
LUNCH.
Want to see something SUPER AWESOME FUNNY?
Sure!
SLURP
MILK
MILK
STING!
SNORT!
MILK
Now that is SUPER AWESOME FUNNY!
Ha! Ha!
Ha!
Ha!
Ha!
ZAP!

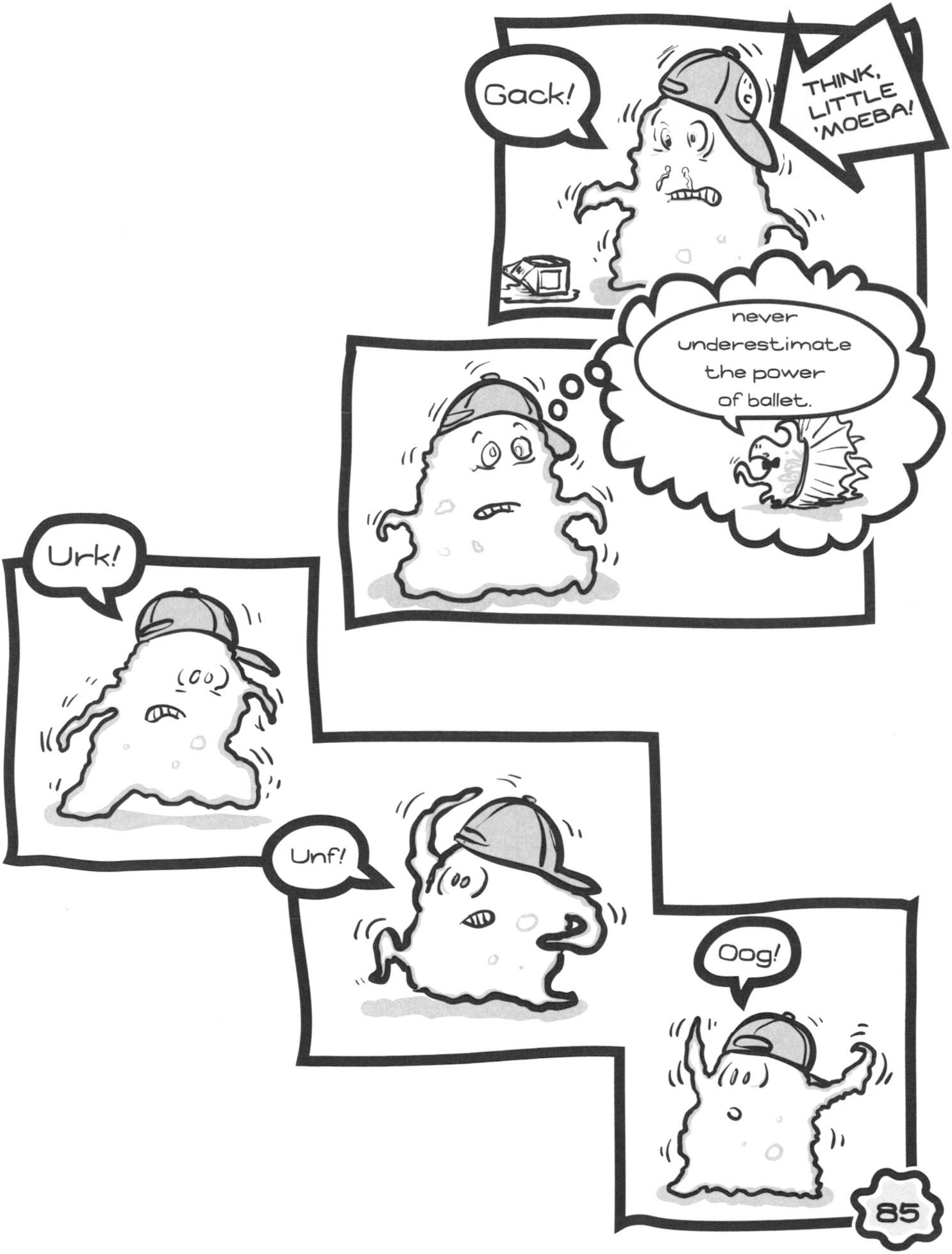
Gack!
THINK, LITTLE 'MOEBA!
never underestimate the power of ballet.
Urk!
Unf!
Oog!

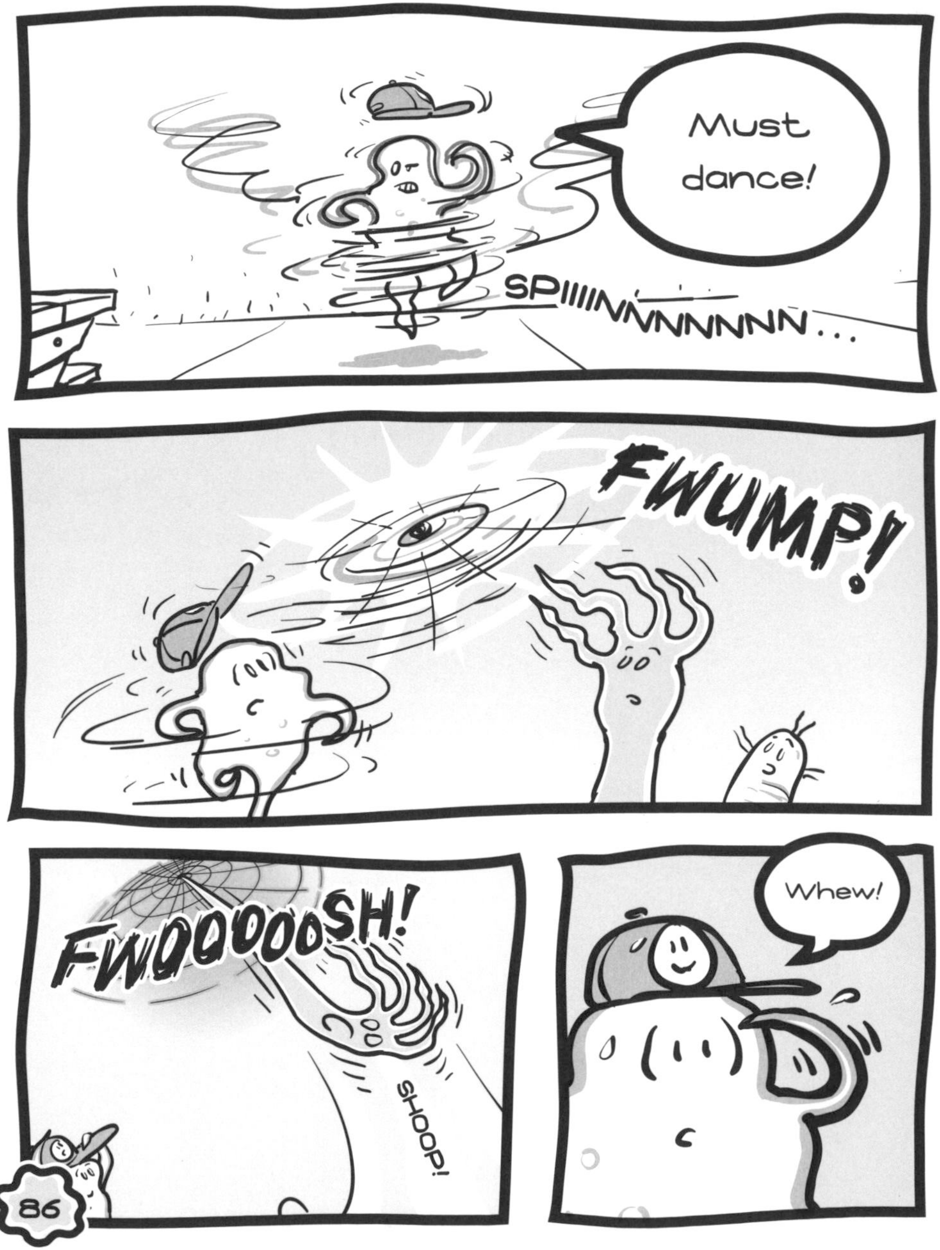
Must dance!
SPIIIIINNNNNNNN...
FWUMP!
FWOOOOOOSH!
SHOOP!
Whew!

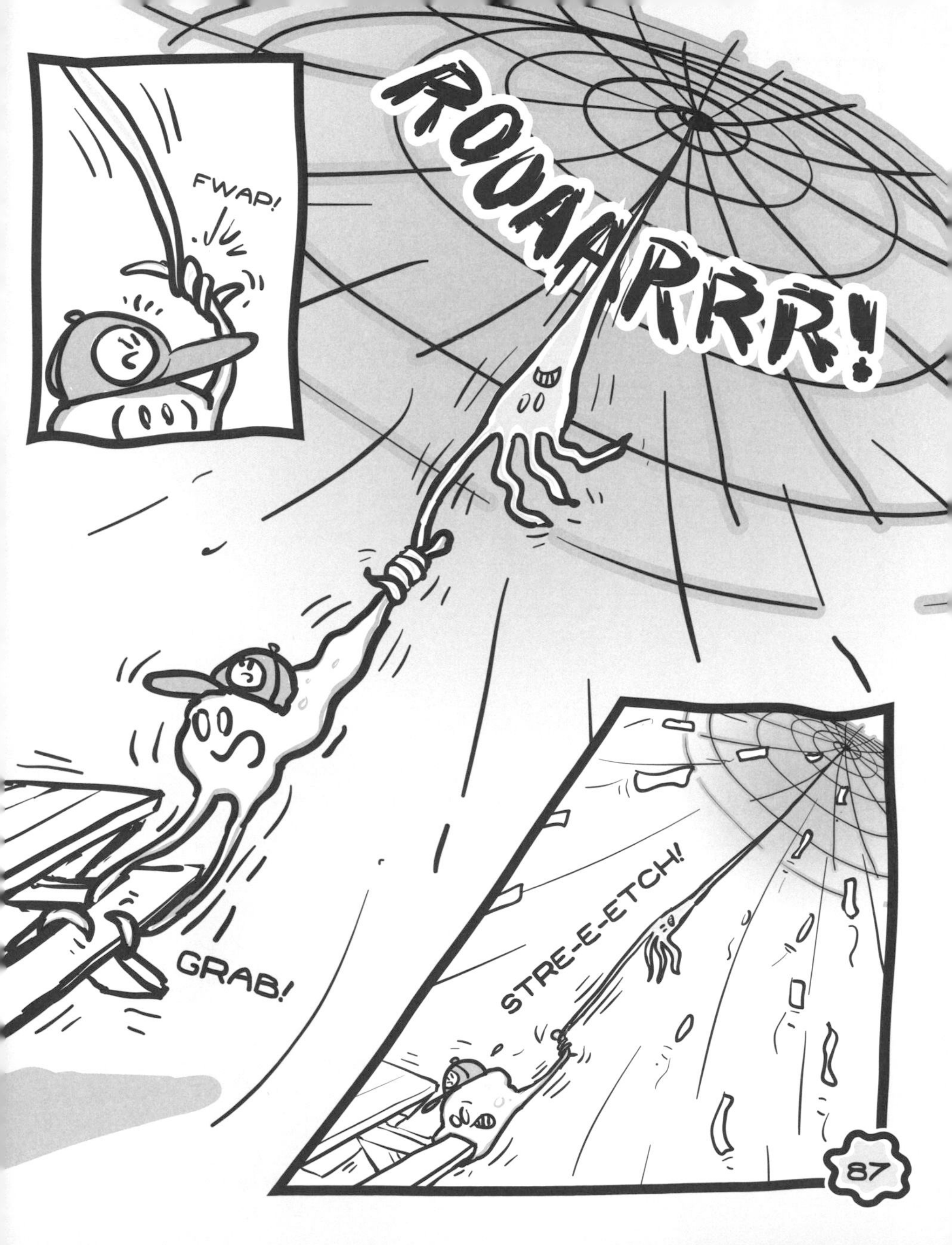
FWAP!
ROOAARRR!
GRAB!
STRE-E-ETCH!

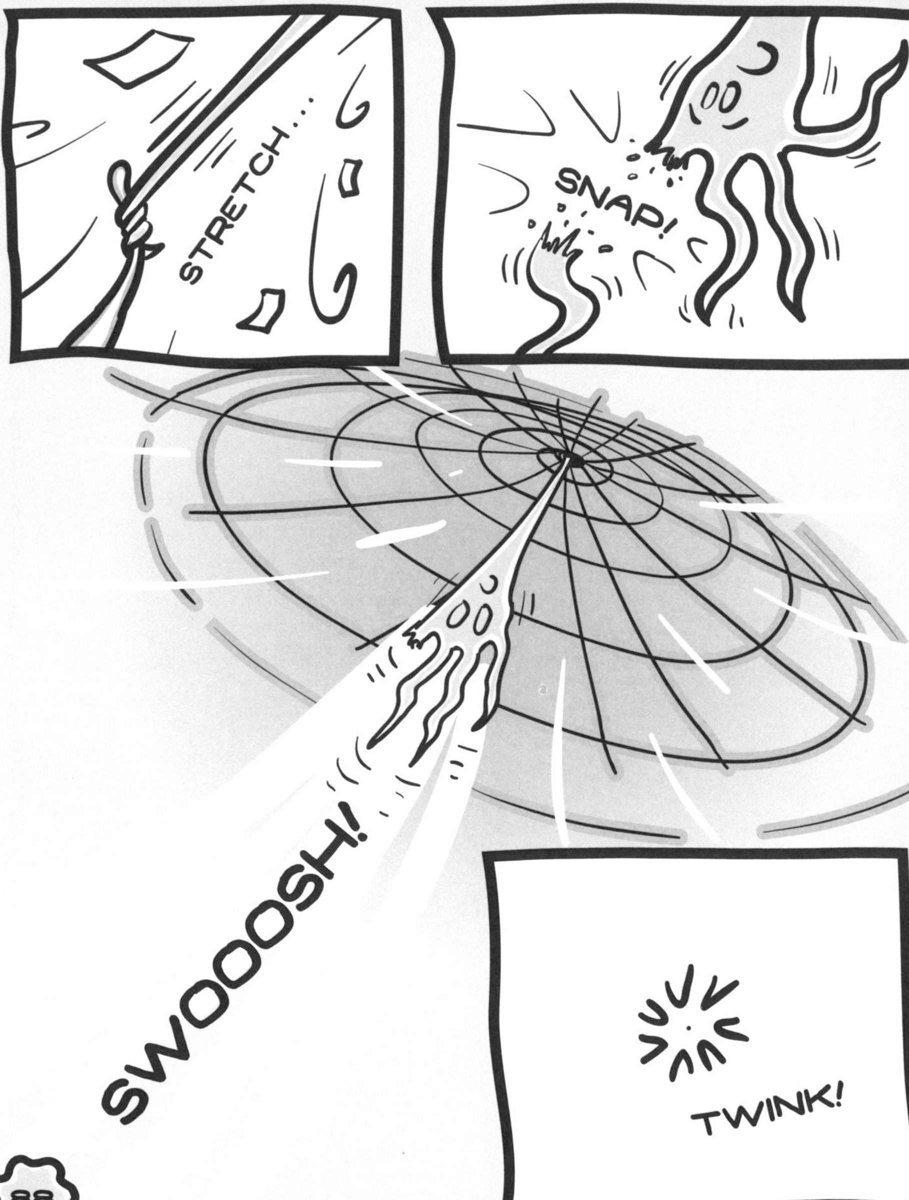
STRETCH...
SNAP!
SWOOOSH!
TWINK!

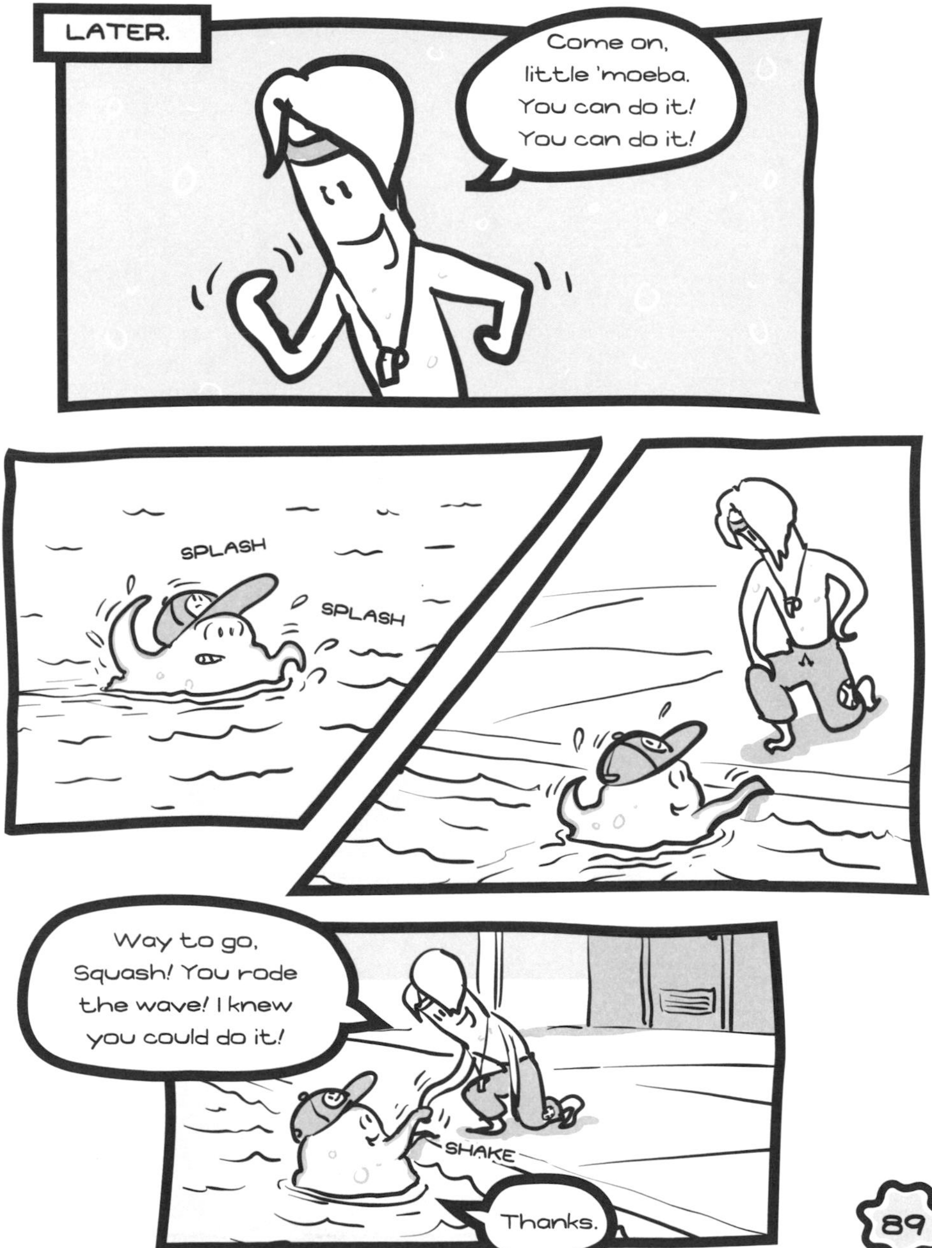
LATER.
Come on, little 'moeba. You can do it! You can do it!
SPLASH
SPLASH
Way to go, Squash! You rode the wave! I knew you could do it!
SHAKE
Thanks.

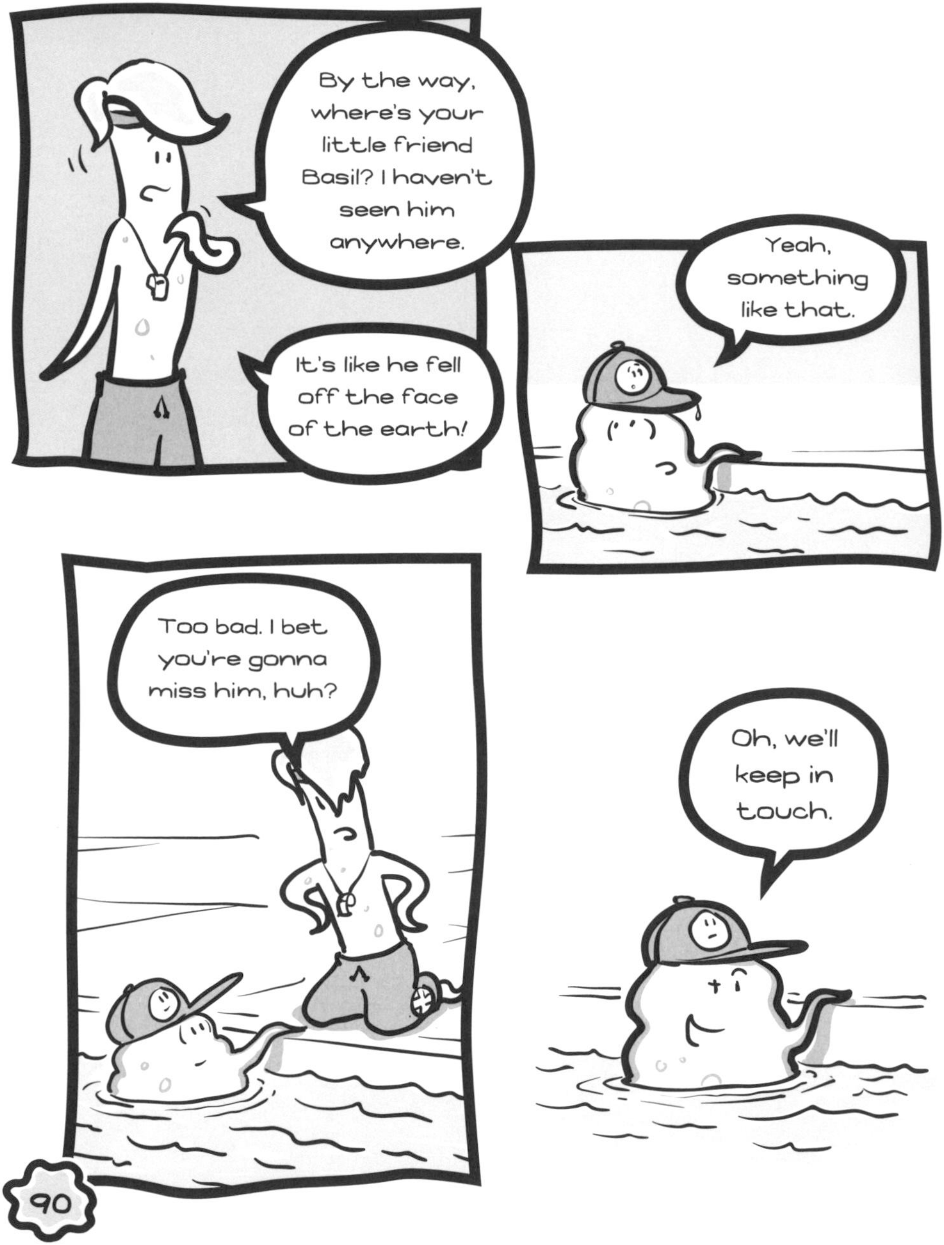
By the way, where's your little friend Basil? I haven't seen him anywhere.
It's like he fell off the face of the earth!
Yeah, something like that.
Too bad. I bet you're gonna miss him, huh?
Oh, we'll keep in touch.

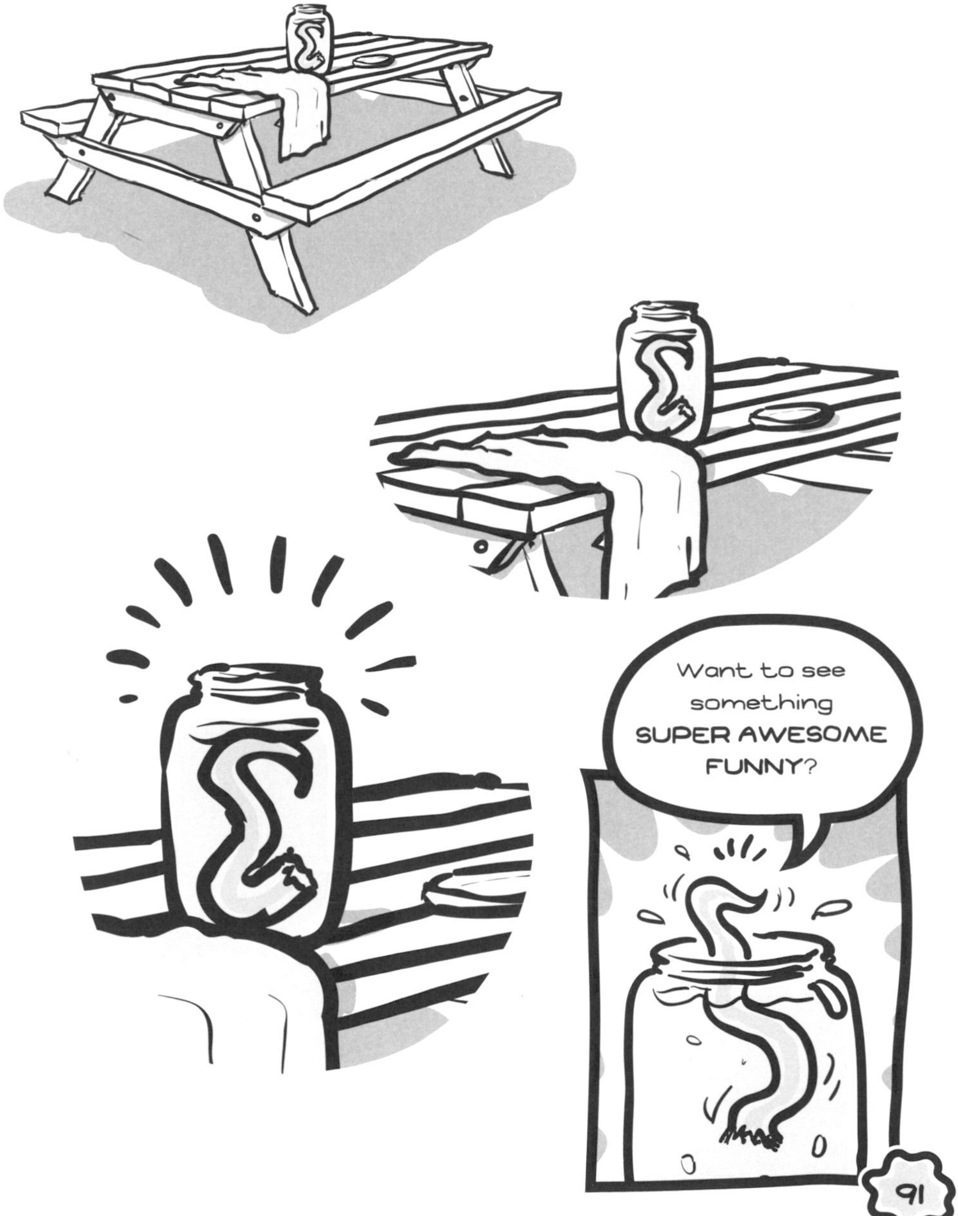
Want to see something SUPER AWESOME FUNNY?

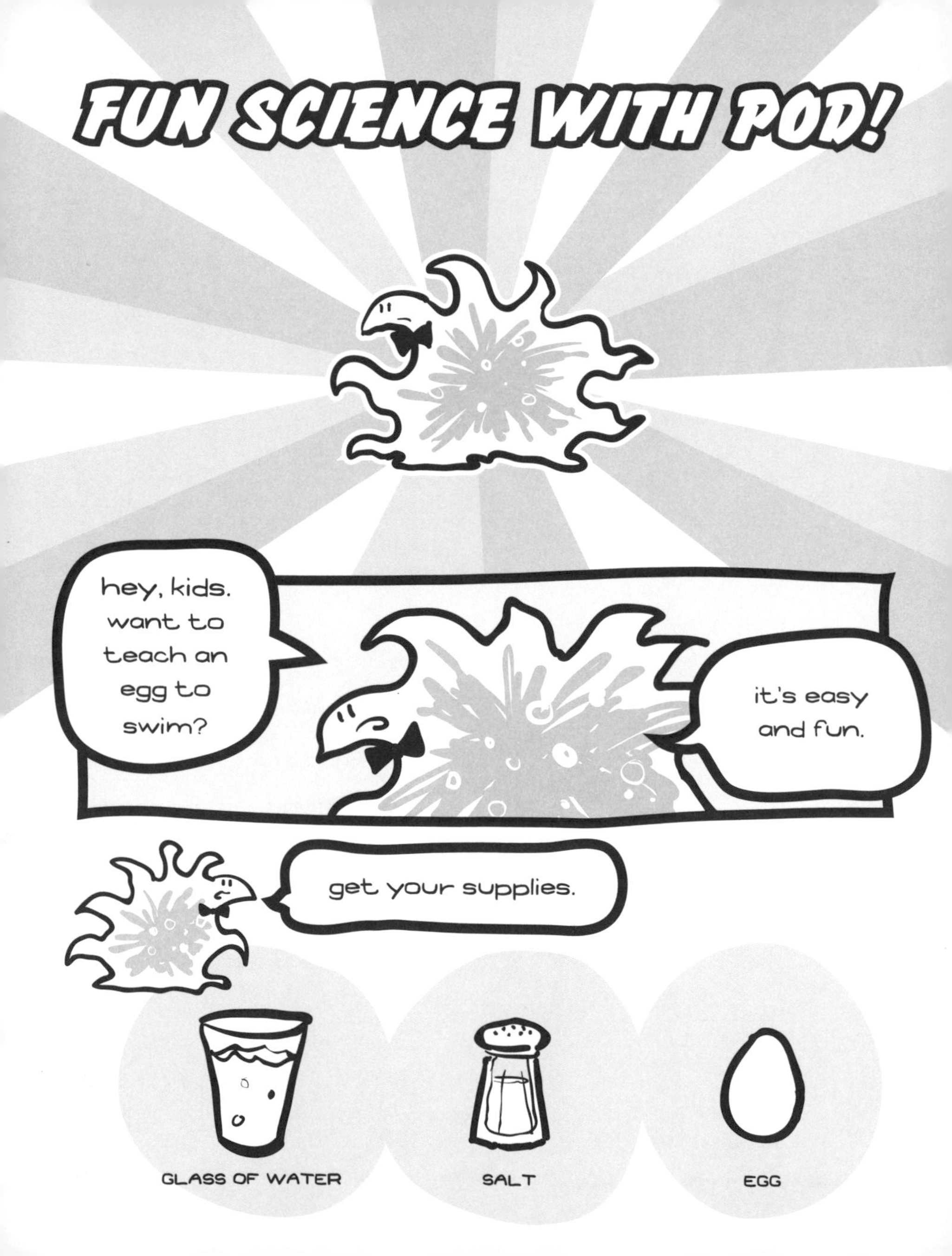
FUN SCIENCE WITH POD!
hey, kids. want to teach an egg to swim?
it's easy and fun.
get your supplies.
GLASS OF WATER
SALT
EGG

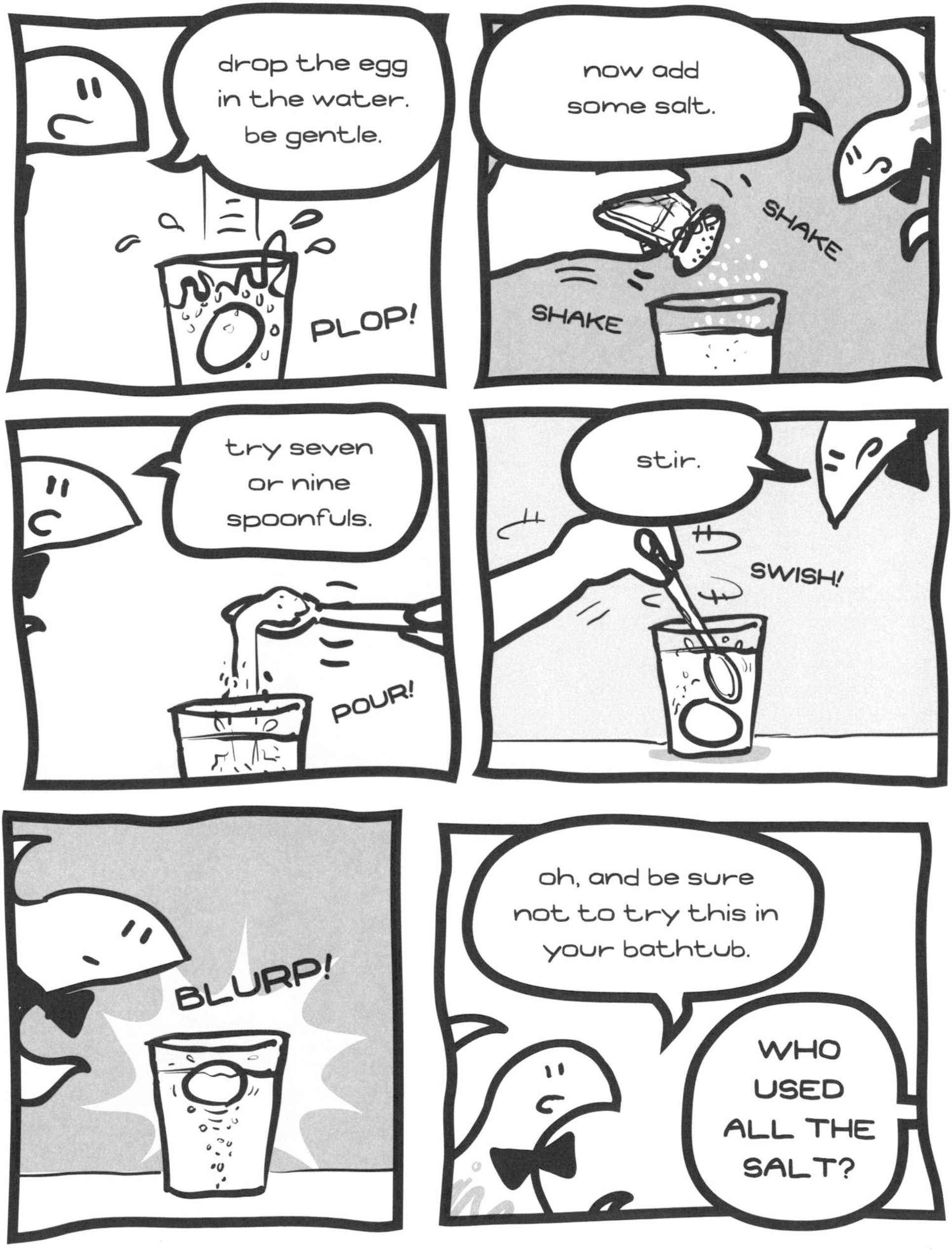
drop the egg in the water. be gentle.
PLOP!
now add some salt.
SHAKE
SHAKE
try seven or nine spoonfuls.
POUR!
stir.
SWISH!
BLURP!
oh, and be sure not to try this in your bathtub.
WHO USED ALL THE SALT?

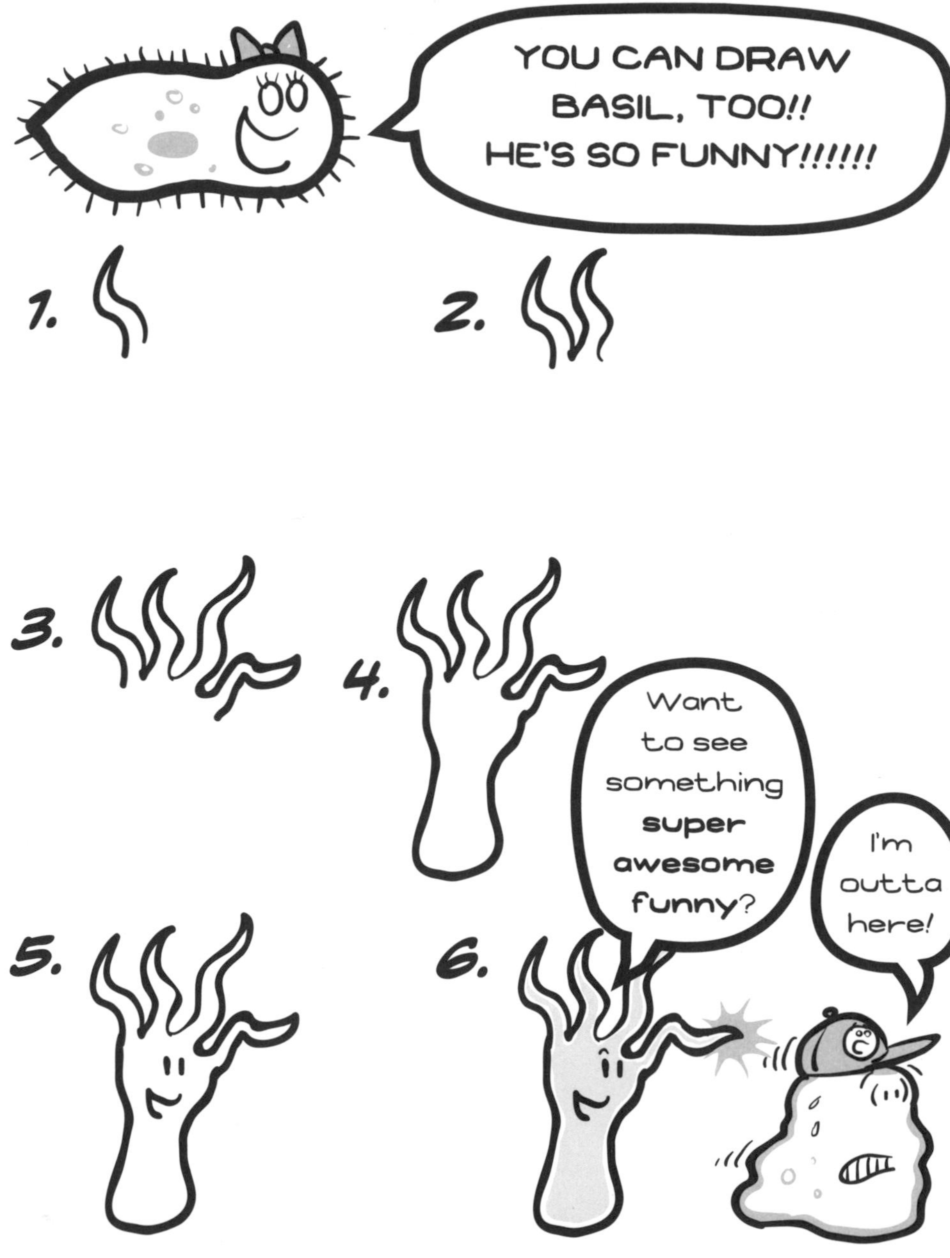
YOU CAN DRAW BASIL, TOO!! HE'S SO FUNNY!!!!!!!
1.
2.
3.
4.
5.
6.
Want to see something **super awesome** funny?
I'm outta here!

IF YOU LIKE SQUISH, YOU'LL LOVE BABYMOUSE!

#1 BABYMOUSE: Queen of the World!
#2 BABYMOUSE: Our Hero
#3 BABYMOUSE: Beach Babe
#4 BABYMOUSE: Rock Star
#5 BABYMOUSE: Heartbreaker
#6 CAMP BABYMOUSE
#7 BABYMOUSE: Skater Girl
#8 BABYMOUSE: Puppy Love
#9 BABYMOUSE: Monster Mash
#10 BABYMOUSE: The Musical
#11 BABYMOUSE: Dragonslayer
#12 BABYMOUSE: Burns Rubber
#13 BABYMOUSE: Cupcake Tycoon
#14 BABYMOUSE: Mad Scientist
#15 A Very BABYMOUSE Christmas
#16 BABYMOUSE for President
#17 EXTREME BABYMOUSE
#18 Happy Birthday, BABYMOUSE
#19 BABYMOUSE: Bad Babysitter

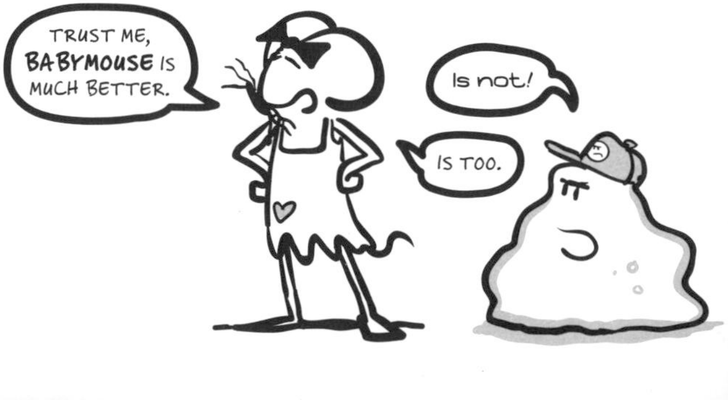
TRUST ME, BABYMOUSE IS MUCH BETTER.
Is not!
IS TOO.